# CAMERON HALEY

"*Mob Rules* is exciting and fresh, with a complex and conflicted heroine who grabs your attention and doesn't let go. This book will make you fall in love with urban fantasy all over again!"
—Diana Rowland, author of *Mark of the Demon*

"*Mob Rules* is an exciting, gritty urban fantasy that stands out in a crowd. Very original, with a compelling plot and an intricately developed fantasy world that on the surface looks very much like our own."
—Jenna Black, author of *The Devil's Due*

"Gangsters and vampires, ghosts and sorcerers, and the mean streets of L.A. Add to the mix a woman who can definitely take care of herself, a plot full of twists and some clever magic, and you've got *Mob Rules.* And a whole lot of fun."
—John Levitt, author of the Dog Days series

Stay tuned for more Domino Riley in
*Harvest Moon*
an anthology also featuring *New York Times* bestselling authors
Mercedes Lackey and Michelle Sagara.
Coming in October 2010
from LUNA Books!

# THE Burning Man WAS AN ANGLO,

tall, black hair slicked back, dark eyes glittering at me under narrow eyebrows. He gestured to the remaining chair and I sat down.

"Welcome, Miss Riley," he said, and offered his hand. I leaned up out of my chair and reached across the desk to shake it. It started burning and I let go. The flames just licked at him at first, then they caught and began to devour his fine old suit.

"Pay no attention to the special effects, Miss Riley. I assure you it's quite beyond my control. A bit of a nuisance, really." The fire had eaten away his clothes and was working on his flesh, blackening it and peeling it away from his bones. I forced myself to watch. I gave a little nod to let him know it didn't bother me if it didn't bother him.

"Tell us what we can do for you, Miss Riley."

"I need a gun. I heard you were the man to see."

book one: the underworld cycle

# MOB RULES

## CAMERON HALEY

LUNA™

www.LUNA-Books.com

LUNA™

MOB RULES

ISBN-13: 978-0-373-80320-0

Copyright © 2010 by Gregory Benage

www.LUNA-Books.com

Printed in U.S.A.

For Mashenka

# one

Jamal James had been skinned and crucified on the home-built bondage rack in his living room.

I knew what to expect before I walked into his one-bedroom dump in Crenshaw. Phone calls had been made, orders had been issued and I was prepared for what I'd find. I told myself the thing on the rack was just a corpse, and the part of me made on the street believed it. The rest of me ran inside and locked the doors.

Anton Shevakov waddled up next to me, rubbing his hands nervously. "Domino, damn, I'm glad you're here. I sit on couch for hour staring at this fucking fillet." A lot of Russian gangsters used their accents to sound hard, but Anton whined enough to dull the effect.

"A fillet is boneless," I said. "Jamal is skinless."

Anton looked from me to the corpse. "Anyway, I'm just glad you're here. It is lonely time for me sitting with him." He sighed and shook his head. "We were going to get the doughnuts."

Anton was fat. He'd come to L.A. from Moscow in 1992

and hadn't stopped eating since. The guys in the outfit called him Heavy Chevy. I wasn't one of the guys, so I called him Anton.

I looked at the body. It was naked, of course—really naked—but a piece of paper was covering the groin. I looked closer. It was a magazine.

"Anton, the *Sports Illustrated* swimsuit issue is stapled to his body."

"Just cover," Anton said, motioning to the coverless magazine on the coffee table. "Jesus, Domino, I'm tired of looking at dick."

"Well, take the damn thing off. I need to see Jamal like you found him."

He moved to the body and paused to consider. Then he shrugged and jerked the magazine cover from the body, returning it to the coffee table. I approached the bondage rack and examined the corpse more closely.

From the top of his head to the bottoms of his feet, Jamal's body was just muscle and bone. Not much fat—he'd been in excellent shape, lean and sculpted like an NBA small forward. Railroad spikes had been driven through his wrists and ankles into the thick wooden beams of the bondage rack. Other than that, there wasn't much to see. No blood. No empty birthday suit lying around.

"You search the apartment?"

"Yeah, nothing."

"Any juice?"

"I didn't find the unusual magic, but Domino, it's not strong point." Like most low-level soldiers in the outfit, Anton's strong point was mostly blowing things up. Even in that, his talent was modest. If something went down, he was usually better off with a gun. "What are you going to do?"

"Object reading. See if I can pick up anything from the stiff, the room." I shrugged. "I'll look for residual juice, just to be sure."

"So you think it was hit?"

"Magic is about the only way you could peel a guy like this and not leave any blood. There's an old Mongolian ritual—you hang a guy upside down by his toes and make an incision like this…" I traced a line across the top of one shoulder, around my head and across the top of my other shoulder. "You open the top of him like that, hocus-pocus, and he just slides out of his skin like a greased hand from a glove."

"Jesus," Anton swore and crossed himself. "And the guy is alive when you take his skin?"

"Yeah, depending on how good you are and how hard you want to work at it, you could keep him alive awhile."

Anton looked at the corpse and shuddered. "But why do Jamal like this? To squeeze him?"

"I don't see why. Jamal didn't have much juice to squeeze. The ritual would burn more than you could get out of him."

Jamal had been good at what he did, but he didn't have the kind of magic that would make someone think about stealing it. Still, you didn't see a ritual execution like this very often. When you did, the guy usually got squeezed. If you just needed him dead, a bullet in the ear was a lot less trouble.

"Anyway," I said, "that's what I'm here to find out. First, tell me what happened."

Anton spread his hands helplessly. "I was to go with Jamal

to shooting gallery in the Jungle. He needs to check tags, make sure they still put out. I go just in case."

Jamal had been a tagger, a graffiti artist who used his craft to tap into the juice—the magical charge—of various places like buildings, freeway overpasses and buses. Anywhere he could lay down his tags and where there was juice to tap.

The derelict hotel in Baldwin Village where junkies went to shoot up was a well-known juice box. The place reeked of pain, hunger, desperation and despair. It was *bad* mojo, but it was still mojo. Jamal's tags were the straw in the juice box. Shanar Rashan, the boss of our outfit, had his lips on the straw.

Like every boss of every outfit in the world's major cities, Shanar Rashan was a powerful sorcerer, probably the strongest in Southern California. The LAPD thought he was Turkish. He was actually Sumerian. Rashan had been in L.A. for almost eighty years, building his organization, expanding his territory and his control of the city's juice, though he'd used many names in that time. The investigations into his activities always seemed to hit the wall. The detectives and task forces inevitably lost interest and stuck the file in the back of a drawer before moving on to something else. Rashan had become more an urban legend than a wanted criminal.

When I drifted into the outfit as a teenager, Rashan noticed me. Unofficially adopted me, became my mentor. I already knew a lot of craft. I'd picked up a bit from my mother, a lot more from the street. But I was raw, unpolished. Rashan taught me discipline, control, finesse. When I was twenty-seven years old, he made me his youngest lieutenant. For the past eight years, I'd been his go-to girl.

And that's why I caught the last phone call when the body

of an executed gangbanger turned up. One of my gangbangers. One of Rashan's soldiers.

"So I come here," Anton continued, "knock on door, no answer, and so on and so on. I have key and I don't want to stand in heat all day, so I unlock door and go in. I find Jamal hanging with no fucking skin. After I look around, make sure no one is here, I call Rafael."

The outfit didn't really have a rigid chain of command, but it did have a pecking order. It was based on how much juice you had and how close to the boss you were. Rafael Chavez sat a little higher in that pecking order than street-level soldiers like Anton and Jamal, a little lower than me. He'd been two phone calls from Rashan, and Rashan had thrown it to me.

"How do you know it's Jamal?" I asked.

"Who else would it be?" That kind of limited imagination was one reason Anton would always be a low-level soldier. He didn't have the head to be anything more. He didn't have the juice. He never would.

You can't get a good ID on a guy when he's been skinned, but Anton was probably right. My instincts told me it was Jamal hanging there. Most of him anyway. If it wasn't, I'd find out soon enough.

Witch sight involves staring at something long enough for your eyeballs to dry out. It's like looking at one of those optical illusions. You look at the pattern, then you look through it, past it, and pretty soon there's a picture of Jesus.

The only thing supernatural about magic is that most people don't believe in it, don't even notice it's all around them. It's as natural, as much a part of the world, as electricity. A rare few can see magic if they know how to look.

I stood by the door of the apartment and looked. I looked

into the room, all the way in, past light, and color, and contrast and shape. I looked behind the visible to the magic that flowed beneath.

I looked first at the bondage rack. I saw the natural juice of the wood, no longer flowing, just pooling in the lumber and slowly evaporating. I saw the juice that soaked into the rack from the pleasure and pain of those who had occupied it.

I didn't think Jamal had really been into the BDSM scene. Most likely he'd been using the rack and its associated activities as a tool. He'd been trying to tap more juice, learn to harness and control it. He'd wanted to get stronger, and he'd been working out. The bondage rack was his magical Bowflex.

There was quite a lot of juice in the rack, but none of it smelled like the murder. If this had been a ritual execution, the wood should have been dripping with the black magic of the spell used to kill Jamal. If I could have gotten a taste of that juice, I could have identified the ritual. Because magic is personal, I might have been able to identify the sorcerer who performed it. Failing that, I might have been able to use the juice to recreate the murder, just as Jamal had experienced it. It wouldn't have been pleasant, but I might have gotten a look at the killer, might have been able to learn something useful from the details of the ritual.

But I didn't get any of that, because the juice just wasn't there. The rack had been cleaned. Scrubbed. On the surface, what I got was mostly the pain and terror of the victim. I also got the brute fact of his death, which stained the wood like mildew on bathroom tile. Deeper still I found only the old juice that had soaked all the way into the wood and the natural juice that had been there since it was a sapling.

I found enough juice in the corpse to confirm that it was

Jamal, but I didn't find nearly enough of it. A person's magic clung to the body after death, evaporating at a measured rate until there was nothing left. This was especially true with sorcerers. If you knew how old a sorcerer's corpse was, you could get a pretty accurate idea of how powerful he'd been by how much juice was left in the body. In the old days, graves and tombs were even violated to get at the juice trapped in the moldering corpses of powerful sorcerers.

Jamal hadn't been a powerful sorcerer, but even a civilian's corpse would have more juice than remained in the kid's body. The skinless corpse was like a desiccated husk, sucked almost dry of the magic that had made Jamal a valuable if limited member of our outfit. He had been squeezed.

Whoever had done the ritual was good. It was complex magic, and most sorcerers—guys like Jamal and Anton—didn't have the craft for it. But the really impressive part was the way the killer had scrubbed away the magic after the deed was done. It isn't easy to clean up magic with magic. It would have been simpler just to obscure it, contaminate it—stir in enough random juice that you couldn't get anything useful from it. Instead the murderer had wiped away every magical trace of the ritual spell that killed my guy.

I let my gaze pan around the small living room, and my luck turned. The carpet in front of the bondage rack was stained with black juice. I knelt by the stain and touched it. It was roughly circular, about two feet in diameter, cold to the touch, damp and sticky.

I dug my fingers into the stained carpet and reached out for the juice, tapping it, allowing it to flow into me. I leaned down and tasted it.

The juice began to resolve itself into a pattern in the part of my mind or soul that makes me a sorcerer. The black stain had been left by a small rectangular box. I didn't get any sense of exact dimensions—it just doesn't work that way—but it was about the size of a normal cookie jar, maybe a little smaller. From the taste and texture of the juice, it was probably made of clay or ceramic. It was very old and somewhat crudely formed. I could see symbols, like hieroglyphs, carved into its sides, though I had no sense of their meaning.

Mixed in with the box's juice, I tasted faint notes of living human magic. Most of it was very old, and there was no way I could identify it. Some of that juice was fresher, though. It was Jamal's.

I stood up and caught myself rubbing my hands on my jeans, as if it could somehow rid me of the black juice that had soaked into my skin. I let my gaze slip back to the mundane world.

"You find anything?" Anton asked.

"I'm not sure. The killer cleaned up after himself. It's definitely Jamal, and I think he was squeezed. I might have a line on the murder weapon."

"What do you do next?"

I thought about it a moment and shrugged. "I'm leaving. I can try to contact Jamal, but I'm not going to do it here."

Anton's eyes widened. Even guys who had been around the game a while got a little creeped out by necromancy. "Tell him I'm sorry about it, Domino. Tell him I wish I got here sooner." Anton crossed himself again. "Tell him goodbye."

"Well, I'll try to get Jamal to talk to me. Probably I won't be able to say anything to him at all. If I do, I'll tell him for you."

As touching as Anton's request might have been, I knew

his real motivation wasn't just the bonds of friendship. He and Jamal hadn't been that close. He was mostly worried that Jamal would blame him and stick around to haunt his ass.

Anton gestured at the corpse. "What about…?"

"Get rid of it. Clean the place. It's dark and this is Crenshaw. Shouldn't be much trouble."

It wouldn't be real messy, either, given the complete lack of blood. I took one last look at the skinned corpse hanging on the rack, and I was still glad I didn't have to do it.

"And Anton," I added, "put the word out. Tell everyone to stay sharp."

In the underworld, you never find just one skinned and crucified corpse.

I can speak with the dead. It comes up in my business. Gangsters with interesting stories to tell are often deceased. Jamal's corpse didn't have much to say, but his shade might. Once you've killed a guy it's not easy to keep him from talking. It's not a foolproof spell—sometimes the dead don't want to talk—but I had decent odds to contact Jamal. He hadn't been dead long, and I didn't expect him to be happy about getting murdered.

Most spellcraft is just will and power. You tap into a source of juice and manipulate it using a pattern you've learned. The spell is the pattern, a kind of cookie-cutter template you channel the juice through so it does what you want it to. That doesn't mean it's easy. You have to be able to create and sustain a complex, multidimensional mental and spiritual pattern, and you have to be able to tap and channel enough juice to produce the result you want.

Most people don't have the will or the power. If it was easy, everyone would be doing it.

Still, the words of the spell can be just about anything you can memorize. It doesn't have to be some cryptic verse in a dead language. You don't have to invoke the four corners or the forces of earth, air and fire, or any of that stuff. You just want something that makes sense to you, something that will help you stabilize the pattern and flow the juice.

I know dozens of spells, and each one is associated with a famous quotation I've memorized. Other sorcerers use nursery rhymes or hip-hop lyrics, dead languages, invoking the saints, or pagan mumbo-jumbo. Whatever works.

To contact Jamal in the Beyond, I needed some real craft, a spell backed by an easily repeated ritual. Again, the traditionalists use black candles, séances, Ouija boards, that kind of thing.

I use FriendTrace.com.

I sat down at my desk and brought up the Web browser on my laptop, then typed "Jamal" into the search box on the site. I tapped the ley line running under my condo and said, "In heaven all the interesting people are missing." Then I hit the search button and released the spell.

My laptop went crazy. Random windows opened and closed faster than I could follow, like pop-ups at a porn site. A disharmonic, cacophonous squall blared from the speakers. The screen went black and the sound died. Without the juice, you just get personal ads.

A few seconds passed and a Web page flared to life on the screen. It was one of those slick Flash sites, and I had to stop myself from clicking the Skip Intro option.

Grainy, distorted, black-and-white images appeared, one

after the other. A noose dangling from the twisted branch of a dead tree on a barren field. The indistinct silhouette of a man standing in a backlit doorway. An extreme close-up of a fly feeding on raw flesh. A blood vessel bursting. Jamal's face pressed against the LCD, his mouth open in a silent scream.

The laptop speakers crackled, hissed, and I heard a voice.

"Domino," it whispered, the word stretching out like a dying man's last breath. It was Jamal's voice.

"I hear you, Jamal. Tell me who did this to you. Tell me who killed you." The dead usually weren't in the mood for small talk, so you might as well get to the point.

Instead of an answer, the frozen image of Jamal's face was replaced by the Blue Screen of Death as my computer crashed. I shut it down, counted to ten and rebooted.

I tried again, but I wasn't optimistic. A mundane crash wouldn't exactly have been a freak occurrence, but in this case, I knew I'd lost whatever connection I'd had to Jamal. It was so tenuous, I couldn't even be sure I'd really had a connection. It could have been an echo, a psychic afterimage. After three more crashes, I decided to give it a rest.

My effort to contact Jamal had been a form of divination, the difference being that the spell had to reach all the way into the Beyond. I can use a similar ritual to do other kinds of divinations—say, running a check on an ancient magic jar whose juice I'd tasted.

For that, I use Wikipedia.

I brought up the browser again and typed "magic jar" in the site's search box. I conjured up that magical image of the artifact I'd absorbed from the juice in Jamal's apartment and powered up my divination.

The title of the entry was Soul Jar, and it featured a digital reproduction of an old lithograph. In the photo, a black woman who looked to be about a hundred and twenty years old sat behind a simple wooden table. Her withered hands clutched the clay jar resting on the table in front of her. Four other figures, all black men of various ages, stood behind her. The caption read, "Voodoo Queen Veronique Saint-Germaine, New Orleans, Louisiana, 1849. Saint-Germaine was the soul jar's last known owner."

I'm pretty good at this stuff. I quickly read through the rest of the entry.

This item is one example of a class of artifacts known as soul jars. Crafted in Egypt during the Old Kingdom period (c. 2650 to 2150 BCE), the artifacts were designed to contain the ka of the exalted dead.

"Ka" was hyperlinked, so I clicked on it and skimmed the new screen that popped up.

While ka is commonly translated as "soul," to the ancient Egyptians it more properly represented a person's magical essence.

I closed the pop-up and went back to the main entry.

This soul jar was crafted for Pharaoh Bakare (c. 2500 BCE), who desired that the priests of his inner circle would continue to lend him their power in the afterlife. The priests were ritually executed at the pharaoh's funeral ceremony. Their magical power was contained within the soul jar and their bodies were mummified. The mummies and the soul jar were entombed with the dead king.

Like many artifacts, Bakare's soul jar faded from history for many hundreds of years. It reappeared when a French knight returning from Crusade brought it back to Europe from the Holy Land. It disappeared again, only to emerge in Haiti, and later in New Orleans, in the possession of Veronique Saint-Germaine.

The voodoo queen was murdered in 1854, the apparent victim of infighting within the occult underground of antebellum New Orleans. The current whereabouts of Bakare's soul jar are unknown.

I shut down the computer as the spell faded and leaned back in my chair. I had a pretty good idea of the soul jar's current whereabouts. I also knew the identity of its current owner. I recognized one of the men in the photo of Saint-Germaine—a gangster called Papa Danwe. I didn't know him, but I knew of him and I'd seen him a couple times. He apparently hadn't changed much in the last century and a half.

Papa Danwe had come to L.A. in the early 1900s, by way of New Orleans, Haiti and some coastal sandpit in West Africa. I'd heard his first racket had been trading slaves and ivory to French pirates for guns. His outfit was much smaller than Rashan's and we'd never had any trouble before.

It seemed we had trouble now.

Ninety-nine percent of my job is pretty simple. I'm a fixer, a problem-solver. I make sure the outfit is operating as it should. When it isn't, I step in and make the necessary adjustments. I have no day-to-day routine, no ongoing managerial responsibilities. It's a nice gig.

This looked like a one-percenter. In the outfit, shit flows uphill but it doesn't flow all the way to the top. It stops with me. Rashan is at the top of the hill, and he never even gets a little on his shoes.

I grabbed a glass and a bottle of wine from the kitchen and curled up on the couch. Most of the problems I have to solve are pretty simple. There's a body, get rid of it. Someone's skimming juice, make so they don't do it anymore. The cops are working too hard, pay them or put the hoodoo on them so they leave us alone. Action, reaction. Most problems have easy solutions.

This wasn't one of those problems. Jamal had been executed by another outfit. It had been an act of war.

Ordinarily, if a rival gangster hit one of our guys, I'd hit *him* and make sure his boss got the message. Problem solved. I wouldn't enjoy it, probably, but I'd do it because that's the way this thing of ours works.

That wasn't going to be a quick fix this time. Even with all the juice and testosterone on the street, L.A.'s underworld is surprisingly peaceful. There's violence, but most of it happens within the outfits, not between them. There's competition, but overt confrontation is rare. No one wants a war.

I was pretty sure Papa Danwe was responsible for Jamal's murder, but I couldn't prove it. My divination spell allowed me to build a pretty strong circumstantial case against the sorcerer. But as powerful as magic is, it also has its limitations. By its very nature, magic is ephemeral, intangible and subjective. My divination might be enough for me, but it wouldn't count as hard evidence to anyone else. Even among sorcerers, "Wikipedia told me so" isn't a compelling enough reason to touch off a gangland war.

I didn't plan on taking Papa Danwe to court, but we would need the support of at least some of the other L.A. outfits if we wanted to make a move against him. We wouldn't need their help, but we would at least need them to stand aside. There were a dozen major outfits in Greater Los Angeles, and plenty of smaller ones, but only a few really had a stake in South Central. Those were the ones that mattered, and they'd be the hardest to convince.

It was also unlikely that Papa Danwe had done the hit himself. It wasn't his style. He'd have a henchman to do the dirty work, though it would have to be someone pretty good.

And finally, while I could connect Papa Danwe to the soul jar, and I could connect the soul jar to Jamal's murder, I didn't have even the glimmer of a clue about motive.

I'm not a detective. Most gangsters have it in them to do a murder, but it's a rare thing if one of them is clever about it. Elaborate plots and cunning schemes are for normal people. A gangster usually kills a guy because someone else told him to and he thinks he's covered. Mistakes get made—gangsters are prone to them—and that's where I step in. There isn't a mystery to solve, just an error to be corrected.

Most of what I knew about detective work came from cop shows and buddy movies. Look for clues. Develop a theory and find a suspect you like. Spend time with the family of your partner, who happens to be only a couple weeks from retirement.

Despite my lack of investigative experience, I wanted the killing to make some sense. It didn't. Why would Papa Danwe be making a move against our outfit? If he was, why did he do it by hitting a guy like Jamal? The kid just didn't merit the attention. Why squeeze him? He didn't have the juice to make it worthwhile. And why leave him hanging in his apartment? If Papa Danwe was sending a message, we weren't speaking the same language.

If I wanted to answer the "Why Jamal?" question, I needed to connect the kid and Papa Danwe. Maybe Jamal crossed him somehow. Maybe he'd even been working for Papa Danwe on the side and the relationship went sideways. Unless Jamal was a random victim, which seemed unlikely, there would have to be a connection. It sounded like a plan.

I stared at the vintage movie posters hanging on the living-room wall. I stared at the wall. I turned on the TV and turned it off. I had a couple more glasses of wine and fell asleep on the couch.

That night, I dreamed that Jamal was on the balcony outside my condo, trying to jimmy the French doors with a crowbar.

# two

When he wasn't tagging or tying someone up in his apartment, Jamal could usually be found on a playground in Crenshaw, shooting hoops with his homeboys. I parked on the street by the court and went in through a gap in the rusted chain-link fence.

There were seven guys playing full-court, all of them young black males. The oldest might have been twenty-five. A few girlfriends and hangers-on lounged courtside on the cracked concrete. They leaned against the fence and watched the game. They passed a blunt around and smoked. The court and both backboards were decorated with tags Jamal had put down.

The game stopped as soon as my car pulled up, and everyone was watching me as I stepped through the fence. The guy holding the ball walked toward me. He was a six-foot-ten, three-hundred-pound horse named Marcus. He'd come off the bench on a full-ride at UCLA for two years. He would have started his junior year at power forward, but he got collared for dealing crack and lost his scholarship.

"Yo, Domino," he called. "We need a skin."

It was going around. "You've got four skins and three shirts, Marcus."

"Nah, D, Shawan gonna go shirts." He nodded to one of the brothers. The kid jogged over to his gym bag and dropped a tank top over his head.

I was always a skin. Watching a five-foot-seven Mexican-Irish girl in her thirties trying to play ball with these guys wasn't enough entertainment. Jamal's boys always needed me to go shirtless. I'd learned a somewhat embarrassing lesson the first time this happened, so I was wearing a sports bra.

I stripped to the waist and handed my jacket and shirt to Marcus's girlfriend, a young twentysomething with an elaborately styled weave and gold fingernails. She smiled and folded them neatly in her lap. I passed her the shoulder holster with the forty-five and she tucked it under my jacket.

"Don't take Marcus money, Domino," she whispered. "We got rent."

"Yo, D, you been workin' out?" Marcus asked, laughing and elbowing the kid named Shawan. "You lookin' ripped, girl!"

"My people weren't bred to pick cotton." Casual sexism and racism were social etiquette in Crenshaw. I hear it makes some people uncomfortable.

"Nah, that's right. Your peeps bred skinny to crawl under the fence." Everyone laughed.

"I'm only half-Mexican," I said, and gave up the straight line. "My dad was Irish."

"Someone get this skinny bitch a potato," said Shawan. The game was delayed another couple minutes so he could be congratulated for his wit with chest-bumps and fist-pounds.

"Okay, Shawan, I got you. Bitch." I'd been cheating on the playground since kindergarten. This time, I only used enough juice to make sure Shawan didn't score and to throw down a two-handed jam in his face on an alley-oop from our point guard. Skins still lost, and I coughed up my twenty so Marcus could make his rent. After the game, I joined them along the fence for Red Bull and weed.

"So what you doing, D?" asked Marcus. "You come down here just to give your money to us poor black folks?"

"Yeah, Marcus, I don't pay taxes and I was worried your welfare check might bounce."

"Fuck that, D. I got a job."

Marcus, like most of the guys on the court, was a part-time criminal. No juice, no serious gang affiliation and no real connection with our thing. They were the handymen of Crenshaw's ghetto economy. If a small-time rock-slinger turned up dead or incarcerated and his boss needed someone to fill in, he'd have a ready labor pool waiting at the playground.

"Actually, I was just wondering if you knew what Jamal has been up to."

"You ain't seen him, neither, huh?" said Marcus. "Word is he got a new ho." Marcus's girlfriend scowled and drove an elbow into his ribs.

"Sorry, baby," he said.

"You know who she is?"

"Nah, girl, like I said, we ain't even seen the brother. The woman, you know, that's just what he said she said and whatnot."

"Any new friends, besides the woman, I mean?"

Heads shook.

"Maybe you've seen some new faces hanging around. Maybe some guys in Papa Danwe's outfit."

"Nah, D, Papa Danwe got most of Inglewood and Watts,

but he don't got Crenshaw. Everyone know Crenshaw belong to the Turk."

Rashan was known as the Turk on the street, at least by those who didn't know him well. The outfit's turf is shaped like a crescent, running from Santa Monica around the southern edge of downtown, up through East L.A. and reaching into Pasadena. Rashan controlled Crenshaw, but there was only a nebulous border separating his territory from Papa Danwe's turf.

"All right, you give me a call if you hear anything else." Nods all around.

"Jamal in some kinda trouble, D?" Marcus asked.

"I think y'all might need to recruit another player," I said. "Jamal won't be going skins anytime soon."

I left Crenshaw and drove back to civilization. I took Santa Monica Boulevard into Beverly Hills. I've always liked Beverly Hills. The outfits exist by virtue of the fact that most people don't pay any attention to what's going on around them. It's charming. No other place has reached Beverly Hills's level of clueless perfection, with the possible exception of Vegas.

A vampire can walk down Rodeo Drive, window-shopping and pausing for the occasional snack, and no one will even notice as long as he's wearing the right suit. A sorcerer would have to turn a demon loose in Gucci to attract attention.

The art opening was like any other of its kind. When I walked in, the gallery was bustling with the young, rich and fashionable in-crowd. This was L.A., though, so everyone had two out of three working—they were all faking the third.

I was there to meet an associate, a connected probation officer on the outfit's payroll. His name was Tommy Barrow and he was twenty-nine years old. He used his secondary income, drug connections and gangster stories to circulate with the art-opening crowd and chase women who were out of his league.

I spotted him standing by an abstract painting in animated conversation with a salon blonde. Her swimsuit-model body and pouting lips advertised one of the many nearby clinics.

"Hi, Tommy," I said. "Who's your friend?" The blonde wore a diamond-and-ruby pendant that nestled in her prodigious cleavage. A red arrow painted on her chest wouldn't have drawn more attention to her neckline.

"Sandy, this is Domino, a friend of ours," Tommy said, his voice low and conspiratorial.

Sandy's tastefully decorated face brightened and the pouty lips stretched into a sunny smile. "Oh, so you work for Tommy in, you know, the business?"

I looked at Tommy and raised an eyebrow. He shrugged apologetically. "Not exactly," I said. "You could say we answer to the same boss."

"Oh, I see," Sandy said. "Can I ask what you do, or would you have to kill me?" She giggled, bringing a delicate and bejeweled hand to her mouth but making sure I could still see her perfectly straight and whitened teeth. In the outfit, I didn't get any real sexism from the guys and I didn't deal with cattiness from the girls. I had juice, and that's all that mattered on the street. I only ran into that kind of shit from civilians.

I laughed, turning from her to Tommy, and then back to her. I put the smile away. "I wouldn't have to."

She stopped in midgiggle, and I could almost hear the little wheels in her head turning as she tried to figure out if I was joking or not.

Tommy laughed loudly and put his hand on my arm. "That's

a good one, Domino! Sandy, why don't you run along so we can talk business?"

Sandy lit up again and the smile reappeared. "Oh, okay!" she bubbled. "It was nice to meet you, Domino." She bounced away and I turned my attention to the painting on the wall, some kind of abstract brown swirl on a yellow background.

"Looks like shit."

"It is," Tommy said, following my gaze to the painting. "Dog, I think."

I looked closer. It was. The artist had lacquered it to the canvas.

"Let's go outside for a smoke."

Tommy nodded, grinning. "Those things will kill you, Domino."

I have a purification spell that rules that out, but I didn't mention it. It's the kind of thing that pisses people off. They don't really mind if you smoke as long as it kills you. Out on the sidewalk, I drew a Camel and lit up.

Tommy immediately began scanning the area for attractive female pedestrians. "So what can I do for you, Domino?"

"Jamal is dead," I said. Tommy's gaze immediately snapped back to me. I wouldn't be able to keep the murder a secret, and Tommy would need to know eventually.

"When? How?" Tommy asked. His store-bought tan had lost a little color.

"Last night. Probably a hit."

"Jesus. Who did it?"

"Hard to say. Jamal isn't talking."

"How did he die? Where did you find him?" Tommy was fishing for all the details that would allow him to spin a good insider report to impress his friends.

"Skinned and crucified in his apartment, magical ritual. Squeezed."

Tommy let out a low whistle. "Damn. Hell of a way to go."

"Yeah, Tommy, not the best."

"So what do you want from me? You want me to call it in?"

"No, just report him AWOL the next time he comes up on your schedule. I don't need a police investigation, even if it is half-assed."

Tommy nodded.

"What I really need is information. I already ran Jamal's homeboys through the paces. They don't know much."

"Okay," Tommy said, thinking hard. "Like what? I was his PO. It was my job to keep him out of Chino. I guess I knew Jamal about as well as anyone." For once, I didn't think Tommy was exaggerating, at least not much. A probation officer was the closest most outfit guys ever came to a confessional. Jamal probably told Tommy Barrow things he'd never tell his friends or family.

"I need to know if he was up to anything unusual. Maybe he had something going on the side, maybe he made a new enemy."

Tommy shook his head. "Far as I know, Jamal was a standup guy. The outfit was his life, and he wouldn't try to run something under the radar. He thought he had a future with the outfit…and more to the point, he didn't think he had a future without it."

That fit with what I knew about the kid. He was smarter than most, and ambitious. It wasn't exactly helping me connect him to Papa Danwe, though.

"Any new habits? New friends?"

"Yeah," Tommy said, after a moment biting his lip. "He was hanging out at the Cannibal Club. He had this thing he was trying with bondage and that kind of stuff, to work on his craft. He said it was a good place to find girls who were into that."

The Cannibal Club was a nightspot in Hollywood that was popular with the black leather and porcelain fangs crowd. It was hard to picture Jamal there, and once you did it was a funny picture. Hollywood wasn't Papa Danwe's turf—none of the outfits controlled it. Still, maybe Papa Danwe had something working at the club. Maybe Jamal had gotten in the way.

"What about family?" I asked. It bothered me that I hadn't thought about it before. Jamal had been a person before he'd been a corpse and a problem for me to solve.

Tommy shook his head. "You know the story. Father split, mother OD'd when Jamal was fifteen."

"Okay," I said. "You got anything else?"

"I don't think so, Domino. If I remember anything, I'll let you know."

"Do that. Have fun with Sandy. You make a great couple." I guess I can be a little catty, too, sometimes. I flipped my cigarette into the street, drawing a contemptuous sniff from a middle-aged woman in a white dress, saucer-size sunglasses and a ridiculous hat. I smiled at her and tapped a little juice, vaporizing the butt where it lay on the asphalt. She didn't even notice.

About eleven o'clock that night, I left my condo and drove into Hollywood. It was a Saturday night, and as usual, traffic was a bitch. Fortunately I have a spell that allows me to weave through even the worst snarls with a little lane-jockeying.

Technically, the incantation I think of as the traffic spell is chaos magic—the old school would call it a luck spell. It's one of my favorites. It's subtle, and practical and complex enough that most sorcerers can't manage it. In simple terms, it isolates and adjusts probability lines such that you just happen to find an open route through even the heaviest traffic. I surfed the probability waves through the Hollywood night and found the club on Sunset Boulevard.

I pulled up out front and spun my parking spell, muttering the words of the incantation. "Any place worth its salt has a parking problem." I eased my car into a spot right by the door of the club just as a yellow Honda tuner pulled out. What luck.

There was a line of pasty, black-clad kids winding around the block, but sorcerers don't wait in lines any more than we settle for lousy parking or sit in traffic jams. I walked up to the bouncer and smiled.

"I'm on the list," I said. I wasn't. I didn't even know if there was a list. The bouncer's meaty, clean-shaven head didn't even budge as he checked me out from behind his wraparound sunglasses.

I reached out and touched the juice, channeling it through my imagination and rearranging it according to the pattern I'd learned.

"I have with me two gods," I said. "Persuasion and Compulsion." I released the magic and let it wash over him. Behind the sunglasses, the bouncer blinked.

"Oh," he said, stepping aside to let me pass, "you're on the list."

I met the chorus of protests from the waiting kids with a smile and a little shrug. "I'm on the list," I said.

Metal detector, pat down, cover charge and then I was inside and heading to the nearest bar.

The Cannibal Club was black decor, chain-link fencing, head-splitting techno-industrial you can dance to, blacklight and the smell of sweat and patchouli. It was teenagers and twentysomethings in black leather, black rubber, black nylon, black vinyl and black velvet. It was body piercings and tattoos, black hair dye and white clown makeup. Flat-panel monitors offered a live feed of the writhing, thrashing, swaying bodies on the dance floor. An electronic ticker scrolling at the bottom of the screens announced that sunrise was at 5:41 a.m.

I went to the bar and ordered a beer. I used a little juice, or I'd have stood there for hours without attracting a bartender's attention. I took a lengthy pull from the longneck and scanned the club. I wasn't sure exactly what I was looking for. I guess I was hoping to spot one of Papa Danwe's guys hanging around, looking suspicious. I didn't see anyone I recognized, but then it was dark as the Beyond and everyone was dressed like the Crow.

After a few minutes of fruitless squinting into the strobe-pierced gloom, I relaxed and tried my witch sight. A few of the kids in the club had a little juice. That was normal for a place like the Cannibal Club. None of them had the kind of juice to be my killer. I sensed stronger magic in the VIP area that ran along one side of the dance floor, but I didn't have a clear view from where I was standing by the bar. I dropped the sight and headed that way.

The guy holding court in the semicircular booth was a prince among the pretenders. His glossy hair flowed to his shoulders and draped his white collar in black silk. He'd elected not to conceal the natural beauty of his caramel skin in the hideous clown makeup that seemed mandatory for most of the club-goers, male and female alike. His dark eyes were at once soulful and boyish, and the combination made my knees a little weak.

I'd been in the outfit most of my life, so I'd run into Adan Rashan on more than one occasion. I'd always thought he was attractive. Cute, even as an awkward teenager when his father had first introduced us. That night in the club, I thought he was the most beautiful thing I'd ever seen.

I don't have a spell to counteract the intoxicating effect of a truly gorgeous man. If I did, I probably wouldn't use it anyway. Even if it means I one day get sucker-punched by some seductive creature of the night, I say to hell with it. Some risks are worth taking.

So, yeah, Adan was hot. The Goth posse that flanked him in the booth was pretty much indistinguishable from the rest of the crowd, from where I was standing. One long-haired pale face sitting next to Adan stared at me menacingly. He leaned over and whispered something without breaking eye contact with me, and then he sneered. I hated him already.

I went back to the bar, juiced the bartender again and had her send over a couple bottles of Cristal. A waitress delivered the champagne, pointing in my direction. I raised my bottle and smiled, wishing I'd ordered something classier than a beer. Adan recognized me and returned the smile, then waved me over. The Gothtard next to him scowled, which I liked.

The VIP area was roped off, and I gave the bouncer the same Jedi mind trick that got me in the club. I handed him my empty before making my way over to Adan's table.

He stood as I approached. He was wearing a tailored black suit, the ivory shirt unbuttoned at the collar just enough to be interesting. The rich fabric draped his slender frame like…

well, like an expensive suit on a young male body that's just about perfect.

"Domino," he said, "thanks for the champagne." He leaned across the corner of the table—and across Gothtard—to give me a hug and a chaste kiss on the cheek. He smelled like musk, and apples and cinnamon—and like sweat and patchouli, but that was just the fucking club.

"Hi, Adan," I said. "You're welcome. I'll send the bill to your father."

He laughed, and it echoed around the table, though the posse probably had no idea what I was talking about. Gothtard didn't laugh. He just stared at me and brooded dangerously.

"I've never seen you here before," Adan said. "Do you come here often?" Then, laughing, "Jesus, I can't believe I just said that."

I'd planned to play the tough girl and outbrood Gothtard, but I found myself laughing, too, because Adan's dark eyes sparkled and because he had the tiniest little dimples in an otherwise classically sculpted face.

He introduced the posse—Edward, Louis, Armand, Elvira, Wednesday Addams, yada yada yada. I nodded, smiled and then politely ignored them.

Adan sat back down and turned to Gothtard. "Manfred, can you pour the champagne?" The intensity of his brooding deepened momentarily, but he slid out of the booth to do the honors.

"Thanks, Fred," I said, and took his seat beside Adan.

"It is Manfred," he growled. He had a cute little German accent, probably affected. I nodded absently and turned to Adan.

"Anyway, no, this is my first time here," I said. Fred handed him the first glass of Cristal, and he passed it to me. Fred scowled and I smiled.

"And what do you think of the Cannibal Club?" he asked. He took the next glass from Fred and nodded politely.

"It's growing on me."

Adan grinned, flashing those dimples again, and we touched glasses. "So what brings you here?"

I waited until Fred finished pouring the champagne and wedged himself in at the other end of the booth, and then I stood up. "I want to dance."

"That works," Adan said and laughed. I could feel Fred brooding as we made our way to the dance floor.

I know gangsters who use their magic to dance. I even know the spell. It's actually a variant of a nonlethal compulsion that neutralizes an opponent, with the secondary benefit of making him look goofy. You cast the spell on yourself, relax your body, and with the help of a little juice, you literally let the music move you.

That's just weak. Using magic for parking spots and prompt bar service is one thing, and I'll admit to using my purification magic in ways that will keep me away from cosmetic surgeons indefinitely. But I draw the line at using it for sexy dancing. As far as I'm concerned, that's just cheating. Maybe it's nothing more than a different brand of vanity, but whatever sexiness I've got is all-natural, baby. Mostly.

In fairness to the weak-ass sorcerers who use the spell, club dancing does present a bit of a dilemma. If you really have no idea what you're doing, you'll look like an idiot. But if you try too hard, you'll look like you're trying too hard, and you'll still look like an idiot. The key is to look like you have no idea what you're doing, but sexy just comes naturally to you.

Out on the floor, I did my best to still my body, mind and

soul and settle into this Zenlike state of nondancing dancing sexiness. I probably looked like an idiot. Mostly, I just held on to Adan and hoped no one would notice me.

As I moved against my boss's son, I reviewed what I'd learned so far. First, the Goths in Adan's posse were all normal humans, unremarkable but for their poor fashion sense. All except Fred, who was the genuine article. Judging by how much black juice was oozing from his undead hide, he had to be at least five hundred years old.

Adan, of course, was the source of the magic I'd picked up from the bar. Not him, exactly, but his accessories. The small gold hoop in his left ear, the star pendant hanging from a slender chain around his neck, a ring, his Rolex—all of it radiated first-class juice, mostly protective magic, and I recognized it immediately as his father's.

As for Adan himself, well, the parts of his incredible body I could feel were lean, toned and hard, and I could feel most of them. Other than that, there wasn't much to talk about. He had a little juice, about what you'd expect from a young man. He wasn't a sorcerer.

After about ten minutes of dancing, I dropped a sound-dampening spell around us. The music faded into the background. Adan's eyes widened and he smiled. "Are you trying to impress me, Domino?"

"Of course," I said. "Adan, you know Fred is a vampire, right?"

He nodded. "Yeah, I met him here at the club. He's never tried to, you know, fang me or anything."

"How long have you known him?"

"A few months. Really, he's nothing to worry about. He's a little weird, I guess, but you know, he's just a guy at the club."

What did that mean? He's just a guy at the club as in I don't swing that way and he's not any competition for you? Or, he likes me and promised not to drain my blood until my heart stops?

"Okay," I said finally. "You're a big boy…I guess you can choose your own friends."

Adan laughed. Dimples were brandished disarmingly.

"So you like this Goth, emo, industrial scene—whatever they're calling it now?" I asked. "It doesn't really seem like your style."

He shrugged. "It's okay. I go to other clubs, too. I feel like a loser if I hang around Dad's strip clubs too much."

Touché.

"Adan, I heard one of our guys had started coming here, kid named Jamal. You ever see him?"

Adan nodded. "He started coming in about a month ago. I hang out with him sometimes. Manfred doesn't like him, but Manfred doesn't really like anyone. Anyway, Jamal seems pretty cool."

"Who else did he hang out with? Did you ever see him with anyone that looked, I don't know, out of place?"

Adan's brow furrowed. "He leaves with women sometimes, I guess. A lot of gangsters hang out here, so Jamal didn't stick out as much as you'd think."

"Really? This is a gangster hangout?"

"Yeah, mostly Papa Danwe's guys. You know him?"

This detective stuff was easy. "Yeah, I've heard of him."

"A lot of them hang out here. They all seem to know Manfred—at least the big guy does."

"The big guy? Do you know his name?"

Adan shook his head. "I don't know him, but I think he's like a captain or whatever. Like you, I guess. He comes in here the most, sometimes by himself and sometimes with others. Anyway, he's black and just a really big dude."

There was one gangster in Papa Danwe's outfit who matched that description pretty well. Terrence Cole, one of Papa Danwe's lieutenants. He was the kind of guy who made a lasting impression.

"Did you ever see Jamal talking to this guy—or any of Papa Danwe's boys?"

"No, other than the girls and when he was hanging out with me, Jamal mostly kept to himself."

I guess that would have been too easy. "Okay. Thanks, Adan, this is really helpful."

"Why are you asking? Is Jamal in some kind of trouble?"

I decided not to tell him, at least not yet. If his father wanted him to know about outfit business, he could tell Adan himself. He'd eventually hear about it anyway. I changed the subject.

"Do you have a girlfriend?" I groaned inwardly. It had been the first thing that came to mind.

"No. I did in college, but it didn't work out. It's hard to find someone, you know?"

I nodded.

"What about you?" Adan asked. "Boyfriend? Is there a Mr. Domino?"

I smiled and shook my head. "The only guys I meet are gangsters. It's hard to find someone to bring home to Momma."

He laughed, tilting his head back so the strobes danced in his liquid-brown eyes. "Does your mom know what you do?"

"Yeah, she's always known. She's just glad I have a job."

"She probably worries about you. You're her baby girl. This line of work, it's gotta freak her out."

I shrugged. I didn't tell him my mom was a fortune-teller, a good one. Mom probably knew more about my life and my future than I wanted to think. Then again, maybe not— the fortune-telling game is notoriously unreliable, even for Mom.

I'd probably learned as much as I was going to, and really, that was more than I expected. I'd found a connection between Jamal and Papa Danwe's outfit. Maybe Jamal was doing business with Papa Danwe. Maybe the kid had unknowingly picked up one of Terrence Cole's girlfriends and tied her to the bondage rack in his apartment. I could see Jamal getting himself squeezed for something like that.

And then there was the Vampire Fred. I couldn't probe his mind as I could a normal human's, probably because his brain was as dead as the rest of him. But I didn't like him. I didn't like him lurking around my boss's son. I didn't know exactly what Jamal had been up to in the club, but I didn't like the apparent coincidence of an unaligned supernatural creature hanging out in the place—hanging out with Papa Danwe's guys. I was itching to connect Fred to the murder in some way.

Mostly, though, I didn't want the undead piece of shit with Adan. Maybe it wasn't any of my business, but I thought his father would want me to step up. Okay, maybe I had ulterior motives. Maybe it was some maternal, protective part of me screaming to get involved. Or maybe it was the romantically challenged part. I was sure it was what the maverick in the cop shows would do, so it had that going for it.

"Do you think your friends would mind if we got out of here?" I asked. I'd planned to wait until the end of the song to make my move, but I think the same damn song had been playing since I walked into the club.

Adan's arms tightened around me and he breathed in my ear. "I don't think I care what they think, Domino."

We left the club without returning to the table. Fred, of course, was leaning against my car when we got outside. My vintage 1965 Lincoln Continental convertible with the original Arctic White paint. The vampire gave me the Look—the usual vamp shtick that would make a mortal woman his willing slave or whatever. To me he just looked like a really pale and very gay fashion model.

"Scratch the paint and I'll shove a stake far enough up your ass to pick the blood clots out of your teeth." I smiled and tucked my arm inside Adan's. "Fred," I added.

I'd like to say Fred sensed my great power and backed down. I'd like to say he recognized the more dangerous predator and submitted to the law of the jungle. But he didn't. Fred made a move.

There aren't a lot of vampires in L.A. They don't like gathering in large numbers—too much competition for food. But when it comes to vampires, popular culture is so full of shit I don't even know where to begin. I'll mention just two things in passing.

First, humans haven't believed in monsters for a long time, but in the twenty-first century, we've taken it one step further. We've rehabilitated the bastards. These days, vampires aren't really monsters; they're just tragically hip antiheroes with unusual diets. They sip daintily from cherished and willing blood donors and pine away for their lost humanity.

Well, vampirism isn't a disease. It's not a virus, or a genetic disorder or any other ridiculous pseudoscientific rationalization. Vampirism is blood magic. It's a necromantic shortcut to immortality and a limited range of superpowers. Vampires are just ex-human sociopaths who lacked the juice to become real sorcerers.

Second, in the supernatural food chain of the underworld, vampires are pussies.

The instant Fred leaned away from my car, I triggered the repulsion spell stored in the silver gangster ring on my right pinkie. The ring was a preloaded talisman, allowing me to cast the spell with only the barest concentration and no witty quotation.

So when the Vampire Fred launched himself at me with catlike speed and preternatural fury, the repulsion spell met him halfway and used his own kinetic energy—plus a little extra—to throw him over my Lincoln, across the street and into the storefront of an overpriced flower shop.

"This'll just take a second," I said to Adan, and then I went after Fred.

By the time I crossed the street, the vampire was standing up and brushing flower petals and broken glass from his suit. He saw me approach and dropped into a predatory crouch, fangs bared and ready for battle.

Still about twenty feet away, I casually extended my hand, palm up, toward the Vampire Fred. "Vi Victa Vis," I said. That's Cicero—sometimes I bust out the Latin. The force spell hit Fred in the sternum and knocked him through the back of the flower shop into the skin-care clinic on the other side of the drywall.

This time, Fred was a little slower getting up. It's another myth of popular culture that vampires are fucking bulletproof. They're tougher than humans and they heal quickly when they're fed, but their bones still break when you hit them hard enough. Fred's left shoulder was dislocated and his right leg was twisted at an unnatural angle.

"All movements go too far," I said, picking him up with the telekinesis spell and flipping him back through the flower shop and out into the street. There was the screech of rubber against pavement and a double thump as the Vampire Fred was run over by a Mercedes before he could crawl out of the way. Oops.

I made my way back through the trashed flower shop, pausing to pick out a red rose for Adan. The Benz was stopped but the driver wasn't getting out of the car. Fred was struggling to peel himself off the asphalt. I guess five hundred years of owning mortals had made him a little stubborn.

"A great flame follows a little spark," I said, and a grapefruit-size sphere of fusion fire appeared, spinning like a miniature sun above my upturned hand. I let Fred get a good look at it.

"You might want to stay down, Fred, so I don't have to cook your pasty ass."

Fred's jaw clenched, whether in pain or frustration I wasn't sure. I could see the pride and survival instinct, both honed over centuries, warring in his eyes. He looked at me. He looked at the fire. Survival won.

Like I said, vampires are pussies.

"Here's the way it is, Fred. Out of respect for your friendship with Mr. Rashan," I said, turning and smiling at Adan, "I'm going to let you walk away. But Fred, if you fuck with me again, you're going to burn. Clear?"

The Vampire Fred gritted his pointy teeth, and then he nodded.

"Groovy," I said. "Now get the fuck out of here."

Without a word, Fred pulled himself up and hobbled off

down the street. Even with a busted wheel, the vampire limped faster than the human eye could follow.

I pulled in juice and dropped a confusion spell over the street, just enough hoodoo to render any witnesses or inconvenient security cameras useless to a police investigation. I looked in the direction the vampire had fled, then turned back to the crowd of stunned onlookers and shrugged.

"He wasn't on the list."

# three

Adan was annoyed. We were cruising down Santa Monica Boulevard toward the beach, and he was pressed against the passenger door and glaring at me.

"You didn't have to kick his ass like that in front of everyone."

"He started it," I said. "I wasn't going to touch him as long as he didn't scratch my car."

"You sound like a ten-year-old, Domino."

"Well, what should I have done? He's a vampire. You want me to go back and let him take a bite out of me?"

"No, of course not. And I know he's a vampire, but he's been cool to me. Besides, you provoked him."

I shrugged. That was true. I tried a different angle.

"He's cool? You know the magic is in the killing, right? Every human is topped off with ten pints, give or take, but all that's just foreplay. It's the mouthful that stops the heart that keeps him going."

"I know. I just said he's been cool to *me*." He shook his head and snorted. "Anyway, you're a gangster. Where do you get off judging him?"

I scowled. "Yeah, I'm a gangster—in your father's employ, I might add—but that doesn't make me a homicidal undead monster. Come to think of it, I can't even remember the last time I killed a guy and drank his blood."

"No, you just kill guys and have some stooge bury the bodies."

Ouch. That was going to leave a mark. "I don't kill anyone. Usually. And never civilians. If you choose to get in the game, you know the rules and you know the risks. It's not murder when you have to kill an enemy soldier."

Adan laughed. "Oh, yeah, the standard gangster code of situational ethics. That bullshit's an insult to real soldiers."

"That…is probably true. Anyway, it's just a fucking metaphor. Excuse my language."

"Actually," Adan said, "I think it's a fucking analogy."

I glared at him and he laughed. I shook my head, chuckling, and just like that the tension was borne away by the wind whipping through the open convertible.

I wasn't sure why I was arguing with this guy, anyway. His last name was Rashan. He knew the score. The truth was, Adan had pushed one of my buttons. Growing up, I'd always thought I'd end up using my magic for the Forces of Good. Maybe work a quiet job by day and kick evil ass by night, like Batman or the Ghostbusters. Long before I hooked up with the outfit, I'd seen enough of the world to know how things really work.

Adan was right. I clung to that gangster code because it was just about all I had to distinguish myself from psychopathic freaks like the Vampire Fred. I hadn't killed often, but I had killed. I hadn't killed innocents, but I'd taken husbands, and fathers, and brothers and sons. Even some sisters. To stay sane,

I tried to convince myself they were bad guys, just like me, and they got what they deserved.

And still, late at night and usually when I was drunk, I'd type their names into that search box on my laptop and reach out to them in the Beyond. They never answered, but I knew they were waiting for me out there in the dark.

Adan noticed my uncharacteristically angsty mood and laid a hand on my arm. "I've had this argument a thousand times with my dad," he said. "You know what he says? He says the difference between a strong man and a weak man is that the strong man will do anything, even kill, to remain strong… the weak man will do anything, even die, to remain weak. He says that a man who is both strong and good will kill to remain strong, and will hate himself for it."

I looked at Adan, and a little smile teased his infinitely kissable lips. That's about when things started to get really complicated. I knew my little stunt with Fred would have ended my chances with most of the guys I'd met. Not because they felt sorry for Fred or disapproved of violence or anything like that, but because they would have felt threatened and humiliated by it.

The bottom line was that I'd worked over the vampire because I'd wanted to protect Adan. And he didn't seem to mind. The reason for his enlightened attitude was obvious—he knew the outfit. He knew the life. He knew that in the underworld it wasn't about girl power versus machismo or any of that shit. It was about the juice. I had it and he didn't. Adan accepted that. He maybe didn't like it, exactly, but he was man enough to deal with it. For a girl like me, Adan was a miracle.

By the time we got to the beach, I'd forgotten why I went to the club. Sitting with Adan on the sand, listening to the sound of the waves and the wind, I forgot about Jamal altogether.

We were sitting quietly together when I heard laughter drifting across the water. The moon was out, and I could see there were no late-night surfers or swimmers out there.

I nudged Adan. "Watch," I said. I scooped up a handful of juice that washed ashore with the tide and spun a spell of true seeing. Golden, sparkling light cascaded out over the waves. The light revealed figures frolicking in the surf, male and female, their skin so pale it was almost translucent in the moonlight.

"Oh, my God. What are they?" Adan whispered.

"Ocean spirits. Mermaids—merpeople—or something like it. When I was a kid, I used to come down here all the time just to try to catch a glimpse of them. They're more common now than they used to be. I don't know why. Sometimes I'd go months without seeing one."

The creatures noticed us and froze, suspended in the water like seaweed bobbing in the tide. Then, as suddenly as they'd appeared, they were gone. I dropped the spell and the light faded.

"Domino, that was amazing. I had no idea," Adan said, moving closer to me. I shivered, shamelessly, and he wrapped an arm around me and pulled me against his body.

"There's a whole world out there most people never even see," I said. "Some of it is beautiful." Most of it just wants to eat you. I decided to keep that part to myself.

"I want to see you again, Domino."

"I'd like that."

"What about my father?"

"Yeah, I'll have to see him again, too."

Adan laughed. "No, I mean, he probably wouldn't approve."

I smiled. "I'm sure of it. He probably wants you to find a nice professional girl, like a doctor or lawyer or something."

"No, he hates lawyers."

"Well, whatever fathers want for their sons these days, I'm pretty sure a gangster isn't what he has in mind. If you're planning to get involved in the outfit, it could get really complicated."

Adan didn't respond and I looked over at him. He was staring down at his feet, tracing abstract designs in the sand with his fingertips.

"Did I say something wrong?"

He shook his head. "Nah, it's okay. It's just…I can't ever be part of the outfit." He looked up at me, and I thought I saw real pain in his eyes. "I don't have it, Domino. I'm not a sorcerer."

I already knew that, and I felt stupid for being so careless with my words. I'd known he didn't have any real juice the moment I saw him in the club. I'd thought about what that meant for me, but I really hadn't thought about what it would mean for him.

"Damn, I'm sorry. I thought maybe, you know, considering who your father is—"

"It's cool. It just doesn't work that way. Dad says the gift or whatever isn't genetic. He has over thirty living children. None of them have it. He keeps trying because he wants an heir, in case something happens to him. I'm his latest disappointment." Adan laughed and shook his head. "Ah, man, I can't believe I'm telling you all this. Dad would kill me."

I squeezed his arm and smiled. "I won't tell on you."

He laughed. "Thanks," he said, "and I won't tell him you forced me to reveal his secret shame."

I tried to laugh, but really, that shit wasn't funny. It was definitely the kind of thing Rashan wouldn't want anyone to know. I felt like I had a good relationship with my boss, but I couldn't read him, didn't really know him. I couldn't even guess what he'd do if he knew I'd found out about something like this.

"Yeah, let's just pretend you didn't tell me that," I said. "The fewer of your father's secrets I know, the better."

Adan nodded. "Yeah, I'm sorry I told you. I just...I guess I feel like I can talk to you. Maybe it's lame, but it gets lonely, you know? I can't be a part of my father's life, but I never really feel at home in the normal world, either, because of what I know."

I understood how he felt. I'd had that same feeling of being an outcast until his father found me and brought me into the outfit. For Adan, it was worse. He would always be an outsider in both worlds. That was real loneliness. I could even see how he'd reach out to someone like the Vampire Fred—anyone or anything that would accept him.

"Maybe it's a bad idea, Adan, but I still want to see you."

He smiled. "Me, too. It'll be our secret. Dinner tomorrow night?"

"Okay," I said, "I want pizza."

"I'm impressed," he said. "On a first date, women usually restrict themselves to salads they never actually eat."

Okay, I use magic to cheat with dieting, too. "I have a fast metabolism," I said.

"Sounds great—I love pizza. Pick you up at seven?"

I nodded and smiled.

"Give me your cell phone. I'll give you my number and you can call me tomorrow, give me directions."

I handed him my cell and he punched in his number and gave it back to me. I checked the display, and he'd given me both his home and cell numbers. My dating game was a little rusty, but that seemed like a good sign.

"Great," I said. "I'll call you. I'd better get going. Did you drive tonight or catch a ride with someone?"

"I drove," he said. "You can just drop me at the club." I did, and I waited there until he got in his car and drove away.

I'd never been a romantic. I didn't believe in love at first sight, soul mates, star-crossed romance or any of that stuff. I didn't believe that Adan and I were destined to fall in love, get married and live happily ever after. Judging by past experience, he was more likely to screw up my life, make me miserable and hop in bed with an exotic dancer just when I was finally getting used to him.

I grew up in the barrio, fatherless and poor. My life was violent and brutal, and I'd long ago stopped pretending there was anything more to it than getting ahead and getting out alive. Despite that, it wasn't a hard life. With magic, I could have just about anything I wanted. The only thing I couldn't change with a little juice was myself. I couldn't change how I felt, and I couldn't change what I believed. And the worst thing about not believing was that I always knew what I'd lost or what I'd never had.

I was a gangster, and I'd done things for which even God couldn't forgive me. But I was still human. I was still a woman. I *wanted* to believe in that fairy-tale love that little girls dream about, and I hated that I couldn't. The cruelest joke of the underworld was that so many parts of fairy tales were true, but not the ones that really mattered.

Adan made me want to believe. He made me want to believe all those wonderful, impossible things, and that he could somehow make them come true. He made me want all those things with him.

Sorcery is just will and power. So is believing.

Later that night, I tried to contact Jamal again. This time, when the same Flash intro came up, I kept pumping juice into the spell from the ley line below my building in an effort to stabilize the pattern. The squall from the speakers intensified until I was sure it was loud enough to raise the dead, or at least wake my neighbors. My computer slowed to a crawl and the screen flickered dangerously, but the system didn't crash.

I poured more juice into the spell and the noise finally died down, to be replaced by sporadic bursts of white noise. In the intervals between the bursts, I heard voices. There were a lot of them and it was disturbing, like a party that had turned ugly. The cacophony of voices was punctuated by panicked shouts, terrified screams and despairing wails. It reminded me of live video footage I'd seen of a crowded Jerusalem restaurant in the aftermath of a suicide attack.

There was no foreground or background to the noise—all of the voices were just mixed in together. Occasionally, though, one of the voices was isolated enough that I could make out the words. Most of it made no sense to me—names I didn't recognize, languages I didn't understand, mundane phrases so removed from context they had no meaning. The voices were garbled, warped, but a few *did* make sense, and that was worse.

"I can't find my leg," a voice whispered.

"I'm dead now."

"They took my mommy." A little girl's voice.

"I want to go, I want to go, I want to go, I want to…"

"I know who you are." The voice sounded like an old woman. She sounded pissed.

"Help me, Domino. Please, D."

"Jamal?"

"Help me, D…help me."

I channeled more juice into the spell, straining until I thought my eyes would pop. I kept feeding the spell, but the juice kept backing up, into *me,* like blood in a junkie's syringe. It was so cold it burned.

"Jamal, I'm trying. Talk to me. Just keep talking to me."

"I can't…I can't get back, D. I can't get back. It's just dark… ain't nothing here, Domino…ain't nothing but the dark."

"I know, Jamal. Keep trying. I'm here. Keep talking."

"Domino? Are you there, D? Please don't leave. Domino, please don't leave me here." He was crying, but his voice was growing fainter.

"Jamal, keep talking. I'm here." I ground my teeth and reached for more juice, but I had so much of the backwash in me I couldn't push it through and I felt like I was drowning. "Fuck!"

I tried again to force more juice into the spell, but now it was washing back into me faster than I could tap it from the line.

"Jamal! I'm still here. Come back."

Silence, then a few short bursts of static. Then nothing. I'd lost him.

I shut down the computer and went to the kitchen for a beer. I was buzzing from all the juice I'd flowed. I was also shivering and choking on that grave-cold backwash I sucked down. I collapsed on the sofa and drained the beer.

Whatever was happening with Jamal wasn't right. Contacting the dead was never a sure thing—if they didn't want to talk to you, there wasn't much you could do about it. Jamal obviously wanted to talk, but I couldn't reach him. Why? The backwash I was eating when I tried to feed the spell—why?

The only explanation was that someone was fighting me. Pushing back at me. While I was flowing juice into the spell, someone was pumping it back into me. Someone stronger than I was.

Someone like Papa Danwe. It might have been Terrence Cole, I supposed, but I doubted the Haitian had a sidekick with enough juice to shut me down like that. It had to be Papa Danwe.

I felt pretty sure after this experience that FriendTrace wasn't going to get it done. I maybe could have kept flowing juice into the spell a little longer, but I knew the backwash from the Beyond would have killed me before I was able to establish a stable connection with Jamal.

Still, the fact that Papa Danwe was blocking my efforts at communication made me even more determined to succeed. I needed to talk to Jamal. He obviously had something important to say, something the Haitian didn't want me to find out.

Well, if you can't bring Mohammed to the mountain, bring the mountain to Mohammed. That's not a spell formula, just a saying that came to mind. If I couldn't reach Jamal in the Beyond, maybe I could bring him to me.

It was a little after two in the morning, and I still had time. I went down to the garage and put my toolbox and several cans of spray paint in the trunk of my car. Then I drove to Crenshaw, back to Jamal's apartment.

When I got to his door, I juiced the lock and let myself in. Anton had removed the corpse as ordered. The small apartment was empty and quiet. I set the toolbox on the floor beside the bondage rack and went to work.

The rack was really just two fitted timbers bolted together to form an X. I unbolted and separated them, laying them on the floor side by side. I closed up the toolbox and ran it down to the car, then returned for the first of the timbers. The beams were heavy, but I was able to get them down to the car, one at a time, using a little juice. With the top of the convertible down, they fit in the backseat, more or less. It was something to cling to the next time some prick in a Prius smirked at my vintage Motown gas-guzzler.

I went back to the apartment and stuffed some things from Jamal's closet into a duffel bag. On the way out, I grabbed the stapler Anton had used with the magazine cover to protect Jamal's modesty. I went down to my car and drove to the playground where I'd talked to his crew.

There was no one on the playground at that hour, even in Crenshaw. The security lights had likely been broken within hours of being installed, and the concrete was lit only by a feeble moon and the ambient orange glow of the sleeping city.

I hauled the timbers out to midcourt and reassembled the bondage rack. I'd packed some of Jamal's clothes in the duffel bag, and I took them out and stapled them to the rack. There was a Lakers jersey, jeans and a pair of Nikes. Next, I went to work with the spray paint.

The tags Jamal had laid down all over the playground were designed to tap the juice of the place. There was a fair amount of it, and Jamal had done good work. I'd be able to get plenty of power, and best of all, in a way it would be Jamal's juice I was flowing. I just needed to hook up his tags to the ritual I was building.

I used the spray paint to lay down a circle around the bondage rack. When the circle was complete, I grabbed a detailer out of the toolbox and began stenciling symbols into the painted line of the circle and the wood of the bondage rack. Ordinarily I'm not really into symbol work, but in this case I was just copying Jamal's tags, in miniature. When I was finished, I scrounged up some broken boards and garbage and built a fire in front of the rack. Once the fire was blazing, I stripped off my clothes and started dancing naked around the circle.

It was a little pagan, more than a little ridiculous, and not the way I usually roll, but sometimes the oldest magic requires the oldest methods. The fire and the nude dancing would attract spirits. Jamal's tags, the rack and the clothes stapled to it would ensure that the ritual called more loudly to Jamal than to anything else out there in the Beyond.

If the summoning ritual was successful, Jamal's shade would be pulled out of the Beyond to fill his clothes and be bound to the rack. Once bound, I was pretty sure I could hold him there long enough to find out who killed him, and why. Even Papa Danwe wouldn't be able to stop me. At least, not before I got what I needed.

I started chanting as I danced naked around the summoning circle. For hard-core necromantic work, you can't beat Lovecraft. "That is not dead which can eternal lie, and with strange aeons even death may die," I chanted, over and over. I chanted quietly. If anyone saw me doing this shit, I'd never live it down.

I tapped Jamal's tags and started flowing juice into the ritual. The symbols stenciled into the paint and the wood began to glow orange, matching the dancing light of the fire.

The juice flowed around the circle and into the rack, then punched through into the Beyond.

It started to pull. A cold wind blew in from nowhere, and Jamal's shirt and pants began to swell, filling out. A hazy, insubstantial form began to take shape.

Then a huge dog, like hell's own mastiff, burst out of the fire and crashed into me. I went down under the weight of the beast and tumbled onto the rough concrete. The surface did cruel things to my naked body, but I barely noticed. I was too busy trying to keep the creature's massive jaws away from my throat.

The beast loomed over me, pressing me down into the court. Then it lifted its head and howled. The sound sent goose bumps percolating across my bruised and bleeding skin. An answering howl split the night, then another, and another.

"Yield not to evils, but attack all the more boldly," I said, spinning a close-combat spell in my mind.

Nothing happened.

"That's bad," I said.

My summoning spell was still active. It shouldn't have been, but it was drawing all the juice I could flow into the circle, into the Beyond. Unless I could flow some juice into a new spell, I'd just be babbling stupid quotations while the dog ate me. I triggered the repulsion spell in my pinkie ring, but I'd drained all the juice from it when I hit the Vampire Fred.

I cursed and struggled, trying to beat the mastiff down with my fists, but it was pinning my arms to the cracked concrete. Its jaws were wide, drool spattered my face, and its breath smelled like the worm-ridden intestinal tract of a moldering corpse. Maybe even worse. I got one arm free and slammed it into the beast's jaws as it went for my throat again.

Out of the corner of my eye, I saw another of the creatures

slouching through the shadows on the other side of the playground.

With my left forearm still in the creature's mouth, I grabbed an ear with my right hand and pressed my thumb into its eye. I pressed hard, and tried to put a little juice into it. I didn't have enough to power a spell, but I thought, maybe...

The beast's eye exploded. Raw magic, pulsing bloodred, sprayed from the wound, spattering the side of my face. I pushed against the creature and it leaped away, howling.

I heard a low growl and turned in time to get my arm up as another creature lunged at me. I was trying for a kind of stiff-arm move, but it probably looked like I was cowering and trying to shield my head from the thing's gaping jaws. Again, I fought to divert some juice from the summoning spell into the blow.

My arm thrust into the creature's chest, pushing all the way through it and out its back. The beast's momentum carried it into me and we went down.

I didn't have to push this one off of me, because the creature was disintegrating. Writhing, crimson energy burned away its flesh as it howled, and in seconds it was nothing but a smoking grease spot on the court. Tendrils of smoke curled from the concrete and were pulled toward the circle, into the fire, vanishing in the flames. I felt that cold wind on my skin again, and now it seemed to be pulled from every direction at once into the center of my summoning circle.

I raised myself to one knee and looked for the next attacker. The creature I had wounded was circling the battle warily, looking for an opening with its remaining eye and brushing at the other with a massive, taloned paw. The other two beasts were preparing to eat me.

They came at me from opposite directions, crouching low

and baring fangs the length of my hand. There was no way I could keep both of them off me. I still couldn't grab enough juice to spin a spell.

I was screwed.

I had just enough time to fumble my gun out of the shoulder holster and squeeze off a wild shot as the creatures pounced. The shot missed.

The beasts hurtled through the air toward me, and then seemed to stretch out in midflight, their squat, powerful bodies pulled into impossibly elongated shapes. They sailed over my head, yelping in frustration, and incandescent red energy began to devour them as they were pulled into the circle. A moment later, what was left of their bodies vanished into the flames.

I spotted One Eye slouching around the edge of the court, its form rippling and contorting grotesquely as it fought against the pull of the Beyond. I took careful aim and put a bullet in its good eye. Crimson juice sprayed across the concrete and the chain-link fence. The beast seemed to collapse in on itself, and the stuff that flowed into the fire looked more like glowing red plasma than flesh.

In an instant, the wind died, the fire went out and the playground was quiet and still. My connection to the summoning spell was severed, and Jamal's clothes hung empty and motionless on the bondage rack. It was over, and I'd failed. Again.

I didn't think I had another summoning spell in me. I also couldn't see myself driving home with Jamal's bondage rack in the back of my car. Besides, I was hurt, and scared shitless, and I didn't want to take the damn thing apart again. I had my juice back, so I spun up a ball of fusion fire and torched the rack. Next, I ran my housecleaning spell over the circle I'd painted on the basketball court. It left a dark smudge on

the concrete, but at least all the spooky arcane stuff was obscured. Jamal's homeboys would have a hell of a mess to clean
up before their next pickup game.

I stuffed my toolbox and paint cans in the duffel bag, threw
it in the trunk and got the hell out of Dodge. As I drove home,
I chain-smoked and tried to make some sense of what had
happened.

My summoning spell had worked. I'd reached out into
the Beyond and started pulling Jamal's spirit back into the
corporeal world. But somehow, Papa Danwe must have used
the ritual as a beacon to sic those ghost dogs on me. They'd
used my ritual as a bridge, but they hadn't been confined to
my circle.

This time, I knew it *had* to be the Haitian. Terrence was
probably doing the grunt work, but no way could he spin that
kind of juju. Papa Danwe had used my own spell against me,
my own juice, and I'd have been puppy chow if the Beyond
hadn't chosen to reclaim its own. I reached two conclusions
by the time I got home.

First, even if there had been no formal declaration, my
outfit was at war. Second, I was way out of my league.

# four

I was planning to report in to Rashan when I woke up that morning. Or afternoon—it'd been a late night. But Rashan beat me to it. I got a call at a little after eight o'clock summoning me to a meeting at his strip club, the Men's Room.

Rashan was the smartest person I'd ever known. Maybe the guy was Sumerian, but his English was perfect. No accent, huge vocabulary—he always sounded more like an Ivy League professor than a gangster.

Despite all that, he missed some of the nuances of the language that are second nature to a native speaker. When Rashan had chosen a name for the strip club where his office was located, I'd pointed out that, technically, the men's room was where you put your urinals. I'd suggested the Men's Club, the Men's Place...Pussy Galore would have been an improvement.

Rashan wouldn't budge. He liked the name, and that was the end of the discussion. Most of the clientele probably didn't notice anyway. For whatever reason, though, the boss's linguistic blind spot seemed to be at its blindest when it came to naming conventions. I was just glad the outfit didn't have a name, like a street gang. It would have been embarrassing.

I parked my car in the front row of the lot—I had my own space, so I didn't have to use the parking spell. Despite the name, the Men's Room was a nice place. Tasteful, at least by the standards of the pole-dancing industry. The club was closed but a girl was dancing onstage, probably for the boss's benefit. I made my way to the back stairway and ascended to Rashan's second-floor office. It had the traditional glass wall looking out over the bar, and I found my boss sitting at a table and watching the main stage with gray, almost colorless eyes.

"She is one of my favorites," he said, nodding to the dusky-skinned young beauty of pleasantly indeterminate race. "Look at that ass."

I looked. It was a nice enough ass. "Jesus, boss, you're old enough to be her long-dead ancestor."

Rashan laughed and motioned for me to sit down. "You know," he said, "my people understood the importance of naked dancing girls. It is a sign of this country's bankrupt culture that you've made it into something sleazy."

"I have nothing against naked dancing girls. Or boys." My attention drifted to the stage again. "I think it's the brass poles and disco lights that make it seem sleazy. And maybe the bills tucked in their G-strings. The patrons are a little questionable, the music the girls pick doesn't help and perhaps—"

"Dominica, tell me what you've learned about Jamal," Rashan interrupted. Rashan always used my real name. I didn't care for it much.

If you can mentally take a deep breath, I sucked in a cerebral lungful. "It was a hit."

"Go on," Rashan said.

"You know about the skinning and crucifixion already. Jamal had been squeezed. The strange thing was, there were no traces of the ritual on him or at the scene. It was like the hitter scrubbed the place when he was done."

Rashan frowned. "If Jamal was squeezed, it must have been a sorcerer. That suggests another outfit."

I nodded.

"Tell me what you know about the ritual."

"That's what I'm saying, boss, the place was clean."

"And yet, you were able to learn something."

It's hard to play coy with a Sumerian sorcerer. "Yeah," I said, "the hitter used an artifact in the ritual. It left a mark that wasn't cleaned up. I was able to get a taste of the juice and find out a little about it." I told him about the soul jar and what I'd learned about it from my divination spell.

Rashan steepled his fingers and tapped them against his black, neatly trimmed goatee. "Veronique Saint-Germaine. I remember her. She was the strongest sorcerer in the Old South. There were more famous voodoo queens in New Orleans during that period, but only because Saint-Germaine didn't work the tourists from New York, Boston and Paris."

"Based on the New Orleans angle and an old photograph I got with my spell, I thought there might be a connection to Papa Danwe."

"Indeed there is. Papa Danwe was one of Saint-Germaine's inner circle. He'd come to New Orleans with her from Haiti, after the slave revolt. He murdered her in 1854."

"Knew she was murdered, didn't know Papa Danwe did it."

Rashan shrugged. "It was something everyone knew and no one could prove. Not that anyone would have done anything about it anyway. Survival of the fittest."

"So I figure, we can put the soul jar at the scene of Jamal's murder. We can connect Papa Danwe to the jar's previous owner. He's got the juice, so he had the means and opportunity."

"Your theory is tenuous and circumstantial at best," Rashan said. I started to protest, but he waved me off. "That doesn't mean you're not right."

"Yeah, but it doesn't make any sense. Jamal was good at what he did, but his talents were pretty much limited to tagging. I can't see how he had enough juice that the Haitian would get anything from squeezing him."

Rashan shook his head. "There are very few instances in which you would squeeze a sorcerer for power. Any sorcerer strong enough to do it wouldn't gain anything from doing it, just as you suggest. The usual exception is a group of sorcerers or coven that works together to squeeze a more powerful magician and divides the spoils amongst themselves. In any event, there are much easier ways to acquire power." Rashan gestured expansively at the strip club. The club was a juice box, and like I said before, Rashan's lips were on the straw.

"Then what's the point of squeezing a guy? I guess I wouldn't call it common, exactly, but it does happen. Everyone knows about it."

"You squeeze a guy not to procure power in the abstract. As you say, Jamal had precious little of that. You squeeze him to steal his *specific* power, his unique arcane talent and craft. You take another sorcerer's juice, it isn't like taking it from a tag or a line. It's *his* juice. You squeeze him to make it yours."

This was all news to me. "So, Jamal was a tagger. You're saying Papa Danwe squeezed him to steal his way of doing graffiti magic."

Rashan nodded. "There can be no other explanation."

"But why? Jamal was good, okay, but he's not the only tagger in town. It seems like it'd be a lot easier to just recruit a guy, even if he needed a little training. Why take the risk of hitting a connected guy?"

"Two connected guys," Rashan corrected, "which is why I called you in. Jimmy Lee's body was found floating in a storm runoff this morning."

I'd been expecting another body to turn up, but I hadn't been expecting it so soon. "Damn," I said. "No skin?"

Rashan nodded.

"I don't know this guy, boss. What was his thing? Another tagger?"

"No. Jimmy Lee was a warder—defensive magic. He designed protections, locks, alarms, minor defensive spells, that kind of thing."

I arched my eyebrows. "Important stuff?"

Rashan shook his head. "No, in that respect, Jimmy Lee was rather like Jamal. A valuable asset, but not a critical one."

"It's a pattern," I said. "Jamal was a tagger. He tapped and flowed juice on the outfit's territory. Jimmy Lee was a defensive guy. Put the two together. Papa Danwe is going after our defenses. He's making a move."

"It is the beginning of a pattern, Dominica. Tragically I expect there will be more bodies, and with each one, more of the pattern will be revealed."

"Both of the victims' names begin with *J*," I suggested. "Jamal's last name is James and Jimmy is short for James."

Rashan just looked at me.

"Okay, but I'm on the right track, yeah? The first part, I mean. What other reason could there be to hit Jamal and Jimmy Lee, two guys with those specific talents?"

"The problem with your hypothesis is that it overestimates

the importance of the deceased. I have a lot of taggers and warders in the outfit. As far as our operational security is concerned, they will not be missed. These were low-level guys. Jamal's tags weren't responsible for tapping a significant amount of juice. Jimmy Lee's wards were not protecting anything of great importance."

"So it still doesn't make any sense."

"Not yet. Truly, it's not a bad plan, in principle. If you could squeeze assets in critical positions, and if you could move quickly enough that your enemy couldn't react in time, it's not a bad way to initiate hostilities against a rival outfit."

"But that's not what's happening here. Papa Danwe is hitting low-level guys. He doesn't seem to be in any big hurry about it, either. If I were doing it, I'd hit them all at once, or one right after the other, at least. I wouldn't take my time about it."

"Just so. Which is why I suggested you have discovered only part of the pattern."

"Okay, but whatever it is, the fact remains that Papa Danwe has given us time to react. So what's our play?"

"First, tell me about Jamal. I assume you've made an effort to contact him."

"Yeah, but the Haitian is blocking me." I told him about my efforts to reach Jamal, and my attempt the night before to summon his ghost from the Beyond.

"If Papa Danwe did, in fact, send those creatures to kill you, perhaps his plan is unfolding more quickly than we imagined."

"Any idea what they were? You ever know the Haitian to use something like that before?"

Rashan shrugged. "Just about every culture on earth, living or dead, has some kind of ghost dog or hellhound. In the north of England, they were called barghests, or town ghosts, and they were thought to stalk lone travelers at night. They are denizens of the Beyond, and for that reason they are usually associated with death and appear as minions or messengers of the underworld."

"Well, yeah, I got that much from Wikipedia."

Rashan arched his eyebrows. "I'm sorry, Dominica, I am old but I am not a scholar. If you think it might aid you to know more about them, I encourage you to pursue it."

"The point is, I haven't been able to contact Jamal, and it's pretty obvious Papa Danwe doesn't want me to. But what's the point of keeping Jamal quiet if the Haitian has to launch overt attacks against the outfit—against me—to do it?"

"It seems likely that Papa Danwe isn't aware that you've connected him to Jamal's murder. If he prevents you from contacting Jamal he keeps that connection hidden, from his point of view. And, after all, you have no real evidence that he was responsible for the attack on you."

"It was him."

"Have you found any other connections between Jamal and Papa Danwe, besides the murder?"

"I'm not sure. I don't think Jamal was working both sides. If Papa Danwe needed Jamal's craft for something, maybe he was trying to recruit him. When Jamal wouldn't go for it, they squeezed him."

"It fits what little we know, but of course, we don't know enough. The question remains, for what purpose did Papa Danwe want Jamal?"

"Does it really matter, boss? Papa Danwe hit Jamal and Jimmy Lee. He probably means to squeeze more of our people. He sent those ghost dogs after me. He's making a move. Shouldn't we start hitting back?"

"I am loath to launch a war against a rival organization unless it is absolutely necessary. One doesn't get as old as I am by courting violent conflict impulsively."

"I get that, boss. I'm not Sonny Corleone. We need a measured response, but we do need to respond."

"What I am suggesting, Dominica, is that there is precious little to be gained for either Papa Danwe or myself from a war between our organizations."

"The Haitian obviously thinks he has something to gain."

"Perhaps. Very well, find out what Papa Danwe is up to. You have my blessing to act directly against his interests and his organization, but make every effort to do so in a proportional way."

Seeing how the Haitian was responsible for two murders and a magical attack against me, that would give me plenty of leeway.

"I'm on it, boss. What else?"

"We can begin making certain preparations, quietly. For example, if there is to be war, we need to know which of the others will stand with us. We also need to know where we are vulnerable, should Papa Danwe launch an overt attack."

Rashan got up and went into a back room, returning with a rolled-up parchment. He spread it out on the table. It was a map of Greater Los Angeles and looked hand-painted, almost archaic. Rashan touched an area in South Central and it expanded above the table into a three-dimensional image, like the holograms in sci-fi movies and CNN.

"This is Crenshaw. It is the area where our territory borders most closely with Papa Danwe's."

"Which just happens to be where Jamal lived and worked."

A thought occurred to me. "What about Jimmy Lee, also Crenshaw?"

Rashan shook his head. "No. Jimmy Lee lived in Chinatown and did most of his work in East L.A.—your old stomping grounds, Dominica."

"Well, maybe Papa Danwe is making a move on both Crenshaw and EasLos." I looked at the map. It was a stretch.

"Perhaps you will find out. However, I think it's clear that the most likely place for Papa Danwe to attack is here, in Crenshaw."

"I'll tell Chavez to beef up the security there. We can put more guys on the street, get some surveillance up."

"Tell him also to get the taggers working. He can bring in help from other neighborhoods if he needs it. I want all our rackets working at full capacity, and I want enough tags that we can channel the juice anywhere in Crenshaw at a moment's notice."

"What about police? The increased activity is going to be obvious to anyone who looks. We don't need Five-oh getting in the way, taking guys off the street."

"Leave that to me. I'll make sure that Vice and the Task Force stay away from Crenshaw. There may be elevated patrol activity, but our people can handle uniforms."

"We'll deal with it, boss."

"Good. I know you'll be busy, but I'd also like you to make contact with the Russians and the Koreans." Rashan touched two more locations on the map: one south of Crenshaw and the other northwest, near Santa Monica.

I nodded, looking at the map. We could handle Papa Danwe, but we needed to make sure our flanks were secure. If the Haitian wanted a war, it sounded a lot less insane if he had support from other outfits in the area.

"You want me to put out the word for the guys to go to the mattresses?"

"I think not. Everyone will have heard about the killings by now, but I don't want any special precautions to be taken. Unfortunately, I think we need to leave the bait in the water to draw out our fish."

Rashan was a pretty nice guy, but whenever I forgot that he was also a cold, calculating, mobbed-up Sumerian sorcerer, he said something like that to remind me.

"Okay," I said, "what about Lee?"

"The body was removed immediately. Even in L.A., the authorities will eventually notice a corpse floating in a canal. Ringo is down at the bar—he can give you directions if you'd like to investigate the scene."

"Yeah, but I probably won't find anything more than I did at Jamal's apartment."

"Is there anything else you wish to report?"

I thought about Adan. I could tell Rashan I'd met his son at the club and I wanted to date him. I could tell him about the Vampire Fred. I could tell him Adan had seen some of Papa Danwe's boys at the club where Jamal had been hanging out. He probably deserved to know.

"That's all I've got."

"Very well, then, Dominica. I will leave you to continue your inquiries."

The old man turned away. I left him there watching the stage, and my sins of omission chased me from the club.

I drove out to the place where Jimmy Lee's body was dumped, one of the many concrete runoffs that crisscross Los Angeles County. It was in Hollywood, near the reservoir. It wasn't outfit territory—most of the tags on the sloping concrete walls were mundane Crips-and-Bloods or Mexican Mafia shit.

I didn't know exactly where the body had been found, or even if it had been found in the same spot it was dumped, so I just scanned the area with my witch sight. At the bottom of the spillway, tangled in some debris, I spotted a bedspread stained with Jimmy Lee's juice. I guessed it had been on Jimmy's bed the night before, and the killer had wrapped his corpse in it.

I waded down into the shallow, stagnant water and inspected the cover. Not all of the juice on the bedspread was Jimmy's—it was black and it didn't smell human. I leaned in and tasted it. Mostly it tasted like filthy canal water, but I was able to get a little magic from it.

I got an image of a tall, slender man in dark clothes scrambling down the side of the canal. Jimmy's corpse was wrapped in the bedspread and slung over the man's shoulder. The guy didn't seem to be struggling much under the weight. It was impressive because he was injured, bleeding black juice into the cloth of the bedspread. Maybe one of Jimmy's wards had gotten a piece of the bastard.

When he got to the bottom, the man flipped the bound corpse into the water and climbed quickly back up to where a pair of headlights marked a waiting car. I had the sense that someone else was standing there, a silhouette by the open driver's door.

That was all I got. I considered taking the blanket with me, but I didn't really want to fish it out of the canal, and I didn't really want to ride around with physical evidence of a homicide in my car. I crab-walked my way up from the canal and returned to my Lincoln.

I hadn't seen enough to identify anyone—certainly not the figure standing by the car, and not even the guy carrying

Jimmy's body. I knew who the guy was just the same—I recognized the juice. It was the Vampire Fred. Call it a hunch, paranoia or wishful thinking, but I'd known when I saw him at the Cannibal Club that I'd connect him to the murders.

The problem was that he couldn't actually be the killer. The murderer had definitely been a sorcerer, and a pretty accomplished one. The vampire might be many things, but a sorcerer he was not. I'd known that the first time I saw him. The only juice he had was what he got from sucking blood out of people's throats.

So the Vampire Fred was an accomplice. The figure standing by the car had probably been Papa Danwe. I was a little surprised the Haitian would take a personal interest in disposing of dead bodies. The figure might have been Terrence Cole, the henchman, but I didn't think it was large enough.

So why was Papa Danwe using a vampire as an accomplice? Vampires could occasionally be useful as straight muscle, but that's about it. If the Haitian needed someone to dump dead bodies for him, surely he had plenty of worthy candidates in his own outfit.

Vampires are somewhat resistant to a sorcerer's subtler magics. I couldn't probe Fred's thoughts the way I could if he'd been human. If you knew you were going up against other sorcerers, that would be a pretty strong qualification in an accomplice.

I drove into Chinatown and let myself into Jimmy Lee's apartment. One of the wards on the front door had been discharged, and I found a little more of Fred's juice there, staining the wood and the hallway carpet. Jimmy had definitely put up more of a fight than Jamal. Good for him. It occurred to me that the killer hadn't cleaned up the vampire's juice. For that matter, he'd missed the stain on the floor of Jamal's apartment, the one left by the soul jar.

Why? If he was good enough to scrub away all traces of his ritual magic, why not clean up the rest of the mess? I tried to think about it like he would. If I were the killer, all I really cared about was protecting my own identity and the details of my rituals. I didn't want anyone to find out who I was, and I didn't want anyone to find out why I'd chosen to squeeze Jamal and Jimmy Lee. Those were the big secrets, and as long as they stayed that way, I was covered.

Papa Danwe had really screwed the pooch when he left the stain from the soul jar, though. I'd been able to use that juice to identify the artifact, and I'd been able to connect the soul jar to the Haitian. This in itself wasn't hard to believe—gangsters screw up all the time—but it seemed out of character for a cunning son of a bitch like Papa Danwe. Maybe he could only clean up his own magic. That was a lot more than I could do. Maybe he didn't clean up the juice from the soul jar, or the juice that leaked out of the vampire when the ward popped him, simply because he couldn't.

It occurred to me that he might have *wanted* me to find the stain and track the soul jar, but that idea didn't lead me anywhere useful and I put it away. Clues had been hard to come by, and the soul jar had been the biggest one I got. I wasn't a detective, but I knew I could paralyze myself if I started to second-guess all my leads.

But why had Papa Danwe left Jamal hanging in his apartment, and then made a feeble attempt to dispose of Jimmy Lee's body by dumping him in a canal? I felt like I was in a poker game where I was sure I was being outplayed, but I wasn't sure exactly how or what I should do to escape the trap.

★ ★ ★

I searched the rest of Jimmy's apartment, but I didn't find anything more than I'd found at Jamal's. Maybe a real investigator would have had more luck, like those forensics experts on TV. Fingerprints, fibers—there could be all kinds of evidence that I had no way to find, and no way to analyze if I did find them. Not for the first time, it occurred to me how limited magic was, especially when dealing with another sorcerer who knew how to cover his tracks and block me at every turn.

I found myself wondering, again, if I was in over my head. Rashan obviously trusted me to handle this situation, but why? I had to admit it really wasn't magic that was limited—it was me. Rashan could probably step in, get involved and take care of this little problem in the time it would take me to drive back to my condo from Chinatown.

So why didn't he?

When it came right down to it, what use did Rashan really have for someone like me? I had a habit of looking down on people lower in the organization than me, but the truth was that guys like Jamal and Jimmy Lee at least had a specialty. There was one thing they did better than just about anyone else. They were specialists, and they'd found a niche for themselves.

What was my niche? I was just Rashan's gofer. It was my job to clean up the messes Rashan couldn't be bothered with. Okay, fine, I could live with that. Where I grew up, people didn't count on having any kind of job—or any kind of future—at all. I knew I had it pretty good, and I was grateful for the opportunities Rashan had given me.

I had nothing to complain about, personally, I just had to wonder if I hadn't outlived my usefulness as far as this situation was concerned. Papa Danwe, or a sorcerer connected to him, had hit two of our guys. For all practical purposes, we were at war. More of my people were probably going to die, and I couldn't even figure out why they were being killed.

I realized what really bothered me was that their deaths would be on me. It came as something of a surprise. I'd killed before and I'd do it again. I wasn't one of the good guys and I didn't pretend to be. At the end of the day, I could live with myself and that's all that really mattered.

But having someone die, someone close to you, one of your fellow soldiers, because you were too weak or too stupid to stop it…that was a lot worse than killing someone who had it coming. I thought about what Adan had said after our argument about the Vampire Fred.

"The difference between a strong man and a weak man is that the strong man will do anything, even kill, to remain strong," he had said. "The weak man will do anything, even die, to remain weak."

Those were the rules of the underworld. Mob rules. Good and bad, right and wrong—those are problems for other people, normal people. Strong or weak? That was the question that mattered for a gangster. Survive. Pick a side and do whatever it takes to win.

That was the crux of all my self-doubt. That was the meat on the bone. I was losing, and I knew it, and every other player in the underworld would know it, too. I was being tested, and I was coming up short. And then where would I be? What would I be? I knew the answer.

I'd be just another victim.

I resolved that no matter what happened, I wasn't going out like that. I wasn't afraid of dying—I'd had to make peace with that possibility on the street, before I even hooked up with the outfit. There was really only one thing I was afraid of, and that was being the helpless little girl.

So maybe I was out of my league. Maybe Papa Danwe had more experience, more moves and more juice. Maybe I'd be dead long before I figured out what was going on. If the Haitian was smarter and stronger than me, I was going down, and that's the way it should be. Welcome to the underworld.

But I didn't have to make it easy. I could make it hurt.

On the drive home, I got on my cell and started mobilizing for war. I told Rafael Chavez to crank things up to eleven. I wanted Crenshaw buzzing with juice, and that meant putting our criminal operations into overdrive.

There's really only one source of magic in the world—the world itself, the earth, like the ley line that runs under my condo. That's why territory is important to the outfits. The more you control, the more and better access you have to the rivers of power flowing through the world.

That power can be amplified by human activity, though, and nothing amps up the juice like hedonistic human activity. The outfit caters to that, cultivates it and takes some off the top of every transaction. Sex, drugs and gambling are the three pillars of the trade and always have been. It's what we do best, and people can never get enough of it. The rest of the organizational infrastructure, like Jamal's tags or the juice boxes, is maintained in support of those core rackets.

A sorcerer can't change the natural supply of magic in the world. She can expand her territory to control more of it, and she can find new and better ways to tap, reroute and harness it, but she can't fundamentally increase or decrease the quantity of natural juice in the universe. It isn't physics, but they do share some of the same rules.

A sorcerer *can* control the human-modulated potency and

geographical distribution of the juice, but it's labor intensive and requires organization. That's why there are outfits. Turning up the juice in Crenshaw was a matter of ramping up the supply of extralegal self-gratification on the street—more sex, more drugs, more gambling. People would do the rest.

All of this would require manpower. The soldiers and gang associates could work overtime, but we'd need to bring in more guys from the other neighborhoods, too. I gave the orders and delegated all the boring managerial shit to Chavez. He promised to get things rolling right away, but cautioned me that it would take time for some of our operations to get up to speed.

"We need this done yesterday, Chavez. What's the problem?"

"Drugs. After we run through current inventories, our timetable is going to depend on suppliers. Then, you don't get any juice just putting drugs on the street. It takes a couple days for the extra supply to work its way down. People gotta buy 'em and use 'em, then you get your juice."

"Okay, Chavez, I see that." Sometimes I think I should spend more time on the street, overseeing day-to-day operations. Maybe then I wouldn't sound like an amateur. "Just make it happen as quickly as possible. Overpay for the product and give the shit away if you have to. Just make sure both ends know it's a temporary arrangement."

Our tags were the next order of business. The extra juice wouldn't mean anything unless it was accessible to us and could be channeled wherever we might need it. That's where graffiti magic came in. Rashan had authorized a major infrastructure project, and we needed taggers on the street expanding the network throughout the city. Anyone who's been to Crenshaw knows there's lots of graffiti already, but we didn't have full coverage and the increased flow of juice through the grid was going to cause bottlenecks and blackouts.

This was an easier problem to solve, and it just reinforced how replaceable Jamal was, and how meaningless his murder seemed as a result. Chavez told me we had twenty-seven taggers working in Crenshaw. He wanted to double that number, bringing in people from the surrounding neighborhoods. That's a lot of kids with spray cans and some juice. Jamal just wouldn't have made that big a difference.

"The only trick with the taggers is we need to move 'em out there fast," Chavez said. "There's no point turning up the juice if we can't do anything with it. We need the tags in place before everything else starts jumping."

"Get whoever you need, but bring them in from EasLos, Pasadena, maybe Santa Monica. Stay at full capacity in the hoods around Crenshaw."

Chavez was quiet for a few seconds. "You think this thing is gonna escalate, Domino?"

I thought about my instructions to leave the bait in the water. Then I thought about letting my people die without even warning them of the danger. The hell with that, it was lousy bait anyway. I already knew I wasn't going to learn much from another murder scene. Papa Danwe might miss a couple crumbs, but he'd keep the big secrets hidden.

"I don't know for sure, but I think it might. We've lost two guys already. If there has to be a next one, he goes down fighting. Put the word out for everyone to man the battle stations."

"Consider it done, boss. And Domino?"

"Yeah?"

"You lit up Crenshaw like a five-alarm fire with that shit you did on the playground last night, *chola*."

"Well, tough shit. I did what I thought I needed to do, and I tried to clean up—"

"No, boss, that's not what I mean. The fucking playground was still glowing this morning. Most of the guys have never seen anything like that, and that includes me. No one really knows what you did out there, but everyone knows you're going all-in for Jamal and Jimmy."

I wasn't sure what to say, so I didn't say anything.

"The thing is, and I speak for everyone—if it's gonna be war, I'm glad you're on our side."

After I wrapped up the war preparations with Chavez, I called Sonny Kim and Ilya Zunin to arrange a sit-down. Both were lieutenants in their own outfits, more or less my counterparts. Like Terrence Cole, I guess, but unlike Terrence, I'd actually worked with these guys in the past. Relations between our outfits were about as cordial as they got in the L.A. underworld, and I needed to know if they'd come down on our side in a war with Papa Danwe.

We met in a corner booth at a dive bar in Hollywood. Zunin, the Russian, got there first, a little after noon. He was in much better shape than Anton, and his track suit had about three fewer Xs on the tag.

Zunin slid into the booth and reached across the table to shake my hand. His knuckles, wrists and forearms were decorated with intricate tattoos. There were Orthodox crosses, Russian eagles, Cyrillic characters and a lot of other things I couldn't decipher. More tats curled out of his collar around his neck. The Russian outfits were even more into tattoos than the gangbangers in South Central.

"Domino, is good to see you. You look beautiful, almost as good as Russian girl. I am becoming to be thirsty. We must drink." Zunin may have exercised more than Anton, but his English was a lot worse. He flagged down a waitress and ordered a bottle of vodka. The waitress started to protest that they didn't offer bottle service, but she changed her mind when Zunin peeled a couple hundreds off his roll and stuffed them in her apron.

Sonny Kim walked in as the waitress was leaving. He was small, Asian, wearing cheap slacks, a short-sleeved dress shirt and sneakers. He looked about fifty, but I knew he was older.

"Three glasses," I called to the waitress. Zunin looked over his shoulder and saw Kim, then frowned at me.

"I thought this is private meeting, Domino."

I stood and shook hands with Kim, gesturing for him to sit by Zunin. I wanted to watch both of them while we talked, and didn't want them watching each other.

"You know Sonny Kim, Ilya," I said. The two men looked at each other for a moment and then shook hands.

"I asked you both to meet me here because I wish to discuss matters of interest to all of our organizations."

Kim spoke up. "With respect, Ms. Riley, from what I have heard, the problems you are having are regrettable, but I do not think they concern us."

"Da," Zunin said. "Your dead African is no business of ours." Political correctness hadn't yet reached Russia—at least not the neighborhoods Zunin had come from.

"Two dead," Kim corrected him. "And the one this morning wasn't African, as you so crudely put it."

Zunin scowled at him, but then looked to me for confirmation. I nodded.

"That's right. Two unsanctioned and unprovoked attacks on Shanar Rashan's outfit." I used the boss's full name for effect. Rashan had more juice than the guys they answered to. I belonged to the stronger outfit. I knew it, and they knew it. The waitress returned and set out our drinks, and that gave them both time to think about it.

"These offenses will not stand, of course," I continued once the waitress had gone. "There will be a response. In uncertain times like these, Mr. Rashan needs to know who his friends are."

"Do you know who is the hitter, Domino?" Zunin asked. He was eyeing the vodka bottle, but I was the host and he'd wait for me to pour. He ordered, he paid, but I had to pour the booze in his glass. I decided I'd make him wait for it.

"We know the outfit that's responsible. At this stage, I'd like to know if either of you have heard anything that might be of assistance to us."

"You think we have something to do with it?" If Zunin was offended, he wasn't showing it. His pale eyes were steady and utterly devoid of emotion.

"Not at all, Ilya. Mr. Rashan has long valued the friendship of your organization."

"We have learned of the murders, of course," said Kim, "and something of their nature. There are many secrets in the underworld, Ms. Riley, but sometimes fewer than we might wish."

*Your spies are everywhere, in other words.* I didn't hold it against him. If he didn't know what had happened, I'd have lost some respect for him. He'd scored a couple points on Zunin when he revealed that he already knew about the second hit.

"So you've learned nothing else about these events, Sonny?"

"Sadly, that is correct. To be completely frank, Ms. Riley, we were not just surprised, we were shocked."

"No one is wanting war, Domino," said Zunin. "And what else could this mean? Is very bad."

"Mr. Rashan doesn't want a war, Ilya. But if it comes to that, what is your organization's position?"

Zunin remained silent, staring at me with those cold blue eyes. I knew he was thinking it through, playing through scenarios in his mind. In the underworld, there are no real friendships between the outfits. But that doesn't mean there aren't mutually beneficial alliances, however temporary.

Kim cleared his throat. "Speaking for my organization, we consider Mr. Rashan our honored friend. We will treat any attack on your outfit as an attack on our own, and we are confident Mr. Rashan will prevail if conflict cannot be averted."

That was probably the opposite of the calculation Kim was really making. If there was a war, he believed Rashan was likely to win, and that's why his outfit would back us. It was good enough for me.

"We are friends with Rashan longer than the Koreans," Zunin said, sparing a cold glance at Kim. "We stand with you, Domino."

"Mr. Rashan will be very pleased to learn of your support and friendship," I said, speaking to both of them. "It is greatly prized and will be richly rewarded."

I poured the shots and we raised our glasses.

"To friendship," I toasted.

"To victory," Zunin said.

"For honor," added Kim.

We all put some juice in it, and just like that, an alliance was forged.

# five

A lot of Angelinos think of South Central as a war zone. Maybe not Baghdad circa 2006, but the kind of place where drive-bys are routine and white folks regularly get dragged out of their cars and curb stomped.

The truth is, South Central is a lot of different towns and neighborhoods, and most of them aren't any worse from day to day than the sprawling trailer parks in the Valley and a whole lot less sleazy than most of Hollywood. Still, much of the God-fearing, law-abiding, and more sheltered citizenry thinks of South Central as a powder keg, even if they never speak of it in polite company. They think of it that way because the fuse has been lit before, in 1965 and again in 1992. A lot of people figure when the Big One finally comes, it won't be a quake—it'll be a meltdown in the hoods and barrios.

I got the same vibe as I drove through the streets of Inglewood that afternoon. It was riot weather in South Central L.A.

People were out on the streets, and not just lounging on porches or lawns, or hanging on the street corners. They were moving in packs with nowhere to go and nothing to do but evil. Most were young males, but not all, and the gang colors, wife-beaters and chinos were joined by nursing whites and work coveralls. They were angry crowds, just a bad wind away from becoming mobs.

The people on the streets didn't know what was driving them, but I could see it easily enough. It was the same thing I was trying to do in Crenshaw. Juice was flowing through the streets like floodwater. It had been building for a while, and it put a hateful edge on everything and everyone in the city.

Humans stir up the potency of magic, but it doesn't really agree with them. Magic sparks up some ancient, animal part of the human brain, makes a person feel like there's something they can't see out there in the dark, something bad, something they should fear. It's not an irrational fear—it's older than rationality, and in this case, it's right on the money.

It's the same kind of unease teetering on violence that slithers through the city when the Santa Ana wind blows that old, dry, baleful juice in from the desert. But what was happening in Inglewood was a hell of a lot worse.

Juice was pounding through the concrete of the city like a bad migraine. I'd have to do more than drive around to see what was pumping it, but I had a pretty good idea anyway. Papa Danwe was into most of the same stuff as Rashan, but maybe a little more, a little worse—a few home invasion and carjacking rings, even some street-level extortion. The Haitian allowed independents to set up on his turf—small-timers like my mom—but he kept most of their take for himself. When they didn't come up with the juice, sometimes it got ugly.

The juice Papa Danwe had put on the street was giving people a bad trip, and it was intensified by the spiking crime and violence that was driving it. A perfect storm of negative energy, both magic and mundane. Riot weather.

At Crenshaw Boulevard and West 88th, a car was burning on the side of the street. A small huddle of people stood around it, staring in apparent confusion. Their eyes were glazed, reflecting the light of the fire, and their arms hung limply at their sides. They didn't speak or even look at each other.

A block south, a group of young men were working at the steel shutters of a pawn shop with crowbars and baseball bats. A small figure was crumpled on the ground near them—an old man or woman, probably the owner of the shop. Alive or dead, I couldn't tell.

I kept driving. To my left, I saw another prostrate form curled into a fetal ball, half on the sidewalk and half in the street. It looked like a homeless man. A fortyish woman in a cheap business suit, purse in one hand and cell phone in the other, was kicking him repeatedly, jabbing her spiked heel into his midsection.

I tore my eyes away from the scene just in time to see a ragged figure stumble into the street in front of my car. Ratty clothes hung from a stick-figure frame. His dark skin was drawn and pale, almost waxy, and his lips were cracked and gray. His Afro was an unkempt tangle atop his head, and he was pulling hair out in clumps. The junkie sprawled across the hood of my car as I slammed on the brakes to keep from running him down.

I got out and pulled the guy away from my car, and he collapsed in the middle of the street. I was trying to decide whether to drag him to the sidewalk when there was a crash behind me. The windshield on the passenger side of my car was shattered, and a brick was lying on the hood. People lined the sidewalk, watching me. Any of them could have thrown the brick. None of them looked like they wanted to be friends. I jumped back in my car and sped away. Fifty feet farther down the street, I stopped and retrieved the brick. I'd run it through Wikipedia and track it back to the thrower if I couldn't buff the fucking scratch out of the hood.

I put the car in gear and cruised slowly down the street, watching as the city went mad. As I approached the signal at West 120th, a patrol cruiser sped through the intersection ahead, making for the nearest on-ramp to the freeway. Running from the storm.

I got on my cell and called Chavez.

"Inglewood's going to burn," I told him when he answered the phone. "There's enough juice on the street to feed an army a hundred times the size of anything Papa Danwe has."

"We've gotten reports from Watts, too, Domino. More of the same. He's flooding the fucking torpedo tubes, *chola*."

"And we're flooding ours, only we've got bigger torpedoes."

"We're getting it done, D."

"I know you are, Chavez, but I don't want riots in Crenshaw."

"There's not much we can do about that. We pump up the volume like you want, people are going to wig out. You know how it works."

"Yeah, we can't prepare for war without amping up the juice, and probably things will go to hell. But we don't have to stand around watching people get killed. We can try to control it."

"What you want me to do, D?"

"Bring in more soldiers—whatever you need. I want to put more people on the street. Protect civilians, homes, businesses.

And put everyone on a shift rotation if you can. We don't want our own guys going ape-shit."

"It'll be complicated, boss. It might slow things down—"

"Bullshit, Chavez. You need more resources, you tell me. I'll get you what you need. But don't tell me you can't do it."

"Okay, Domino. I'll make it happen."

"I know you will. I want to know when everything's in place. Call me."

I clicked off the cell and tossed it on the seat. I turned left onto El Segundo and kept driving, though I wasn't really sure what I was looking for. I knew Papa Danwe had ramped up his operations, but most of that would be safely hidden from view unless I really went looking for it. Anyway, the juice was all I needed to see.

The juice.

All that juice was pointless unless Papa Danwe could do something with it. Just like our outfit in Crenshaw, the sorcerer needed to channel it, contain it, so it could be tapped when and where he needed it.

I stopped on the side of the street and got out. I dropped a protective spell on the Lincoln. It wouldn't hold up long if people started chucking bricks at it or set it on fire, but it was better than nothing.

It wasn't easy to get at the juice. There was plenty of it, but it wasn't mine, wasn't flowing on my territory. The tags were pulling it out of the air and the asphalt and channeling it somewhere else, for someone else.

I started walking, following the graffiti and the magic that flowed through it like blood through arteries. It didn't take long to see the patterns. All the juice from the surrounding blocks was flowing to a central location, like the drain at the bottom of a swimming pool. Papa Danwe was filling Inglewood with magic and then sucking it dry.

I followed the juice to an old factory that hadn't been used since the American economy had a manufacturing sector. Almost every inch of the grime-darkened brick was covered in layers of intricate tags. A row of large windows, many of them broken out or painted over, extended the length of each side of the building just below the roofline. Back in the day, they'd probably provided what little ventilation the factory enjoyed. Chain-link fencing topped by razor wire surrounded the site. Unlike the sorry excuse for a building, the fence looked new.

I ducked into the dark recess of an empty storefront across the street. "It is natural to give a clear view of the world after accepting the idea that it must be clear," I said. The eye in the sky spell is like my own invisible skycam, and I can even rig it for audio. I sent it flying toward the factory at an altitude of about fifty feet.

When it drew even with the chain-link fence, the eye stopped, like it had run into a wall. That, of course, was exactly what had happened. The factory grounds were warded.

Even so, the eye allowed me to see plenty from the edge of the site. The first thing that caught my attention was the metal tower extending from the roof of the building, maybe a radio antenna or satellite tower. Like the fence, the tower looked new and the unpainted metal dully reflected the sunlight. There were no power lines leading to the tower that I could see, but there did seem to be some kind of gadgetry at the top. I zoomed the eye in as far as it would go but still couldn't make out any details.

I couldn't see magic through the eye, but I could sense the ley line running under the factory, and I could feel something pulling at that magic, drawing it up through the earth to the surface.

I could also see that the entire site inside the fence was crawling with gangbangers. Papa Danwe had thugs out front, guarding the gate in the fence. There were patrols moving along the perimeter of the fence and the walls of the factory. There must have been at least thirty outfit guys in there, and those were just the ones I could see. They were armed to the teeth, in broad daylight. Even in Inglewood, that kind of thing draws attention. Clearly Papa Danwe felt the time for subtlety had passed.

I had no idea what this place was, but I knew I didn't like it. I also knew I'd have to get a better look at it, and that meant getting inside. I dropped the eye and spun my wallflower spell. It wouldn't make me invisible in any physical sense, but I'd go unnoticed by the gangbangers as long as I didn't get too close.

The warding spell was encircling the factory site, forming a massive cylinder of invisible force. The spell was powered by a small portion of the juice flowing into the site, tied into the graffiti network in four places—north, south, east and west—along its perimeter.

The ward was solid work, but it wasn't the kind of first-rate craft I would have expected from Papa Danwe. More likely, one of his henchmen had constructed the spell. That was good, because it meant I had a shot at disabling it. The simple approach would be brute force. If I hit the ward with enough chaos magic to undermine its structural integrity, it would come apart like a spiderweb in a strong wind.

Of course, the simple approach would be really stupid. It would drop the whole barrier and it would probably set off alarms. It would likely alert all the gangbangers that they were under attack. And while it would be simple, it wouldn't be easy. It would take a lot of juice, and I wasn't sure there was much left that wasn't already being pumped into the factory.

The easy approach was to pull the plug. If I severed each of the four connections between the warding spell and the graffiti network that was feeding it, I could probably drop the whole thing. I didn't really want to do that, either. In a best case scenario, it might be interpreted as a failure rather than an attack, but I didn't think the best case scenario was very likely.

Fortunately I had another option. I went around to the east side of the building and crept up to the fence. A gangbanger stood on the other side about thirty feet away from me. He had a MAC-10 slung over his shoulder, and his rings, gold chains and even some of his tats were juiced. He didn't look to be a particularly strong sorcerer, but he was prepared.

The gangbanger looked right through my wallflower spell as I went to work on the ward. The endpoint of the graffiti network charging the spell was a telephone pole about ten feet outside the fence. It was layered in tags, grabbing juice from the incoming flow and rerouting it into the spell. It was decent work, but I couldn't help noticing it wasn't as elegant or efficient as the tags Jamal had put down. Some of the juice was bleeding out of the glyphs, evaporating into the air. I started pulling in that lost energy to power my spell.

The chaos magic I hit the graffiti node with was about as complicated as a typical computer virus. It infiltrated the arcane structure of the tag and overrode it with conflicting instructions. It wasn't sophisticated enough to actually reprogram the tag. It just made it stop working.

The warding spell was still taking in juice from three of the four points, so it didn't go down. But the loss of one of the graffiti nodes was enough to weaken it at the point of failure. I spun my levitation spell and floated over the fence, punched through the compromised barrier with a little juice and landed inside.

I crept up to the building, being careful to keep as much distance as possible between me and the gangbanger on guard duty. I dodged a roaming patrol and approached the wall of the building, angling for a side door that didn't look like it saw a lot of traffic. I peered at the door with my witch sight and saw that it, too, was warded. The protective spells were being fed by the tags laid down on the brick walls around the door, and I used the same chaos magic I'd used on the perimeter ward to defeat them. I waited until another patrol went by, then I spun my B&E spell, opened the door and slipped inside.

Whatever the factory had manufactured at one time, all of the machinery had been torn out and removed. What was left was essentially one huge, high-ceilinged space the size of a modest airplane hangar. There were another dozen or so gangbangers inside, but most of them were lounging on cots that had been lined up along the walls, or sitting at folding tables eating, playing cards and generally wasting time. Whatever this place was, it seemed Papa Danwe's boys planned to stay a while.

When I'd first seen the antenna outside, I assumed it was just fixed to the roof of the building. Now, I saw that it was actually anchored to the floor in the middle of the factory. It extended up through a crude hole that had been cut in the roof.

The tower rose from the exact center of a metallic ring about fifty feet in diameter that had been set into the concrete floor. I used my witch sight and followed the flow of juice from the graffiti network into the ring. The magic surged around the ring like some arcane particle accelerator.

I moved farther into the building to the edge of the ring. I knelt down and examined it more closely. Silver metal glinted in the light from the overhead industrial fixtures. The ring was about two feet wide. I couldn't tell how far down into the concrete it went. For all I knew, I could have been looking at the top edge of a cylinder that extended all the way down to the ley line deep below the surface.

Whatever its actual dimensions, a lot of juice was flowing through the ring. I reached out for the juice, and I could sense that it was fed both by the graffiti network and the ley line. There was more juice coursing through the ring than I'd ever seen in one place, and I couldn't reach any of it. It was completely contained within Papa Danwe's ring, and I didn't have the access codes.

The tower was obviously meant to draw power from the ring, but I couldn't see any mechanism for it. There were no lines or spokes connecting the two. I got a mental image of raw magic arcing from the ring through the air and into the tower, like an arcane Tesla machine. Whether this was some uncommon design insight or overwrought imagination, I couldn't tell.

I decided I needed to get a closer look at the tower. This was tricky, because there were four gangbangers clustered around its base, standing guard. I crept close, willing myself to remain silent and unseen.

When I was still about twenty feet away, my right foot broke a concealed warding circle surrounding the tower. I hadn't felt it as I approached. I hadn't spotted it with my witch sight, and I should have been able to. Maybe I was dazzled by the magic show created by all the juice flowing through the silver ring.

The instant I broke the ward I was hit with a true seeing spell that dropped my wallflower, and an alarm bell began to sound. It tolled like Notre Dame at noon on Sunday.

I froze in place, looking about as stupid as a cartoon character who just followed his nemesis over the edge of a cliff. There was a long second in which nothing moved and there was no sound but the tolling of the alarm bell.

Then a dozen gangbangers unloaded on me.

I was just a little faster. I hit my jump spell and leaped to the tower, grabbing onto the superstructure about twenty feet above the ground. The hail of bullets and offensive magic turned the factory floor where I'd been standing into a smoking crater in the concrete. If the tower had been protected by a second barrier ward, I'd have continued with the cartoon theme, slamming into it and sliding to the ground.

There was no barrier, though, and I started climbing as soon as I landed in the gridwork. The gunfire and spellslinging ended abruptly when I made the tower. The gangbangers were well trained and disciplined, and their instructions were probably pretty simple. "Shoot intruders. Don't shoot the tower."

I climbed quickly, and I was about halfway up the tower when the first group of thugs started climbing up behind me. I didn't have the same concerns for the tower, so I paused long enough to lob a force spell down at them. It was hard to find the juice, even for the simple spell. I had to reach all the way down below the building and pull the juice from the ley line, before it was drawn up into the ring.

The force spell knocked all three of the gangbangers off the tower. They didn't fall far enough to suffer proper injuries, but no one rushed forward to take their place. I grinned and kept climbing.

When I finally got to the factory ceiling, I discovered metal spikes like lightning rods extending from the tower, and I thought my image of the Tesla machine hadn't been far off. I squeezed between two of the spikes and continued climbing through the hole in the factory roof.

Once outside the building, I kept right on climbing. I could have run across the roof to the edge of the building, and from there made my escape, but I wanted to see what was at the top of the tower.

I climbed another twenty feet and arrived at a circular platform ringing the tower that allowed me a more secure perch. Like the ring below, it was made of silver, and there were arcane runes and glyphs engraved in its surface. They were the old-school equivalent of the graffiti tags and served much the same purpose.

A silver bezel was anchored into the center of the platform, and a crystal about the size of a beach ball was set into the bezel. When I looked closer, I could see that the crystal wasn't actually set in anything—it was suspended in midair. The bezel was charged with enough juice to keep the crystal in place, but the crystal itself was dormant. It didn't take a theoretical genius to figure out that the crystal would be charged by the juice coursing through the ring below. The juice would arc into the lightning rods extending from the tower, flow up into the bezel and be drawn into the crystal. Then something bad would happen.

It also didn't take a genius to recognize God's own magic wand. The tower was clearly an arcane weapon of some kind. It was a weapon that could draw a hell of a lot of juice, not just from the magic contained in the ring but from the ley line and the graffiti network that fed it.

I had a few options, and my first choice was to knock the whole tower down. The problem with that option was that I couldn't reach enough juice. My second choice was to circumcise it. I didn't know much about magic wands, but the big crystal on the tip had to be pretty important.

I do a better job of learning from mistakes than the average cartoon character, so I took a good look at the contraption with my witch sight before blasting it. There was plenty of juice in the bezel, but I could get a good enough sense of its pattern to be sure it was just holding the crystal in place. No ward. I shrugged, placed my right palm against the cool surface of the crystal and blasted it.

The ward that wasn't there turned my spell around, punched me in the chest and sent me hurtling into the blue California sky.

This sounds bad, but there was an upside. The ward hit me hard enough that I cleared the fence and the barrier around the site completely. In fact, by the time gravity started to bend my trajectory into the ground, I was a good two or three blocks away from the factory and the gangbangers who wanted to kill me.

Even the downside, so to speak, wasn't as bad as it might have been. I can't fly, but I can levitate, and I could use the spell to at least take some of the crash out of my landing. Unfortunately I was tumbling through the air having just been hit by some fairly painful combat magic, and I couldn't pull enough juice out of Papa Danwe's turf to properly execute the levitation spell.

This being Southern California, I might have hoped for a swimming pool or at least a fucking palm tree to land in.

Instead I got a gravel parking lot. My half-assed levitation spell was enough to get my feet right side down. I hit the gravel, stumbled, fell, tumbled a few times and then skidded across the parking lot to slam into the brick wall of a body shop.

I lay there for a few moments, squinting into the sun and waiting for the pain to hit. It didn't take long. I couldn't tell if anything was broken, because my whole body hurt. My hands, knees and back were torn, and the abrasions had picked up most of the gravel from the parking lot. I'd managed to skid along on my face for a stretch, and my chin, nose and forehead were bleeding. Despite the haze of pain, I was able to focus well enough to confirm that my nose wasn't in the usual position. All of these new injuries were neatly layered over the ones I received from the ghost dogs the night before.

I forced myself up and started making my way back to my car. I might have lain there and died, but there were a lot of factors arguing against it. I needed to warn Rashan about the big-ass magic wand, and anyway, Papa Danwe's boys would probably find me before I managed to die. But there was something else that really got me up and moving.

I had a date with Adan that night.

## six

The first thing I did when I returned to my condo was grab the bottle of aspirin out of the medicine cabinet in the bathroom. I don't need a spell to treat pain. If I flow enough juice, I can numb myself into oblivion. But the injuries I'd sustained in the last couple days were serious enough that I needed a little more than pain relief. The aspirin was a useful prop and I had a spell that would, in principle, fix everything from broken bones to a critical appendix.

Sadly, I really suck at healing magic. Sorcery is funny that way. Even when you have all the pieces to the puzzle, sometimes you just can't seem to bring them all together. I could handle other spells just fine, ones that on the surface would seem to be closely related, like the purification spell that let me suck down Camels without regard for the Surgeon General's warning. That spell wasn't real healing magic, though. It was equal parts destruction and protection mojo, designed to vaporize the bad stuff and shield healthy tissue from harm. If I actually got cancer, it'd be about as much use as acupuncture. Probably less.

So I gave the aspirin spell a shot, but my expectations were low. I stripped off my clothes and chased a handful of Bayer with a glass of wine.

"We are healed from suffering only by experiencing it to the full," I said. The spell, as it came together, looked more like a tangle than a pattern, and the more juice I poured into it the uglier it got. I put my glass on the edge of the sink and examined myself in the mirror. My nose looked a little straighter and most of my cuts and scrapes were no longer bleeding. The pain had subsided to a dull, full-body throb, but that might have just been the juice. By my standards, the spell was a rousing success, but I still looked like hell. I topped it off with a purification spell to nuke any infections that might want to set up shop and called it good.

I caught a quick shower, taking care not to undo with the loofah what little work my spell had done. When I was out, dried and dressed, I put in a call to Rafael Chavez. I briefed him on what I'd found at the factory in Inglewood, and ordered him to put some boots on the ground in the neighborhood to keep an eye on it.

"We should hit it, Domino. Why wait for Papa Danwe to use it on us?" Chavez had juice, but he was still a man.

"Did I mention the wards, Chavez?"

"Yeah, but—"

"Did I mention that I couldn't even see a couple of them, including the one that almost knocked me into the OC?"

"Yeah, boss, it's just—"

"That's what I thought. We send guys in there without knowing what we're up against, chances are good this war goes hot, on the Haitian's terms, and our people wind up dead."

"You're right, Domino. I just don't want to give him time to use the fucking thing on us. Whatever it is."

"Neither do I, Chavez. If I was sure we could take it out

without knowing what it is, how it works, how it's protected, I'd say fuck it and send in the Marines."

"Okay, D. I can have some theory geeks look at it."

"Good idea, but make sure everyone knows this is strictly surveillance. No one goes inside that fence, Chavez."

"Thing is, boss, this is some fucked-up shit. Guys getting squeezed by another outfit, that I can get my head around. Making a move on Crenshaw, trying to push Rashan out, that I can understand. Maybe it's not exactly business as usual, but yeah, sometimes gangs go to war. We do shit like that, you know? We don't build the fucking Death Star in the middle of Inglewood."

It seemed obvious, but Chavez made an important point. The outfits survived by existing on the margins. We got away with a hell of a lot by not attracting attention to ourselves, keeping our heads down well below the veneer of civilization. But we did not, under any circumstances, draw unnecessary attention to ourselves.

The craziest thing about this new development was that Papa Danwe had apparently decided he didn't care. There would never be one hundred percent agreement on the rules of our thing, but you don't build a magic cannon in Inglewood. It was so far beyond the pale it would have seemed ridiculous if I hadn't seen it myself, hadn't felt the juice Papa Danwe was pumping into it.

It was like the Cosa Nostra deciding to build a battleship in the Hudson River. Apart from the fact that it seemed like a really stupid idea, there could be no doubt that someone wasn't just changing the rules, they were changing the game.

"I hear you, Chavez. It doesn't make any sense. Even if you can build it, I don't see how you can use it. You light the fuse on something like that, this whole party's over."

"Unless…" said Chavez, his voice fading out. "Unless you think the party's already over. Maybe it's like the nuclear option, *chola*. You only bring out the nukes when you know it doesn't really matter anymore."

"Maybe, but the party isn't over. It's not even winding down. Papa Danwe isn't being threatened. Not by us, not by any of the other outfits. Why go nuclear when life is good?"

"I don't know, boss. Maybe I'm wrong. Or maybe the Haitian doesn't see it the same way."

"Okay, here's what we do. I'm still not willing to hit that thing until we know what's going on, but I want you to put a strike team together. Have them standing by. If Papa Danwe tries to go nuclear, we take it out."

"How big a team you want, boss?"

"Jesus, Chavez, I don't know. Just some big hitters, bring them in from wherever. And send a few guys to run some tags in there, as close as you can get without blowing the lid off this thing. It won't do us any good to send in the heavy artillery if they can't get any juice."

"Okay, boss, I'll get it done. You coming down here?"

"Not yet. I'm going to try to get a sit-down with Terrence Cole. I don't know the guy, really, but I know him better than anyone else in Papa Danwe's outfit."

"I don't know, boss. I don't like the idea of you sitting down with those cocksuckers. They ought to come to us."

"Even Nixon went to China, Chavez. This is getting out of hand. If sitting down with Terrence means I can cool this out, I'll do it."

"If you say so, boss."

"Plus, I think he's into this thing up to his earrings. Maybe I can learn something."

My next call went to Sonny Kim. The Koreans had come down on our side, but they'd previously had a cordial relationship with Papa Danwe. They shared some of the same ghettos and generally managed to do it without killing each other. I knew Sonny Kim knew Terrence, and he was a good candidate for a go-between.

Kim promised he'd do what he could, and congratulated me on my clearheaded diplomacy in a time of crisis. Ten minutes later, he called back. Terrence Cole would meet me in Hollywood at the same bar where I'd sealed the deal with Kim and Zunin.

Unfortunately, there was no way I'd be able to meet with Terrence and still make my dinner date with Adan. Kim had arranged the sit-down for nine o'clock, and it would probably take an hour or so, plus drive time.

Then there was the whole question of whether I should be going out on a date with my boss's son when my outfit was at war. I considered it and decided I definitely wanted to see Adan if I could find the time. I'd made all the preparations I could. Sitting around my condo waiting wasn't going to do anyone any good, and besides, I had to eat. I was also still concerned about the Fred connection. I knew the vampire was involved in the escalating conflict with Papa Danwe, and I was concerned he had plans to somehow use Adan to the Haitian's advantage. So, really, I'd still be working if I kept my date with him. Sort of.

I decided I could make it work if Adan would agree to a late dinner. I called, and he did. He understood I sometimes had to keep odd hours—he reminded me who his father was, as if I might have forgotten.

I got to the bar at eight-thirty. I'd asked for the sit-down, it was on neutral ground, so I should get there first. Pick my spot, mark my territory, that kind of thing. Terrence was already there, waiting for me at a table in the back. He stood to greet me as I approached.

Terrence was the kind of guy you want to describe in one word. His word was *wide*. He had a wide forehead, wide-set eyes resting on wide cheekbones, a wide nose, wide mouth and a wide chin. He had no neck to speak of, but his muscular body was wide, too, all the way down to his feet.

Based on this, a person might think the guy had roughly the same shape as a city bus, but he was put together well. His skin was the color of strong coffee, his head was shaved, and all those wide features were pulled together in a round skull that was undeniably handsome, if a little imposing. His body *was* more or less the same shape as a city bus.

"Glad you could make it, Domino," he said, as if he had set up the meeting and I was running late. His voice sounded like a city bus would sound if it could talk.

"You, too, Terrence. Hope you didn't have to wait long." I offered my hand, and it was swallowed by his bus-size one. We sat down and ordered drinks. When the waitress had come and gone, we toasted our health and got down to business.

I was never a big fan of sit-downs in a situation like this. It always had a certain sting to it, like you want to talk while some guy is holding you down and doing something impolite. Most guys overcompensated for that by talking tough, so there were a lot of hard words flying back and forth without much being said. That got old fast, and with Adan waiting, I didn't have the time.

"Before we get started, I want to make something real clear. I'm not here to talk you out of anything, Terrence. If Papa Danwe wants a war, we'll give him one. But I don't see the profit in it."

"There isn't any war, Domino, isn't going to be any war. No one wants that."

"I got two dead soldiers and a lifetime supply of road rash says otherwise."

"We know about your boys that got themselves hit. Everyone does. What makes you think Papa Danwe had anything to do with it?"

I looked at my watch and stood up. "You sit there and pull your own cock, Terrence. I'm not going to do it for you. I got better things to do, and you're not really my type."

Terrence held up his hands, maybe in surrender, maybe to show me he wasn't pulling anything. "Sit down, Domino. We all just following orders. You know that."

"That's all you got? Maybe I'm talking to the wrong guy."

"It is what it is. All I know is Papa Danwe don't want a war. The Haitian told me this shit that's going on, it's to *stop* a war."

"How does any of this stop a war?"

"I don't know that." Terrence looked up from his glass and held my gaze. "Your boss tell you everything he's up to, Domino?"

"So you don't know what any of this is about?"

Terrence shrugged. "If Papa Danwe knew I was sitting down with you at all, I'd be in that mummy box with your boys."

"How does Papa Danwe think this is going to go? All the hard-guy bullshit aside, Terrence, if it comes to war we both know who's going to be left standing."

"Rashan's gotta go, Domino."

I laughed. "Papa Danwe can dream it, but that doesn't make it real. He doesn't have the juice to take down Rashan."

"The way Papa Danwe sees it, it's him or Rashan. I don't know why. I don't know if there is any why. I do know Papa Danwe ain't stupid. This thing goes a whole lot deeper than you or I can see."

"It's not that deep, Terrence. I can see the bottom pretty well. There's a lot of dead bodies down there, and I'm pretty sure one of them is yours." I said it like it made me feel bad, even though it didn't.

"The thing is," Terrence continued, "it's not your outfit that's gotta go. It's the Turk. Papa Danwe don't tell me shit, but he made that clear as day."

I could see where that went, so I didn't say anything.

Terrence locked eyes with me again. "If your outfit had new leadership, there wouldn't be no war. Not now, not ever. Papa Danwe would back the right guy, the right person. He'd back you, Domino."

My first impulse was indignant outrage, but I managed to swallow it. My second impulse was pride, but I put that away, too. My best bet was to play along.

"Let's say someone in my outfit was willing to stage a coup, Terrence. That brings us back to square one. The Haitian can't take down Rashan. Neither can anyone in my outfit. No one has the juice."

"With the right help, you could do it. You can get close. We can give you the opportunity."

"The opportunity?"

Terrence looked like he might be about to say more, but then he just shook his head. "That's all I can say, Domino. Truth be told, I don't know much more than that."

"It isn't much, Terrence. The thing is, it's not just Rashan. If someone did manage to take out the boss, what then? What about the rest of the outfit? You think they're just going to come along?"

"Yeah, Domino, I do. Everybody gets a bump up the ladder. Everybody gets a promotion. Anything else—what's done is done."

As much as I hated to admit it, Terrence was probably right. There was loyalty in the outfit, of a sort, but it only went so far. If you had the juice to make room for yourself at the top, the rank and file would fall in line. Everybody loves a winner.

I shook my head. "Jesus, Terrence. I'm not sure what to do with this. What would you do if you were in my shoes?" I gave him plenty of rope and even wrapped it around his neck for him.

"I'd take my shot, Domino. Didn't no one ever promise you'd ever get one. If you do, you take it."

I nodded. "I'm glad you said that, Terrence. You say Rashan's got to go. I say the Haitian's gotta go, too."

Terrence's eyes got a little wider than they usually were, but the rest of his face remained impassive. He stared at me a long time. If we didn't both have wards up, I'd have thought he was trying to get in my head. Finally he nodded.

"That might work. Like I said, no one wants a war. Maybe if you're a boss you think you can stay alive just by being the last nigger to die. I never signed up to take Papa Danwe's bullet."

Mob rules—Terrence and I were both working from the same playbook. We couldn't trust each other, not really, but at least we had a common ground to work from. "So what happens next?"

"I'll try to keep my boys on our side of the line. You do the same. We buy time. Events have been put in motion, Domino.

We can't change what we can't change. But we can make sure South Central doesn't blow up, at least for a while."

By that, I took Terrence to mean more of my guys were going to get squeezed. That might have pissed me off, but I believed him when he said he didn't know why Papa Danwe was doing it. It was pretty clear he hadn't been briefed on the whole plan. If I had to guess, I'd have said he didn't know much more than I did. If he didn't know what was going on, there probably wasn't much he could do about it. But if I got him to stall for me, slow things down where he could, it had been a pretty successful meeting.

"That's a start, but we also need to share information. We either trust each other in this or we don't. As a good-faith gesture, I can tell you that the Russians and the Koreans have lined up with us. If your boys decide to step across the line, they're going to find themselves surrounded." It was a pretty harmless piece of information to give up. Terrence probably already knew about it. And really, it was more a threat than a good-faith gesture.

Terrence wasn't impressed. "Papa Danwe told me it would go that way. He didn't seem too worried about it."

I shrugged. "I'm just bringing you up to speed, Terrence. Maybe you can do the same for me?"

Terrence looked at me a while, but his expression didn't change. "What else you want to know?"

"Well, how about Jamal? I know he was hanging out at the Cannibal Club. I know you do, too—though I got to say, I'm not sure how you can tolerate the fucking place. What was your interest in the kid?"

"Ain't never been to the Cannibal Club. Didn't know your dead tagger. Don't know what Papa Danwe wanted with him."

"I know you were at the club, Terrence. I've got a reliable witness puts you there."

"Not so reliable, I guess, 'cause I never been there, like I told you."

I searched his face and body language for signs of deceit, but Terrence might as well have been carved from stone. When a good liar decides to lie to you, there's not a whole lot you can do about it—not without using some juice on him. Still, I knew he was lying and he knew I knew he was lying, so maybe I could figure out from that why he was lying to me anyway. Maybe not. I decided to skip it.

"Okay, you were never at the club, but the vampire was. I know he's in this—I can put him at one of the scenes. Why does Papa Danwe need a fucking vampire?"

One of Terrence's eyes twitched a little. Then he shrugged, lifting his wide shoulders and letting them fall. "The vampire is in it, but he don't work for Papa Danwe."

"What does that mean? The vampire is an independent? What's his interest in this?"

Terrence shrugged again. "Never met the cat, myself."

"Or maybe you're saying the vampire is working for someone else? Is there another player?"

"Maybe. I think I said Papa Danwe ain't stupid."

"Who is it, Terrence?" I knew he wouldn't tell me even if he knew, and I got the feeling he didn't.

"It's a dangerous world we living in, Domino. Everyone's got to have friends. You got the Russians and the Koreans. I guess Papa Danwe got someone behind him, too."

It wasn't any kind of answer. Even with another outfit behind him, the Haitian wouldn't have the juice to take down Rashan. And even if he did, he wouldn't be likely to survive the war and enjoy the fruits of victory. But it certainly made things more complicated—assuming Terrence wasn't making all this up as he went along.

"So if our bosses are out of the picture, like we said, what about Papa Danwe's friends? Will they come along?"

Terrence didn't say anything—he didn't even shrug—and I realized he had no idea who the other player was. I was sure of it, and it was actually very useful information. I knew the handful of small-time outfits that were friendly with Papa Danwe. If one of them was the third party, Terrence would know about it. Since he didn't, it wasn't. If none of the other outfits were backing the Haitian, maybe they'd line up with us. But if it wasn't one of the usual suspects...who did that leave?

"Okay, Terrence. We're not going to be able to control this situation unless we know what the situation is."

Terrence nodded.

"So we try to back this thing up, as much as we can, and we try to figure out what the play is. I don't know about you, but I don't like being a pawn in someone else's game."

Terrence nodded and raised his glass. "I'd rather be the motherfucking king. Peace, Domino."

"Peace," I said, and touched his glass. I finished my drink in one long swallow and stood up.

"You in a hurry, girl?"

"Yeah," I said. "I got a date."

"I sat down with Terrence Cole." I was on the cell with Chavez as I drove to Brentwood to meet Adan.

"Did he say anything?"

"He suggested I could make this all go away if I just took down Rashan."

"Doesn't seem like a good career move, *chola*."

"Yeah, that's what I thought. According to Terrence, Papa Danwe doesn't have a problem with the outfit. He'd just like to see new leadership."

"He say why? I never knew there was bad blood there."

"He didn't say. Most likely, the Haitian knows he has no shot at this with Rashan in place, might as well try to get me to do his dirty work for him."

"That makes sense. What'd you say?"

"Quid pro quo. Terrence takes out Papa Danwe, and I take out Rashan. Then we make nice."

Chavez laughed. "Good play, D. And?"

"And, probably we both know we're yanking each other's chains. Still, I don't think Terrence wants this war. He says he'll try to cool things out, play for time."

"That'd be good."

"Best case scenario, maybe he takes his eye off the ball, starts thinking more about his boss than he is about us."

"Maybe," Chavez said. He didn't sound convinced.

"He also hinted that there's another player involved, backing Papa Danwe."

"Another outfit? Mobley's crew? The Rastas don't have enough juice to mean much, D."

"Terrence didn't give anything up, but I don't think it's the posses, Chavez." Francis Mobley ran a small Jamaican outfit, one that was known to be aligned with Papa Danwe. "I'm pretty sure Terrence doesn't know who his boss is allied with, and that tells me it isn't Mobley."

"Or any of the other outfits that bend over for the Haitian," Chavez added. "If it was, Terrence would know."

"If I can believe half of what he said, he doesn't really know much. He didn't seem too happy about it. I guess I believe him. He's got more of it than I do, but not a lot more."

"Fuck him then, boss. What's your next move?"

"I'm working another angle. I got a witness who puts Terrence at a club in Hollywood where Jamal was hanging out. Only thing, Terrence says he's never been there. Plus, there's a vampire I can connect with it. Terrence seemed to think the vampire might be working for the unknown player."

Chavez didn't say anything. Maybe he was waiting for me to say something that made a little sense. I couldn't think of a good way to tell him I was going on a date with Adan Rashan.

"I'm just playing a hunch, Chavez. I can't see what it is yet, but I think there's something there."

I could almost hear Chavez shrug. "Not much for you to do here anyway, boss. We're pulling it together."

"Just make sure no one gets trigger happy. I don't know what Terrence is going to do, but I want to give him a chance to walk this back."

"I'll make sure everyone knows the rules of engagement."

"Let me know if anything changes. And keep an eye on the Jamaicans, just in case. This shit in Crenshaw is bad enough. I don't want to get sucker punched by someone sneaking up from behind."

Miss American Pie is one of the only places in town where you can get a five-hundred-dollar Bordeaux with your pizza. There are fifty-one different pies on the menu, and each one is named after one of the States, plus the District of Columbia.

"What do you think about Maryland?" Adan asked, studying the menu. "It has crabmeat."

"So does Alaska," I said. "I guess it's a different kind."

"Hey, Washington has cinnamon apples."

"Sounds like dessert. How about New York? It's got pepperoni."

Adan laughed. "You can get pepperoni at Pizza Hut."

"Yeah, it's a classic."

Eventually we settled on Louisiana, with Cajun blackened chicken. I insisted on the house white, and Adan's wallet breathed a sigh of relief.

"What shall we drink to?" Adan asked, after the waiter filled our glasses.

"To your father," I said. "He introduced me to gainful employment, and he introduced me to you."

Adan smiled. "To my father." We touched glasses and drank.

"So tell me all about how my father gave you a job," Adan said.

"I grew up in East L.A. My mother still lives in the house where I was born. She's Mexican and my father was Irish— that's how I got the funky name."

"Dominica Riley. I think it's an excellent name."

"Yeah, well, the kids in the EasLos barrios didn't think so. Anyway, you know how the story goes. I grew up hard and fast on the street." I made a face, feigning nausea, and winked at him.

"Yes, but you were different. You could do magic."

"Yeah, there's that." I laughed. "It saved me a lot of ass-kickings."

"When did you know?"

"I've always known. I can't even remember a first time, because I was doing stuff, little things, long before I even realized it."

"But how did you learn the spells?"

I shook my head. "Mostly I didn't know any spells. This was

spontaneous stuff—that's why it was always little things. I was walking home from school and it was hot, so I made myself a little cooler. I didn't do my homework, so I told the teacher the dog ate it and she gave me an A. That kind of thing."

"And other things?"

"Yeah. Some older kids ran a dice game in a vacant lot near my house. I could almost always get my number when I wished for it hard enough. I'd just visualize it, you know, and it would happen."

Adan laughed. "You must have been the richest kid in elementary school."

"Yeah, but it wasn't always funny. The winning led to fights, and I started using magic to win those, too. I'd throw a punch and put a little juice behind it. Or I'd make the gun slip out of a kid's hand."

"And eventually my dad noticed you?"

"Yeah, that was later, when I was fourteen. I'd picked up some craft by then."

"How? You didn't have anyone to teach you."

"Some on the street. There were a couple guys in the neighborhood with a little juice—small-time stuff, but it was a start. I watched how my mom did it, too. That gave me enough of the basics that I could teach myself."

"Your mother is a sorcerer?"

"Fortune-teller, psychic, bruja, whatever. Tarot cards, palm readings, séances, stuff like that. She doesn't have a lot of juice, but she worked it in with the usual hustle and managed to keep food on the table. So I just watched what she did, and I figured out pretty quick that the cards and crystals were just props. They're just different kinds of containers to pour the juice into. I started doing the same thing with my spells."

"Famous quotations?" he asked, smiling. "I recognized one from the club, when you threw Manfred into the street."

I laughed. "Yeah. I think Mom owned three books—the Yellow Pages, the Bible and Collected Quotations."

"Why not the Bible?"

"It was a lot easier to look up good spells in Collected Quotations. And Mom would have kicked my ass for blasphemy if I'd used the Bible."

"So you were already casting spells when my father found you."

"Yeah, I was pretty far into the life, too. You name it, I was probably doing it—shoplifting, some burglary, rigged games like the dice."

"You were a total delinquent."

"Yeah, I was a thug. Really, I just wanted to learn more magic. And that's where it was happening, out on the street. I wasn't going to learn anything in a classroom."

"Did you drop out?"

"No, your dad made me finish. He said he wouldn't hire a dropout. It was bullshit, of course. Most of the guys in the outfit couldn't pass the GED if you gave them the answers."

Adan laughed. "He knew you were different."

"I think he just wanted to teach me how to finish something. It was a good lesson."

The waiter arrived, setting our pizza in the middle of the table on a family-size can of tomatoes. We stopped talking long enough to put away a slice.

"And then?" Adan asked. He reached across the table and pulled a little strand of mozzarella off my chin.

"And then, I'd probably still be out on the street if it weren't for your father. He brought me in, gave me a life."

"He trained you himself."

"Yeah. I already knew a lot of spells—I can memorize quotations all day long. But they were crude, clumsy, and I had a lot of ignorant ideas about how it all works. He didn't make me relearn everything. He just worked with what I already had and helped me put it all together."

"And then you went to work for him."

"And then I went to work for him." I spread my hands. "And here we are."

Adan laughed. I leaned across the table and opened my mouth, and he gave me a bite of his pizza. He sat back in his chair and smiled as he watched me chew. It was probably cute enough to make the other diners lose their appetites.

"And what about you?" I asked. "Who is Adan Rashan?"

He waved away the question. "You know, spoiled, lazy, rich kid who makes absolutely no contribution to society."

"I mean besides that."

Adan threw his napkin at me. "Well, I have a bachelor's degree," he said, with mock pompousness.

"What did you study?"

"I can't say. You'll laugh."

"No, I won't. Promise."

"Criminal justice."

I laughed. "Studying to be your father's consigliere?"

Adan frowned and I remembered the conversation we'd had at the beach about him and the outfit. Very smooth, Domino.

"No," he said, "I wanted to be a cop. Can you believe that? I just thought if I was stuck in the middle, maybe that was the right place for me."

I nodded. "Yeah, actually, it makes a lot of sense. And we could always use another good cop on the payroll."

"You wish," he said, laughing. "I wouldn't have been on the

payroll. I just wanted to help protect the people who deserve it, you know?"

"Sure," I said. "There are still some left."

"Anyway, it didn't matter. I tried everything—LAPD, sheriff, even CHP. No one would even consider me because of who I am."

"That's stupid. You'd probably be the only honest cop on the force."

Adan shrugged and smiled. "So, I could get a job that has nothing to do with my interests, or I could have fun and spend my father's money."

"Yeah, fuck the job."

"Exactly. Can I tell you a secret?"

"You have to now," I said.

"Okay. Sometimes I think I should be desperate to do something meaningful with my life, like teach in an inner-city school or something. But I'm not. I feel like, if they don't want me, then I'm not going to worry about them, either. Does that make me shallow?"

"Probably," I said, and shrugged. "But what do I know? I'm a gangster. At least you're not leeching off the underbelly of society."

"Well, my father is your boss. I guess I am. Anyway, I don't think you're a leech, Domino."

"Okay, then I don't think you're shallow." I smiled, and then watched him for a moment, considering. "You mind if an older woman gives you a piece of advice?

He grinned and shook his head. "You have to now."

"Okay. I obviously wouldn't be doing what I'm doing if I felt the need to contribute to society. I learned pretty quick, you find something you love and you do it—not for them, but for yourself."

"And you love what you do?"

Giving advice is dangerous, especially for a gangster. "I love the magic. I always have. The rest of it—I didn't make the rules."

Adan nodded. "Anyway, you're right. I guess I'm still just looking for something I can love like that." His eyes locked with mine and stayed there until I chickened out and looked down at my plate.

We drank some more wine and picked at the remains of our pizza. We shared stories about life in the outfit, and laughed and played a little footsie under the table.

Adan was telling me about a road trip he'd taken to Cabo with some of his school friends when I saw Jamal. He was wearing a Lakers jersey, baggy jeans and Air Jordans, but he was still skinless. And transparent. He was slouching in a chair a few tables away from us.

When I locked eyes with him, the ghost flipped his head in a quick nod and flashed me a lazy peace sign. He did something with his mouth that might have been a grin, but Jesus, the guy had no lips and didn't need to be drawing attention to it.

Adan was still immersed in animated description of his vacation, and if he was seeing Jamal, he wasn't letting on. The other patrons of the restaurant were talking quietly and enjoying their pizzas, so it was pretty clear Jamal was appearing only to me. I scowled at him and jerked my head surreptitiously in the direction of the restroom. Jamal bobbed his skull, pushed himself out of the chair and faded from sight as he started toward the back of the restaurant.

"Adan, excuse me for a minute. I'm going to powder my nose."

"Okay," he said. "I'll be here."

I pushed through the door of the restroom and saw Jamal trying to press the button on the wall-mounted hand dryer. His hand was passing right through the metal. He didn't really have any facial expressions to read, but he seemed frustrated. I made sure the bathroom was otherwise unoccupied, and then locked the door.

"Uh…hi, Jamal," I said.

"Hey, D, 'bout fucking time you saw me."

"Huh?"

"Girl, I been following you all day."

"Oh. I didn't see you until just now."

Jamal stopped poking his hand into the hand dryer and turned to me. "Yeah, Domino, I get that. Guess it takes some practice manifesting and shit."

"I tried to bring you back across. Last night. Didn't work very well. Sorry."

Jamal shook his skinless head. "It worked, D. It just took a while to get my shit together."

"That's good, Jamal. I'm glad I could help you. But now you have to help me so I can put this right."

"What you think I'm doing, D?" A knife appeared in Jamal's hand, a long, curved blade like hunters use to skin their kills. "I'm gonna go Freddy Kruger on that punk-ass bitch and take his motherfucking skin."

"What bitch is that, Jamal? Who killed you?"

"What you mean, what bitch is that, bitch?" He held up his transparent hands. "No offense, D. Anyway, you brought him here."

I heard what he said, but I couldn't make any sense of the words. I just stood there and stared at him. I think maybe my mouth opened and closed a couple times, but I couldn't think of what to say.

Jamal cocked his skull and looked back at me, that hideous grin slowly stretching his face again. "Ah, shit, girl, you really didn't know. You didn't know it was him." He shook his head and laughed. "You just hot for the cat, D."

"Jamal, are you telling me that Adan Rashan killed you?" It occurred to me that getting himself murdered might have driven Jamal insane. I guess I shouldn't have been surprised. People lose it over a lot less.

"Yeah, D, that's what I'm sayin'. Motherfucker took my fucking skin. Now I'm gonna take his." He flashed the knife in front of me.

"Jamal, you can't even dry your hands."

Jamal nodded, looking at the hand dryer. "Like I said, it's gonna take some practice."

"Okay, let's assume what you're saying is possible, which it isn't. You know I'm on the case, right? You got to leave this to me, Jamal."

"Yeah, I know you on it, Domino. But you didn't even know it was him. No offense, D, I know you got juice and I respect you, but I need some motherfucking justice."

"Okay, Jamal, just tell me what happened. You know, maybe we can work together on this thing."

"What you want to know? I met him at the club. The fucking name of that place—I shoulda known he was into some freaky shit. Anyway, I knew who he was and, you know, he's the boss's son, so we started hangin' out and whatnot."

"And then he skinned you?"

"Nah, girl, not right away. He said he liked my work, said I was an artist. We talked about my tags a lot, you know. That night, I told him what I was doing to improve my game, with the S-M and whatnot, and he thought it was cool. He wanted to check it out, said he might be able to help me hook up with some girls from the club."

I nodded. This was really detailed for a paranoid delusion.

"Okay, so we go to my place and when we get inside that motherfucking vampire is there and he sucker punches me and lays me out. Yo, D, I thought those motherfuckers couldn't go in your crib 'less you said so?"

"Myth," I said, shrugging.

"Damn, yeah, okay, so I come to when the vampire is nailing my black ass to the fucking cross. Motherfucker didn't even use a hammer, just slammed the motherfuckers in there." Jamal made a stabbing motion with his knife hand.

I winced sympathetically.

"So I started screaming and shit, you know, but there wasn't no sound, and I was trying to get my flow on but I couldn't reach the juice. I never was a violent brother, but I thought if I could get my flow I might be able to get away."

"What was Adan doing when the vampire was nailing you?"

"Making a circle and getting ready, chanting and shit over that motherfucking spook box he had."

"He was doing magic, Jamal? He isn't a sorcerer."

Jamal shrugged. "Yeah, well, tell that to my motherfucking skin, D. He was spinning spells all right."

I shook my head. "Maybe it wasn't him. Maybe it was the box."

"No, girl, it was him. I wasn't in your league, D, but I wasn't no rookie, neither. I know what I saw. He was using the box, but he was flowin' juice all right." Jamal's skinless brow furrowed in concentration. "I'll give you this, though, it wasn't normal, like we do it. He was sucking in a lot of juice, but it was different. He wasn't taking it from the street, you know, or tapping a line or a tag or anything like that. He was getting it from somewhere else, D, and it was cold, girl, that motherfucking juice was *cold*."

"Where was he getting it?"

"At the time, I didn't know, and anyway, I wasn't thinking too good with fucking railroad spikes in my fucking arms. But now I know."

I waited.

"He was tapping that shit from the place I been, D. He was getting his juice from the Beyond."

The hairs on the back of my neck stood on end. In my defense, they pretty much had to given that a skinless ghost was telling me about some kind of spooky death magic.

"There was something else, D," Jamal said. "I think those spikes they nailed me with might have been magic, too. He didn't want to even look at them, let alone touch them. Made the vampire do all the spike work. Maybe those spikes come from the Beyond, too, you know, and that's why only the undead motherfucker could touch them."

I shook my head. "Maybe, but they were just spikes when I looked at them. How did they feel?"

"How you think they felt, motherfucker? They felt like fucking spikes!" He showed me the ragged holes they'd left in his wrists and ankles, and I probably shuddered.

"Sorry," I said. "I meant, did they feel magic, or, you know, bone-chillingly cold, or anything like that." I saw the irritated look he was somehow managing despite the lack of a face. "Okay, never mind." I considered for a moment. "The ritual, Jamal," I said. "Did he squeeze you?"

"Oh, hell, yeah. He opened up that box on me and I could

feel it, you know, stripping away my magic along with my skin."

"The box…it's called a soul jar. He got it from Papa Danwe."

Jamal nodded. "He was talking the whole time it was happening. Said it held the juice of some King Tut motherfuckers back in the day."

"Yeah," I said, "it's like an organ jar. I saw this show on the History Channel. They'd pull a pharaoh's brain out through his nose and put it in a fucking jar. Only this one was made to hold a guy's juice instead of his brain or whatever."

Jamal rubbed his nose-hole and nodded. "I ain't got cable, D, but that's what he said, too. I'm just glad they didn't do my brain like that, girl. The whole thing with my skin was enough. When he told me that shit, I thought he was turning me into a fucking mummy."

"Is it possible that the killer was someone else, someone using a magical disguise to look like Adan?"

Jamal looked thoughtful. "That don't sound right. We was hanging out for a couple weeks, you know, before. Sometimes I took him home, even chilled in his crib from time to time. That night, when we left the club, he drove. It was his car, you know, that red Porsche. So if it was a disguise, it was someone living in his crib, driving his car and whatnot."

None of it made any sense. Adan couldn't be the killer. It just wasn't possible. And yet, Jamal was certainly convinced it was him. He wasn't lying. He believed it. He just had to be wrong.

"Okay, what about the vampire? Where is he now?"

"I don't know, Domino. I can't haunt his pasty white ass, I guess 'cause he's already dead."

"But you can haunt Adan? So that means he's alive. I mean, he's not a vampire or anything like that."

"Yeah, D, he's alive. He's really alive. Lit up like the motherfucking fire you set off on the playground last night. I figure it's 'cause he murdered my ass."

"What about the Papa Danwe connection? Did you ever meet Terrence Cole at the club?"

"Some of the Haitian's niggers hung out there, seemed like they knew the vampire. I never saw Terrence there, specifically, but you know, I wasn't there 24/7."

"Okay, Jamal. I don't know what this means, but I'm going to figure this shit out, man, so you can rest or whatever."

"Yeah, that's great, D." He pulled out the knife again. "In the meantime, I'm gonna go get me some motherfucking skin."

"Jamal, I can't let you do that. I can't have you interfering in my investigation."

Jamal laughed. "You sound like Five-oh, D. Anyway, how you gonna stop me?" He disappeared through the wall of the bathroom and then stepped back through a moment later. "I'm a ghost!"

I sighed. "Yeah, Jamal, I know. At first cock-crow the ghosts must go, back to their quiet graves below," I said, and bound Jamal's shade to the toilet in the corner stall of the bathroom.

"Damn."

"I'll come back for you when I'm done. Shouldn't be more than a few days. Work on the solidity thing. Maybe practice flushing or something."

Jamal was cursing me as I unlocked the door and went out to rejoin Adan. I tried to hold up my end of the conversation as best I could while my mind worked over the story Jamal had given me.

Adan was the killer. I repeated it to myself, over and over, trying it out. It just wasn't possible. The killer was a sorcerer. Adan wasn't a sorcerer. Therefore, Adan could not be the killer. I'm no Sherlock Holmes, but that logic seemed locked up pretty tight.

And yet, Jamal had seen him do it. If he believed Adan was the killer, what evidence did I have that he was wrong? He should know, after all. And Jamal hadn't just seen him do it—Adan had been hanging out with him for several days at least, maybe weeks, before he hit Jamal. That ruled out the possibility that the killer was an unknown sorcerer who magically disguised himself as Adan long enough to do the killing. Maybe I could see a way to make that angle work if I twisted it just right, but it would take a lot of twisting.

Leaving aside the impossibility of it all, I tried to reconcile all of this with the man I was sharing dinner with. He was kind, and smart, and funny and honest, and his otherwise hopeful and bright outlook on life was tinged with just a little bit of sadness and loneliness. It made him both strong and vulnerable at the same time. It made him irresistible.

And yet, somehow, it seemed that this same man had murdered at least two people with calculating premeditation in one of the most brutal ways I could imagine. He'd used a death ritual, channeling juice from the Beyond, to take their magic before he'd taken their lives.

I didn't work for the Peace Corps. I'd seen plenty of murders and done some myself. Some of my coworkers were sociopaths. But even in the outfit, there were limits. You just couldn't work with someone who likes to skin and crucify people, any more than you could keep a rabid dog as a pet. I'd heard about guys who went over that line, and they always got put down just like the dog.

This was real evil. If most of my world was shades of gray, this was all the way in the black. But what bothered me most was that I couldn't see even the slightest hint of it in this man.

Given my mood, the conversation wound down before long. We were both stuffed, but Adan insisted on ordering a Washington with cinnamon apples for takeout.

"We can save dessert for the next date," he said. Despite everything, I caught myself smiling at him and meaning it.

We drove back to his loft and I walked with him up to the door of his building. It was about midnight, and the air was cool. I was wondering if he would try to kiss me. I wasn't sure I didn't want him to kiss me, even with what I suspected.

Adan ended my speculation when he leaned into me and kissed me on the mouth. His lips were soft, and firm and wet against mine. He tasted like garlic and chicken, but that was just the fucking pizza.

I'm weak. I responded before I even realized what I was doing. I pulled him to me and kissed him harder. He put his arms around my waist and pulled me close. I felt his thighs and hips press into me and I heard him sigh.

Then I heard him growl.

He bit down on my lip, grinding it between his teeth, and I tasted blood. I tried to pull away but his arms were locked around me and he was pressing his weight into me, driving me back against the wall of the building.

He drew his head back and laughed, spraying saliva in my face. It was so cold it felt hot on my skin. His eyes were completely black.

"Maybe I'll fuck you when I take your skin," he said. It wasn't Adan's voice. It was as empty and inviting as death.

I reached for some juice and started to spin a spell. I'd recharged the pinkie ring, but he was too close for the repulsion talisman. The arcane threads of a combat spell started weaving together in my mind.

And just like that, his eyes cleared, his rough hold on me loosened and Adan was back. He hugged me and kissed me on the forehead, breathing in the scent of my hair.

"That was intense, Domino," he said, and laughed softly. "I think I forgot where I was for a minute."

"Uh, yeah," I said, "me, too. I think."

He squeezed me—the nice kind, where I get to keep my skin. "Call me tomorrow?"

"Uh, yeah," I said.

Adan smiled at me and gave me a peck on the cheek. "Bye," he said. Then he unlocked the door and went inside. I watched him go and wiped blood from my mouth with the back of my hand.

Okay, so my boyfriend was possessed.

# seven

I sat in my car all night watching the front of Adan's loft. I wasn't sure exactly what was going on, and I wasn't sure what I could do about it, but I wanted to know if Adan snuck out in the middle of the night to go skin someone.

In a perfect world, I'd have been able to use magical surveillance, like my eye spell. As I'd discovered at the club, though, Adan was heavily warded. The spell wouldn't even get a fix on him, let alone follow him around. So I had to do my surveillance the old-fashioned way. This really wasn't such a bad thing. I liked stakeouts, and I didn't get to do it often enough. I liked following people. I liked sitting in my car, listening to some tunes, wondering what surprising shit a person would do next. The odds were good that Adan was going to do some pretty surprising shit.

About ten o'clock the next morning, the door of the underground garage slid up and Adan's red Porsche pulled into the street. He slid into traffic heading east, and I followed.

I used the traffic spell, but I put a little spin on it. This was a kind of hybrid of the spellcasting I usually did and the completely spontaneous on-the-fly magic that was second nature to a really accomplished sorcerer like Shanar Rashan. It involved altering the spell subtly to produce a similar but slightly different effect. I went with whatever quotation I'd associated with the spell, but changed some of the words to create the modification. The result never sounded as good as the original quotation, but it got the job done.

"Life is too short for red lights," I said. The modified chaos spell snapped into place around me, insuring that I'd be able to stay one car behind Adan without getting cut off by some asshole or hitting an ill-timed traffic light.

Adan's first stop was a driving range about a mile from his loft. He parked the Porsche in the lot and pulled his clubs out of the trunk. If anything, he looked better than he had the night before, even dressed in a T-shirt and athletic shorts. He was beautiful. He was also possessed, but nobody's perfect.

After watching him go inside, I circled the block and fired up my parking spell. I slid into a space-and-a-half across the street that had been occupied by a black Hummer on my first pass. Then I waited.

And waited. Adan had been busy the last couple days, so I wasn't about to begrudge him a little me-time. Maybe hitting little white balls with a metal stick was the perfect therapy for victims of possession.

I was starting to think I should go in and take a look, that maybe he'd been possessed again, when I saw him come out, dressed in street clothes now, and hop in his car. It didn't look like he'd tried out for the PGA Tour or anything, but he did have a healthy glow about him.

The next stop was the mall, which I might have guessed. Shopping is regarded unfairly as a strictly feminine pursuit, but this was L.A. and young men with a lot of money and nothing better to do weren't afraid of a little retail therapy. Besides, a guy couldn't dress as well as Adan did without putting in some time. I parked my car in the garage a few rows behind Adan's and followed him in.

An hour or so later we were only on store number three, my feet were aching, and I'd decided that stakeouts were fine as long as I could sit on my ass in my Lincoln and didn't have to hike all over town. I was sitting by a fountain eating a giant pretzel and watching the entrance of Burberry when I finally admitted that this wasn't getting me anywhere. It was already after two o'clock, and I had no way of knowing when or even if Adan would be possessed again.

I stood up and tossed the remains of my giant pretzel in the trash. I noticed I'd gotten mustard on the cuff of my jacket. Swearing, I dipped a napkin in the fountain and dabbed until the stain was a duller shade of yellow.

I pulled out my cell phone and walked off a ways, lurking behind the mall directory and keeping an eye on the store. Anton answered on the third ring.

"Hey, Domino, you find the guy that skinned Jamal?"

"No, Anton, not yet. Listen, I need you to meet me at Beverly Center."

"Okay, what for?"

"I'll explain when you get here."

"Okay. There is the huge traffic outside, but I should get there in thirty minutes."

"Just hurry, Anton."

"Okay." A few seconds of silence. "Where are you?"

"Jesus, Anton, I'm at the fucking mall. Right now I'm standing by a fucking fountain, but I have no idea where I'll be in half an hour. Just call me when you get here." I usually tried to keep the ghetto out of my language as best I could, but I didn't have a lot of patience where Anton was concerned.

"Okay, okay, Domino, sorry. I'll hurry, and I'll call you."

Twenty-seven minutes and two stores later, I got a call from Anton. "I'm here, Domino. I'm at fountain, but I don't see you. Did you see the pretty girl working at Victoria's Secret?"

"No, Anton, I guess I missed that. I'm outside D&G."

Moments later, Anton ambled up to me, clutching an oversize waffle cone.

I glared at him. "Glad you had time to stop for a bite to eat, Anton."

"Domino, I'm sorry, I came in right by ice cream and they were giving the free samples." He nibbled guiltily on the cone. "It only took a minute."

"Okay, listen. Adan Rashan is in the store. I want you to follow him. If he leaves the mall, you stay on him. He's parked in the garage. You don't fucking lose him, Anton."

Anton let the instructions sink in. He nodded, but he looked doubtful. "You think Adan skinned Jamal?"

Yes, I thought. "No," I said. "Just stay with him. I have to take care of something. You stay on him until I can hook back up with you."

"Okay, Domino." Anton looked around and finally sat down on the edge of a planter, watching the store and eating his ice cream.

"And Anton," I said. "Whatever you do, don't let him see you."

"Okay, Domino." Anton scooted around the rim of the planter until he was partially obscured by the Cretaceous-size fern. He nodded at me and winked.

I found myself wishing for a spell that would pump a few extra watts into Anton's lightbulb. Some days we could all use one of those.

Back in the parking garage, I noticed a man dressed in black standing by a Ford Taurus station wagon parked a few rows behind my Lincoln. I remembered seeing the car at the driving range earlier. It was black except for a primer-gray hood. The man saw me looking and quickly got into his car. When I started walking over to him, he panicked and fumbled with the ignition. He finally got the car started and backed out of the parking space.

"All progress is experimental," I said, and killed the engine.

I leaned down and peered in the window at him. He was maybe twenty years old, with natural blond hair spiking from his head. He had a little blond soul patch on his chin and piercings in his eyebrow, nose and lip. He was wearing black jeans and a black T-shirt with a red anarchy symbol.

"You should probably tell me why you're following me," I said.

"Fuck you, bitch." The kid was scared, but he obviously wasn't going to cooperate.

"Friends have all things in common," I said. The spell would make the kid trust me, feel like he could tell me anything.

"I…I…" the kid stammered. "The voice…it said…" His eyes rolled back in his head and his body jerked once. Then the kid died. A thin line of blood trickled out of his nose.

I swore and quickly dropped the wallflower spell over us. I pushed the kid over in the seat and checked his jeans. No wallet, no ID, nothing. I went around to the other side of the car and checked the glove compartment. A few parking tickets and some CDs, but that was it. I dropped the fingerprint spell on the car and walked away. The wallflower would last for maybe fifteen minutes. With a little luck, I'd be out of the area before someone noticed him and called the cops.

I'd recognized the magic on the kid immediately. I knew

the smell of that black juice, and anyway, I'd run into vampire compulsions before. Fred was onto me.

When I got back to my condo, I went directly to my office—really just the second bedroom where I have a desk for my laptop—and fired up the TV.

I have two televisions in my house. The first is a forty-six-inch plasma bolted onto the wall in my living room. The second is a little thirteen-inch Zenith black-and-white that I've had since I was a kid.

One of the first real lessons Rashan had taught me when I joined the outfit was that a sorcerer needs a familiar. A familiar is a minor spirit the sorcerer binds to herself, a spirit that aids her when there's a big job to be done. The familiar's most useful role is to flow a little extra juice on the sorcerer's behalf, allowing her to work with magic that would otherwise be above her pay grade.

Rashan taught me how to summon a familiar spirit and then took me into the desert to perform the ritual. Traditionally you bind the spirit into an animal or an inanimate object such as a jewel, a lamp, a skull or whatever. I didn't have anything like that, so I brought my TV.

And that's how a jinn wound up in the Zenith. There are three things worth mentioning about this. First, I scored pretty high on the familiar-summoning final exam. Most sorcerers come up with a minor spirit with less intelligence than a mouse. The familiar is really nothing more than a spare set of batteries. I got an unimaginably ancient and powerful earth spirit—been around since the dawn of time, knows more about magic than I could learn in, well, do the math.

Second, while I might have hoped for a friendly genie in the Barbara Eden mold, what I got was Mr. Clean. That is, he looks like Mr. Clean, with the bald pate, the bushy eyebrows, the gold earrings, the rumbling voice and the steroidal musculature. His name is Abishanizad. I call him Mr. Clean.

And finally, genies cannot, in fact, grant wishes. At least Mr. Clean can't. Or won't. I tried.

I hit the power switch on the Zenith—this ancient artifact didn't come with a remote control—and the spirit appeared on the screen in all his thirteen-inch black-and-white glory.

"What do you want, mortal? Still wishing for a larger bra size?"

"I was fourteen when I made that wish. Let it go."

Mr. Clean is my familiar, but I don't think he's particularly satisfied with the arrangement. He's arrogant, overbearing, sarcastic, sexist and generally unpleasant. Then again, ancient earth spirit, unfathomable power, dawn of time—it could be worse.

"What do you want? I have things to do."

"Like what? You live in a TV."

"Springer is on." No wonder he's always in a bad mood.

"Tell me everything you know about possession. It's really important."

"It's nine-tenths of the law. Can I go now?"

"No, I mean the other kind."

"Oh. You don't have enough time."

"For what?"

Mr. Clean sighed, and it sounded like the Santa Ana winds wheezing in from the desert. "For me to tell you everything I know about possession," he said.

"How much time do I need?" I said, checking my watch.

"You'll be dead before I get to the good parts."

"Oh. Okay, how about I ask you specific questions, and you

answer them as best you can in terms that a puny and barely sentient mortal woman can understand?"

"Fine. It is not an insignificant request," he said.

And so the bartering began. This is why I don't call on Mr. Clean more often. If there's a downside to having a jinn as a familiar rather than an extra set of batteries, this is it. Everything I ask of him is a favor he says I'll have to repay in kind someday.

The key, here, is someday. I won't have to do a favor for him immediately, and in fact I won't have to repay the favors for as long as he remains my familiar. So the exchange is never a simple "I'll do this for you if you do that for me" kind of thing. The price is set in hypothetical terms of the sorts of tasks I might someday do for him when he's no longer my familiar. It's kind of like using a credit card when you're not really sure how much you're spending or when you'll have to pay it back.

"What are we talking here?" I asked. "Like, I could visit you one day and rake your sand dune."

"I don't live in a sand dune. It's not that kind of desert."

Really, it's exasperating. "Well, what then? How about a Hershey bar with almonds? You like those. I'd bring you one—all you'd have to do is ask."

"One Hershey bar, one question," he countered.

"I'm probably going to have a lot of questions, but I'm not sure how many."

"You could bring me a Hershey bar once a month."

"Once a year, duration proportional to the number of questions."

"Done," said Mr. Clean, crossing his arms. "Ask your questions."

On the surface, this looked pretty cut-and-dried.

Unfortunately I hadn't just agreed literally to bring Mr. Clean a candy bar once a year. I'd agreed to do some similar service, a favor of like magnitude. It was like throwing in a player to be named later in a baseball trade. Of course, there's absolutely no way for me to keep a precise record of these transactions. I figure I'll just try to weasel out of anything unpleasant if and when the time comes.

"I need to know how to protect a victim of possession."

"What kind?" asked Mr. Clean.

"A guy. He's young, gorgeous, he has these little dimples when he—"

"No, monkey brain, I mean what kind of possession."

"There's different kinds?"

"Demonic, ghostly, spiritual—benevolent and malign, to name just the most common instances."

"My bad guy channels juice from the Beyond and rolls with a spooky mummy jar, so I'm thinking ghostly possession." I described the ritual murders.

"If the entity is channeling juice from the Beyond, it is not a ghost. A ghost *is* juice from the Beyond, but it has no power to manipulate that medium. In other words, based on the evidence you have presented, you are precisely wrong. The entity is not a ghost, but it could be a demon or spirit."

I ignored the insult. "A demon—like a fallen angel?"

"A demon is not a fallen angel. The Fallen do not possess people. They are angels. They can manifest in the earthly realm and smite cities. Don't you read?"

"So if a demon isn't a fallen angel, what is it? Because I'm pretty sure I've always heard—"

"A demon is one of the Firstborn."

I just waited. Sometimes I can't bring myself to give him the satisfaction of vocalizing my ignorance. Plus, by baiting me into asking stupid questions, he was angling for more candy bars.

Mr. Clean sighed—again with the wheezing. "The First-born were the pre-Adamic race created and given dominion over the earth. The one created before humans."

I tried to let it sink in and basically came up empty. "Sounds like heresy to me, baldy." Sometimes I throw in an insulting nickname, just because. "You're lucky—back in the day, they'd have your chestnuts roasting on an open fire for that."

Mr. Clean's laughter crackled from the set's tiny speaker. "I am an immortal spirit of earth and air. I believe I will take my chances. Besides, it is in your Book, and once again, you have demonstrated that you are incapable of reading anything more challenging than *Cosmo*."

That was a dirty lie, and yet I knew I would never win a scriptural debate with Mr. Clean. Gangsters, as a rule, are never the ones sitting in the front pew on Sunday.

"Okay," I said, "forget the religious angle for a minute. You said pre-Adamic, as in before Adam. This is the twenty-first century. We know now the whole Adam and Eve thing was just an analogy."

"Metaphor," said Mr. Clean.

"I'm pretty sure it's an analogy," I said.

"Nope."

"You sure?"

"Very."

"Okay, just a metaphor then. Anyway, we evolved. There were lots of species that had dominion over the earth before us, like dinosaurs." A sudden, terrible inspiration struck me. "Dinosaurs didn't get bitch-slapped into extinction by a meteor? They turned into demons?"

Mr. Clean was rubbing his temples. "The physical evolves.

The spiritual, I assure you, was created. Your Genesis story is a metaphorical description of the spiritual creation of your race."

"So you're saying humans weren't the first race given souls?"

"Just so."

"And you're saying these Firstborn guys turned into demons?"

"Yes."

"Why?"

"Because they were given free will."

"So were we. Don't you read?"

"But you were given something else."

"Like what?"

"Conscience. Empathy. The knowledge of good and evil."

"Heresy!" I cried. "Right there, that's big-time heresy, I'm sure of it. Satan, the apple, that's when everything went to shit."

"It all went exactly according to plan. The Morning Star was the fall guy."

I crossed myself and eased away from the TV set. I'm a gangster and a sorcerer, but I was also raised Roman Catholic.

"Satan is evil," I said. "I *know* that's in my Book."

Mr. Clean shrugged his massive shoulders. "Yes, Lucifer rebelled, and he Fell for it. Hard. He tainted the soul of humanity with the knowledge of good and evil. But only because he—and a few others, the rest of the Fallen—recognized that someone had to do it."

"Yeah, pride. See, that's it right there. He thought he knew better than God. That's why he Fell." I noticed that I was shaking my finger at the TV, I suppose in righteous indignation. "Anyway...why? Why did someone have to do it?"

"Because the Firstborn were a disaster. They were created as they had to be created, creatures of pure will. Without conscience. Without empathy. Without that little voice in their heads to whisper to them the difference between good and evil. And so they were ruled utterly by their passions— they literally did whatever they wanted, when they wanted, without regard for the pain and suffering it might cause others. They didn't know any better. It was inevitable."

"So then, why didn't God just give us a conscience?" I asked. "I mean, assuming for a moment I believe this heretical bullshit that He didn't." I was starting to understand why my religion generally warns people off trafficking with spirits. I felt my soul getting a little overheated just having this conversation.

"The whole point of creating both you and the Firstborn was that you would have free will. You would be made in the image of the Creator. That is what distinguished you from all the other beings that had been created before, including the angelic host. This in itself is evidence that the Rebellion was part of the Plan. Lucifer, being an angel, had no free will. Ergo, he could not have chosen to rebel. Likewise, only beings with free will could be given dominion and bring the Divine Plan to fruition in the earthly realm."

"Okay, but version one-point-oh didn't go so well, so God had to try again."

"Yes. But the Eternal does not make mistakes. There is only one way it can do a thing. It is bound by its own perfection, by its own Plan."

"So, then...version two-point-oh, us, was going to end up

the same as the Firstborn, created without knowledge of good and evil."

"Yes."

"But God's hands were tied, so to speak, and He would just have to keep trying, the exact same way, every time."

"Correct. And everyone knew it. The Infinite could not directly constrain the free will of humanity—"

"So Lucifer did it for him," I finished.

"Yes. Just as the Creator knew he would. As I said, it was all according to the Plan. This is why there had to be a War in Heaven. This is why the Morning Star had to Fall. It was his destiny."

"Wait, God knew Lucifer would betray Him?"

"Of course the Omniscient knew it. Duh." Mr. Clean didn't usually go in for slang. He must have been especially frustrated with my sluggish cogitating. "All that unfolds does so in accordance with the Will."

"But," I said, flailing desperately for Sunday school lessons, "something isn't right, here. Before Adam and Eve ate the metaphorical apple, everything was perfect. It was paradise."

Mr. Clean shrugged. "It's all fun and games until someone loses an eye. Things started out okay with the Firstborn, too, but they went downhill fast. Humans took the apple. They had but one rule, and they broke it. Free will without constraint— it always leads to the same place."

"But they only took the apple because Lucifer interfered!"

Mr. Clean nodded. "Indeed."

My head hurt. "It seems like a paradox."

"Things do get complicated when one contemplates the motivations and intrigues of eternal and omniscient super-beings."

"What were we talking about again?" I asked, rubbing my eyes.

"Demonic possession."

"Oh, yeah. So the Firstborn, demons, they do that sort of thing?"

"Yes. They were cast out before humans were made, and they still lust for the dominion of the earth that was denied them."

"So if my friend is being possessed by a demon, how do I get rid of it? Exorcism?"

"He's not."

"He's not? After all the heresy, now you tell me he's not?" I was pissed, but this kind of thing is par for the course with Mr. Clean. Like I said, I try not to turn on the TV any more than I have to.

"Demons were created of this world. When they possess a host, their corrupted, physical forms—forms you would call monstrous—assert themselves. This tends to have pronounced and readily visible effects on the victim." He shrugged. "You've seen *The Exorcist.*"

"Yeah, green vomit, uninhibited head rotation, that kind of stuff."

"And more, if the possession persists. Eventually the host will be completely replaced by the demon, in both body and soul. From what you have described, your boyfriend does not exhibit any of these characteristics."

"No, he's hot," I agreed. "All I got were the black eyes and the creepy voice. Okay, not a ghost, not a demon, that leaves spirits. How did I know we'd have to run through all the options?"

"Not all. As I said, only the most common forms. If you

would like, we can also rule out animal possession, sorcerous possession—"

"Sorcerous possession? What about that one? How do we know it's an evil spirit and not an evil sorcerer?"

"Because the possessor was channeling magic from the Beyond. Can *you* do that?"

I frowned. "Not that I know of."

"Of course not. A sorcerer's magic comes from this world."

"Okay, fine, an evil spirit then. How do I get rid of it?"

"Benevolent or malign?" asked Mr. Clean.

"Definitely malign. As in, ritually skinning and crucifying guys."

"In this case, the distinction I make refers to the effect on the host, rather than the moral quality of any actions that are performed in the course of the possession."

"Well, I don't think Adan's getting any good vibes out of it, if that's what you mean. As far as I can tell, he isn't aware of it at all."

"Malign, then. He probably will not be aware of it until the spirit gains full control and his soul is consigned to the Beyond."

"How does the spirit gain full control?"

"The spirit will continue possessing the host, as frequently as it is able. You can expect more rituals. I have no way of knowing how many it will require. The more powerful the spirit, the more difficult it is to sustain itself in the mortal world."

"So the more powerful it is, the more time I have before it gains full control?"

"Yes."

"Great." Wimpy and slow would have been even better,

but at least this gave me some time. "So why is it squeezing the murder victims?"

"I have no idea."

"What?"

"I do not know the answer to your question." This was the first time Mr. Clean had said this to me. I'd have expected him to admit it reluctantly, but it didn't seem to bother him. "I can speculate, if you like."

"Will that cost me extra?"

"Of course."

"Damn. Okay, go ahead. But only a candy bar or two worth of speculation."

"If the spirit is very powerful, it may need to prepare its vessel for permanent inhabitation."

"I thought you said all it needed was full control?"

"In this instance, such a spirit would require full control of a host that was capable of sustaining it. The spirit may need to first prepare the host in order to possess it completely without unwanted side effects."

"What kind of side effects?" I asked.

"Destruction of the host."

"Oh. So why would it need to squeeze my guys for that?"

"The spirit needs to prepare the host, but filling it with juice from the Beyond would also destroy it. Think of it as interior decorating or home improvement. The host needs fresh paint and flooring, maybe some new cabinetry and granite coun-tertops in the kitchen, but the spirit has no such materials of its own. It has to acquire them from somewhere else."

"You watch way too much TV."

"I'm missing Springer," said Mr. Clean, the barb passing safely over his shiny dome.

"Okay, this is good. So how do I stop the spirit from gaining full control?"

"You could kill the host," Mr. Clean suggested.

"I'd really like to go out with him again. Next?"

"You could find the spirit and destroy it."

"But it's not possessing him all the time. Do I just follow him around and jump him if he tries to skin someone?"

"No, you cannot destroy the spirit in the mortal world without also destroying the host. You will have to confront the spirit in the Between."

"What's that?"

"What does it sound like, ape-girl?"

"Uh, the place between this world and the Beyond?"

"Right."

"There's a place between this world and the Beyond?"

"Yes."

Damn. That one was going to cost me a Hershey bar.

"Fine. How do I get there and find the spirit?" I mentally congratulated myself on the twofer.

"That is two questions."

Damn. "Fine, just answer."

"I can show you a spell that will allow you to walk in the spaces Between."

"Cool, and?"

"Where the host is, the spirit will be. The Between is a shadow of this world. Find the place where the spirit possesses the host."

"Like his loft?"

"Probably."

"Okay, let's do it."

"You will need a guide." Mr. Clean arched his eyebrows. "I could arrange one."

"I can't find his apartment on my own?"

"Yes, the Between is an analog of this world, so you should be able to find this place. But something will probably find you first."

"So it's dangerous?"

"It's the kind of place inhabited by evil spirits that possess mortals, and many other such things."

I remembered the ghost dogs that attacked me when I tried to summon Jamal. "Yeah, I can see that. A guide then. More Hershey bars?"

Mr. Clean shook his head. "No, this is more along the lines of a fatted calf, once a month."

"Pizza, once a year."

"Extra-large Texas on the solstices."

"Is that the one with refried beans and salsa?"

"Yeah."

"Done."

The spell turned out to be difficult. It was probably the most complex magic I'd ever tried, and it took me the rest of the day to get the knack of it. Mr. Clean, I had to admit, was a big help, but he wasn't very nice about it. Once I had the basics down, I picked a quotation for it and ran through the incantations until the pattern imprinted itself in my mind.

The guide was a lot easier. "When you arrive, call Honey," said Mr. Clean. "She owes me a favor."

"I can use my cell phone there?"

Mr. Clean glowered at me, his eyebrows bunching like two charging caterpillars head-butting each other. "No. Just call her name. Put some juice into it."

"Who is she?"

"A friend of mine," answered Mr. Clean. That's all he would say, but his eyes twinkled. That made me nervous.

I still had Anton following Adan around town, and it was getting late. Mr. Clean said it would be best to cross into the Between during the daytime.

"There's daytime in the Between? I assumed, you know, shadow world, it was probably always night. Maybe twilight, that sort of thing."

"I would ask you not to be daft," offered Mr. Clean, "but I know you can't help it. As I have already told you, the Between is an analog of this world."

"Analog, yeah, so it's like an analogy."

"It's not funny anymore, Dominica," said Mr. Clean.

I called Anton to find out where he was, and then met him in the parking lot at Gold's Gym. Adan was inside working out, and Anton was eating a chili dog he'd bought from a street vendor.

"I didn't lose him, Domino," he told me when I pulled up. "And he didn't see me."

"That's good, Anton. Where has he been?"

Anton shrugged. "We were at mall. He was looking at the suits, but I don't think he bought them. Then we come here." He nodded to the gym. "He goes in maybe twenty minutes ago."

"Did he meet anyone?"

"No, he is alone when he goes in. I didn't follow him in there, because I thought he would spot me."

Good thing, too. Anton wouldn't exactly blend in at the fitness club.

"Okay, nice work, Anton," I said, slipping him a hundred. "Keep this quiet and get yourself another hot dog, on me."

Anton smiled and nodded. "Thanks, Domino. It's pretty fucking good." He jerked the hand holding a napkin over his shoulder. "You want me to get you one?"

I declined, and Anton drove away in his Monte Carlo. I saw him pull up by the vendor and order two more hot dogs like he was at the drive-through.

I settled back in my seat and watched the gym, where Adan was lifting, treading or stepping his way to cardiovascular fitness. Or pretending to—his father's magic probably had more to do with his delicious figure than the elliptical trainer.

While I waited for Adan to finish his workout, I looked for a way to fit this new development into my theory. Papa Danwe wanted to make a move against Rashan's outfit. He summoned a spirit from the Beyond, or maybe the spirit contacted him. The Haitian made a deal, just like I bartered with Mr. Clean. He agreed to help the spirit possess a host in the physical world, and loaned out his soul jar so the spirit could do some remodeling on its host. Papa Danwe got to pick the host—Rashan's son—and the ritual victims. The spirit was okay with that—it needed victims with some juice, and at least in L.A., that meant gangsters. It also needed a host who could get close to connected guys. Adan had to look like a pretty good candidate. Papa Danwe also got a pledge from the spirit to back him when he moved against Rashan. He got a powerful ally deep inside his enemy's organization.

It fit pretty well—hell, it was right out of the evil wizard's playbook. It matched what Jamal told me, too. He'd said the killer was flowing juice from the Beyond. That was the same reason Mr. Clean had ruled out sorcerous possession. A sorcerer's magic comes from this world, he'd said. I'd been wrong—the killer couldn't have been a sorcerer. In fact, the killer couldn't have been anything other than a spirit from the Beyond.

I sat there for thirty minutes, wondering what I was doing. I didn't really want to leave Adan alone, on the off chance the spirit might stop by for a visit. But I couldn't be in two places at once. For a moment, I regretted sending Anton home. I could have kept him on Adan—he seemed to have done an okay job of it, despite the constant distractions provided by junk food. But if the spirit wasn't coming, there wasn't much point in it. And if the spirit did come, I knew Anton would just get himself killed. I really didn't need to see him without his skin.

The simple fact was that I couldn't watch Adan twenty-four hours a day. The only way I could stop the possessions and derail Papa Danwe's scheme was to cross into the Between and destroy the spirit. And I didn't like my chances at that if I stayed up all night following Adan around. I had to sleep, and Adan would have to take care of himself for a while. I took one last look at the gym, then pulled out of the parking lot and headed home.

The next morning, I prepared myself to cross over into the shadow world. Mr. Clean explained that I wouldn't be taking anything with me but me, so this really just amounted to a few minutes in the bathroom. Then I sank into my recliner in the living room, relaxed my body and mind, closed my eyes and worked my magic.

"I have harnessed the shadows that stride from world to world to sow death and madness," I said, and unleashed the juice.

I opened my eyes and found myself sitting in my recliner in the living room. The spell had worked, though. There was no moment of disorientation, and no precious seconds were lost thinking the spell had failed.

The colors in my living room were all wrong, mainly in that there weren't enough of them. Everything had a kind of washed-out yellow tint, like an old sepia-tone photograph.

Plus, there was an old woman screaming in my face and trying to strangle me.

"Jumpin' Jesus!" I yelled, for the first time since I was eleven. I grabbed the bony wrists and shoved the crone away from me. She flew across the room and landed in my fichus tree, a tangle of spindly limbs both human and arboreal. At first, I was surprised at my own strength, but then I realized I'd put a little juice behind the shove. Apparently, the effect was magnified in this place.

The woman was moaning and untangling herself from the tree. She looked to be at least eighty, and her clothes were elegant Jackie-O specials from the early sixties. Her hair was a chaotic white halo around her skeletal head, and her eyes might have been a pale blue if everything hadn't been painted in some variation of yellow or brown.

And she was cursing me. I was a slob. I was inconsiderate. I came in at all hours of the night and woke her up. I brought men into her home and made her watch the unspeakable things I did to them. And so on. I wasn't sure why she had to watch.

"Sorry," I said. "I didn't know I was sharing my condo with a ghost."

The woman stood up and straightened her dress. She sniffed disdainfully—of course, more sniffing. "I was here a long time before you, young lady. I was here before there were any of these wretched condominiums in the building."

"Well, yeah, I can see that now. Anyway, like I said, sorry. What's your name?"

"Mrs. Robert Dawson," she said haughtily. I suspected she'd say everything haughtily or disdainfully, at least when she was talking to me. "My Christian name is Margaret, but my friends call me Maggie. You may call me Mrs. Dawson."

"Nice to meet you, Mrs. Dawson. I'm Dominica Riley. Sorry about throwing you into the tree."

"I know who you are. I've been living with you since you began squatting in my home. In my day, there were no wetbacks in this neighborhood unless they were cleaning house or tending the lawn."

Great. I was sharing my condo with Maggie the Bigoted Ghost. She'd probably fit right in on the playground in Crenshaw. "Yeah, well, nothing much has changed. These days it's mostly white folks with a few of us gangsters to add some color."

"It's tragic," she said. "In my day, we kept the criminal riffraff in the ghettos where they belong."

"Yeah, we've gotten uppity, lady. Anyway, now I know you're here, I'll try to be a little more considerate. I can't make any promises about the men, though."

"Flowers," said Mrs. Dawson.

"Huh?"

"You could brighten the place with some flowers, Miss Riley. It's so terribly drab, what you've done with this place."

I looked around the washed-out living room. "Yeah," I said, "something in a nice yellow, I think. Tulips or carnations, perhaps."

"That would be lovely."

I stared hard at her, but there was no trace of sarcasm on

her wrinkled face. I shrugged. "Done, first thing when I get back. Right now, though, I have some business. Nice meeting you."

"Goodbye, Miss Riley," she said, and sniffed. Jesus.

I left the building and walked out onto the sun-bleached street. It looked like my neighborhood, like L.A., just with all the color sucked out of it. It looked and felt dry, lifeless—more so than usual, I mean.

"Honey?" I said, putting a little juice into it. Nothing happened. I sat down on the steps in front of my building to wait.

The streets were empty, deserted. I almost expected to see a tumbleweed roll by. There were no cars, which was especially strange for L.A. Occasionally I saw a shadow move in a window or a furtive form dart out of sight around a corner. Ghosts, probably, I couldn't be sure. It was quiet. No sounds of traffic, no birds singing, no children laughing or howling miserably. The only sound was a dry wind blowing, though the fronds of the palm trees lining the street were utterly still. A pale mist or fog clung to the ground and obscured my view of the streets beyond a couple hundred feet.

"Who are you?" a voice asked. It was clear, musical, like a wind chime dancing in the breeze. I looked around and saw... nothing.

"Over here," the voice said. I craned my neck in the direction of the sound. Behind my right shoulder was a tiny woman, about eight inches tall, hovering in the air near my ear. Dragonfly wings were a hummingbird blur at her back. She was cute, in an early Meg Ryan kind of way—short ruff of blond curls, upturned nose, impish mouth, slender frame and golden skin. She was also naked.

"Honey?" I asked. I had to admit, she was a little hottie.

Small, pert breasts—well, really small, but I mean proportionally—toned belly, gently curving hips and long legs, again proportionally.

"Yeah, that's me," she said in her wind-chime voice. "Who're you?" She put her hands on her hips in a Peter Pan pose and thrust her chest out. She was irritatingly perky.

"Dominica Riley," I said. "You can call me Domino. I'm Abishanizad's, uh, master, mistress, whatever." I offered my hand to shake and then, feeling stupid, modified it to a kind of pull-my-finger gesture. Honey just looked at me.

"Abby, huh? I was wondering where he'd been. You got him in a lamp?"

"TV," I said.

"Nice. More to do in there than a lamp, I guess. Still boring, though."

"Yeah, so he says."

"So what do you want?" Honey alighted on my knee and sat down.

"Mr. Clean—I mean, Abby—says you owe him a favor. I need a guide."

Honey laughed. "Mr. Clean, I like that. Not very original, but I bet it pisses him off."

I nodded and smiled.

"Okay, I'll be your guide. That'll clear my debt to Mr. Clean. I'm an excellent guide." She looked me up and down—as well as she could, perched on my knee—and winked. "What are you going to do for me?"

I blushed. "I thought since you owed Mr. Clean, I wouldn't have to do anything."

Honey shook her head, tossing those golden curls across her face. "Nope, doesn't work that way. If I'm your guide, I'm straight with the jinn. But I'm still doing you a favor, so you have to do something for me."

"Damn," I said, "all y'all work this way?"

"Yeah, pretty much."

"You like chocolate?"

"What girl doesn't like chocolate? Anyway, that's not going to cut it. Like for like. I'll show you around the Between, but you have to help me cross into Arcadia."

I waited, on the same principle by which I try not to ask Mr. Clean stupid questions when he says something like this.

"Arcadia. The mortal world. Your world."

"Can't you cross over on your own?" I asked. "You know, fairy circles, Midsummer Night…"

"Not anymore. Now I need help. So will you?"

"You're not going to possess anyone, are you?"

"Of course not! I'm a piskie. We don't do that."

"A pixie?"

Honey frowned. "Piskie," she corrected.

"Honey, are you dyslexic?"

"No, the word is piskie. You meatheads corrupted it, started calling us pixies." She huffed prettily. "It's offensive and insensitive."

"Okay, piskie then. All right, if you promise not to possess anyone, or, you know, do evil, I'll help you cross over." I'm not a complete airhead, and I was feeling a little nervous about this deal. But as far as I knew, pixies—I mean piskies—were friendly fairy spirits that cleaned your house and kept your milk fresh. What harm could it do?

"Done," she said with a little bob of her head. I wondered why I couldn't have gotten Honey as a familiar. Smaller than Barbara Eden, sure, but better than having Mr. Clean in my TV.

"I need to go to Brentwood," I said. I gave her Adan's address.

"Just off Wilshire?" Honey asked. "I know where that is. Let's go. Just keep your head down and try not to look like a tourist." I got up and started down the sidewalk, Honey buzzing along beside me over my shoulder.

"So, Honey," I said, "are you always, you know, naked?"

"Yeah, why? Does it bother you? Piskies can't wear clothes. They interfere with our magic, can't fly. I can wear fig leaves or garlands, if you want."

I looked at her. She had that concerned, does-this-outfit-make-me-look-fat expression women sometimes get when we're feeling a little self-conscious.

"No, Honey," I said quickly. "You look great. I was just wondering. You're very pretty."

She smiled. "Thanks! People say I look like Meg Ryan."

"Yeah, I bet you get that a lot."

I was thinking it was going to take a while to get to Brentwood without wheels when we disappeared into the mist and the world shifted. I found myself standing in front of Adan's building.

"Cool," I said.

"Yeah, things are a little different here. That's why you need a guide."

Just as there were no cars in the Between, neither were there any locks. We went in the front door and climbed the stairs to a short hallway with access to the two second-floor lofts.

"Any magical defenses will still be in place," Honey warned.

"It's okay," I said. "I'm authorized."

Standing in front of the door to Adan's loft, I took a deep breath. I hoped I was authorized. I could bypass all the other wards the outfit used, but I'd never tried to break into Adan's home before. I turned the knob and pressed on the door. It swung open and we went in.

The apartment was deserted. It was the usual L.A. loft, which is to say fake but trendy. The walls were bare concrete and brick, and the floors were dark hardwood. The wall to our left was comprised entirely of floor-to-ceiling windows, and exposed ductwork hung silent above our heads. It was one large room dominated by an open living area, with a small kitchen tucked in one corner. Metal stairs ran along the far wall to a bedroom loft.

I searched the place and found no signs that it was inhabited by an evil spirit. I climbed up to the loft and looked under the bed. I searched the closet and checked the tiny bathroom. I tossed Adan's underwear drawer and rummaged in the table beside his bed. Then I went back downstairs.

"Didn't find what you came for?" asked Honey. She turned away from the wall mirror by the door and flew over to meet me.

I looked at the mirror and back at Honey. "Were you checking yourself out?"

"No," she lied. "Didn't find what you came for?"

"No," I said. "But I think I know where to look."

In the Between, the Cannibal Club looked much as it did in the real world, but yellower. There were a lot of Goth kids standing in line outside the door—that seemed to be a constant on both planes of existence.

"Overdoses and suicides," Honey said and shuddered.

I looked at the ghosts. "They off themselves and then come to the club to stand in line? Don't they have anyone to haunt?"

"Absentee parents, dead-end jobs, empty relationships—they probably felt like ghosts even before they killed themselves."

I turned to Honey and arched an eyebrow.

"Sometimes I read magazines to pass the time. *Newsweek* had an article."

I recognized one of the ghosts standing near the front of the line. It was the blond kid who'd been following me in the Ford Taurus.

"Hey, kid," I said, walking over to him, "small world." He didn't respond, just continued staring straight ahead. I did the usual battery of tests—hand waved in front of the eyes, arm pinch, sharp poke in the ribs—and got nothing.

"He probably doesn't even know you're there," Honey said.

"No way I can get him to talk to me?"

Honey shrugged. I gave it one last shot, clapping my hands in his face. No reaction.

We went inside. The interior of the club was devoid of ghosts. It was also an almost uniform brown, the color of an old cigar. That seemed to be the best this world could muster when blacks were called for.

"What does the Between look like at night?" I asked Honey.

"Like night, only bluer."

"Huh."

I walked across the club to the dance floor and stopped in the middle. I turned around.

"Hello?" I called. "Anyone here?" There wasn't even the barest hint of an echo. The words just died in the air.

"I am here," said a voice from the brownish shadows. I recognized the accent.

"Fred? Is that you? Come on out here where I can get a look at you."

Low laughter, like rats in the walls. I couldn't get a fix on the sound. It was like a theater audio system that kept switching channels.

"Don't make me come looking for you, Fred. Let's have a talk and I won't have to put the beat-down on you again."

"Uh, Domino…" Honey said nervously.

"Oh, I don't think we'll have to worry about that. You're in my world now, Miss Riley."

"Your world, huh? I didn't see your name on it." It sounds weak, I know, but I was just trying to keep him talking, see if I could home in on his position.

I caught a blur of motion out of the corner of my eye, and turned. Something brushed past me, and I wheeled around. Nothing. Soft laughter seemed to float from every corner of the room.

I reached for the juice and started to spin a spell. Nothing happened. I recalled my battle with the ghost dogs on the playground in Crenshaw. Oh, shit.

"Domino, watch out!" Honey cried.

I turned to look in her direction, and the vampire hit me from behind. I never actually saw him, so I'm assuming it was the vampire. The force of the impact whiplashed my entire body as I was launched across the club and through the front door. I hit the pavement, skidded, rolled and crashed into a bank of newspaper machines on the other side of the street. I'd been doing a lot of skidding recently. I was getting pretty good at it.

I lay there, dazed, and heard sounds of combat from inside the club. Actually it sounded more like an earthquake having a go at the place. The Goth ghosts showed no signs of noticing

and remained standing patiently in line. I wondered distract-
edly how many of them the vampire had killed. Finally I got
an arm up on the *L.A. Times* box and dragged myself to my
feet. I started back across the street.

A shape materialized from out of the darkness behind the
shattered doorway and quickly resolved into a giant speaker
from the club's sound system. I dove to the parchment-colored
asphalt as it traced a low ballistic arc over my head.

I looked up just as Honey flew out of the club. She was
holding a tiny silver sword in her hand. Black magic—Fred's
juice—ran down the blade and sizzled when it hit the pavement. Honey was hurt. Glittering green energy streamed from
her wounds and hung in a contrail behind her.

The vampire appeared in the doorway. He paused and
straightened his tie.

"Domino, run!" Honey yelled, zipping over my head.

While I'd more or less missed the fight, a few obvious facts
came to mind. First, as I'd already seen, Honey was injured.
Second, Honey was fleeing. And third, I couldn't put together
a spell.

I got up and ran. The vampire's laughter chased me down
the street.

"See you soon, Miss Riley," he said, as I plunged into the
mist and the world shifted around me.

# eight

We arrived back outside my condo, both Honey and I having instinctively realized that my first sojourn in the Between had reached a logical stopping point. I bent over and grabbed my knees.

"So, what are you doing tomorrow?" I gasped, looking up at the piskie. She'd alighted on the stucco banister that flanked the steps to the front door of the building.

"No plans," she panted.

"Meet me here about ten?"

Honey shook her head. "I'll cross with you. You're going to bring me over, remember?"

"Oh, yeah," I said. "Now?"

"Sure. It's not hard. When you get back, just call me like before. It might take a little more magic, but no big deal."

I nodded. "How bad are you hurt?"

"I'll be okay." Her wings drooped and she was pressing her hand against a wound in her side. "Just need some rest."

"Sorry about that. Last time we met I owned that fucking guy. I can't cast spells here, though."

Honey shook her head. "It's not just that you can't cast spells. He's stronger here."

"Yeah, what's up with that? He's a vampire and it's daytime." I looked around. "More or less. Shouldn't he be sleeping it off in a coffin somewhere?"

"Vampires exist simultaneously in the physical world and the Between. They're active in the physical world at night and in the Between during the day."

"Oh, didn't know that."

"And they're much stronger here, close to the Beyond, than they are in the mortal world."

"Yeah, found that out. So what gives with my spells?"

Honey shrugged. "Spells are for channeling and manifesting magic in the physical world."

"This place sucks."

"In the Between, everything is magic. You're magic. Well, a magical construct, really." I'd added to my road rash collection when Fred threw me into the street, and Honey eyed the glowing blue juice soaking my shredded clothes.

"I'm a magical construct?"

"Yeah. All you can bring here is your magic, so that's what you are."

"So my body is stronger here, but I can't cast spells."

"Yeah, you could probably do all kinds of cool stuff if you knew how to fight."

I scowled. "I know how to fight. Fred just got the drop on me."

"You never even saw him. You're strong enough, but you don't know how to use your power here."

"So are you saying I need to learn kung fu or something?"

"No, kung fu is for manifesting ass-kickings in the physical world. Wouldn't help you much here, seeing as how you don't have a physical body or anything."

"What then? There's something I need to do here, and I'm not going to be able to do it if a pussy like Fred can kick my ass."

"You just need to learn how to control your magic in this place. Like I said, you're pretty strong, just inexperienced. Well, completely untrained, really."

"How do I learn how to control my magic?"

Honey sighed. "I suppose I could teach you."

I laughed. "No offense, Honey, but you're eight inches tall. And you have a sword." I noticed the sword was missing. "Where do you hide that thing, anyway?"

"It's a secret."

"Whatever. Like I said, you have a sword, and you can fly. I'm sure you're quite the little warrior-princess, but I don't think you're—"

Honey blurred, there was a moment of intense pain, and then I was on my back and staring up at the pale yellow sky.

"Ow," I said. I sat up, and Honey was perched on the ban-ister again.

"I am, you know," she said.

"What?"

"A warrior-princess."

"Okay."

"So do you want me to teach you?"

"I guess," I said, climbing to my feet. I felt the instinctive need to rub away the pain, but I couldn't tell exactly where it was coming from. "Can I get a sword?"

Honey laughed. "Of course not, silly girl. Where would you put it? Besides, you'd probably just cut yourself."

"But you'll teach me the kung-fu magic?"

"I suppose," Honey said, cocking her head. "It would be an awfully big favor."

I groaned. "How much?"

"Room and board when I'm in Arcadia."

"Huh?"

"I get to live in your condo. And you have to give me food."

I thought about it. It wasn't like she'd take up much space, and she certainly couldn't eat very much.

"Yeah, okay, that's fine. Mrs. Dawson isn't going to like it, though."

"Who's Mrs. Dawson?"

"Ghost. Real bitchy one."

"Oh. Well, the two of you will barely even know I'm there."

"Fine. So how did you knock me down like that?" I asked.

Honey blurred, there was a moment of intense pain and then I was on my back and staring up at the pale yellow sky. This time she was hovering over me.

"Like that," she said.

"Ow," I said. I got to my feet and rubbed my head, because most of my pain seemed to be settling there. "Jesus, Honey, have you ever taught anyone this shit before? 'Cause so far, your technique really blows."

"Not a human, but we'll figure it out."

"Maybe we can start some other time. I'm not sure how much more training I can take."

She shrugged.

"So you said Fred is active here during the day and in my world at night."

Honey nodded. "Yeah. It's really not much different from

what you're doing, Domino. When you cross into the Between, you leave your physical body behind. So does Fred, but he doesn't have any choice about it."

"Then I have to catch him in my world during the day and take him out. I think he's protecting something I need to get at."

"He must have been using the club as his lair."

I realized for the first time there didn't seem to be a sun in this place, just a diffuse yellow light that hung over the city like an inversion layer.

"I wonder what time it is," I said.

"It's about an hour before sundown," said Honey. "We can travel quickly here, through the mist, but it does funny things with the way you perceive the passage of time."

I mentally calculated how long it would take me to get to the club and search it for the vampire's lair after spinning some spells to distract any civilians that were there.

"That doesn't leave me enough time to get to him before he wakes up."

"He'll be out of there as soon as he opens his eyes. He's going to find a new lair."

"Yeah," I said, "but I know someone who can find him."

"You're going to bring me over with you, right? You promised."

"Okay. But I'll need you to come back here with me, probably tomorrow. I still need my guide. And you have to train me."

"Sure thing," Honey said, and we went inside.

Mrs. Dawson was sitting at the kitchen table staring out the window when we came in. She didn't acknowledge us, and I got the feeling she'd spent a good portion of her life doing the very same thing. It was kind of sad, and I wondered why she was hanging around. I'd always thought ghosts had a purpose.

I sank into my recliner and closed my eyes. There was no incantation this time, and it was a good thing since I couldn't cast any spells. I just let the pattern that brought me over unravel in my mind. When I opened my eyes, I'd returned to my Technicolor world. I got up and spent a few minutes trying to tidy up the place.

"Honey?" I called, pouring juice into the summoning. I felt the magic start to build and the threads of the pattern beginning to assemble, then it fell apart and the juice leaked away.

"Not that big of a deal, huh?" I muttered to myself. Then I tried again.

"Honey!" This time I tapped the line running under the building and squeezed as much juice out of it as I could wrap my head around. The summoning snapped into place, wavered and then held. In the middle of my living room, the world thinned out and went sepia-tone, and Honey buzzed into the room. I let go of the juice and reality reasserted itself.

"Nice place," Honey said, flitting around the room. "Looks better in color."

"Thanks."

"So where are we going?"

"I'm going to see a guy about a thing," I said. "You can do…whatever. Just, no evil, like you promised."

"Sure thing, no evil. Can you open a window for me? Just a crack."

I went into the kitchen and raised the window a couple inches. Maybe Mrs. Dawson would get some air.

"Okay," I said, "I'm going. Not sure when I'll be back. There's beer, wine and tequila in the kitchen."

"'Kay, have fun," said Honey. She was fluttering in the middle of the living room, hands behind her back, like a teenager waiting for her parents to leave for the weekend.

I reached for the door. "Mr. Clean's in the set in the office. You turn on that TV, it's your dime."

"No problem," Honey said. "Anyway, he's your familiar. What would I do with him?"

"Okay then. Bye."

"Bye-bye, Domino," said Honey.

I went out and closed the door behind me.

Screw it. A deal's a deal.


I stopped by a grocery store and then drove to Santa Monica. As always, the pier was crowded with people out to watch the sunset. Tourists took pictures and bums panhandled. Both tossed bread crumbs to the seagulls and dodged the shit bombs that rained down in thanks.

Moon Dog, like all too many bums, was a Vietnam veteran. Like many of his brothers-in-arms, he'd come back from the war without his legs and whatever part of the human mind that makes people give a fuck. Unlike most of his fellow soldiers, he'd also come back with a chronic case of lycanthropy.

Moon Dog had been both a crippled hippie and a werewolf for at least forty years. It might seem that he was doubly cursed (or triply, depending on one's opinion of hippies), except that his lycanthropy gave him back the legs that a North Vietnamese antipersonnel mine had taken. When he changed, Moon Dog, like other lupines, went about on all fours.

It wasn't difficult to pick him out of the throng, even in the twilight. In hippie form, Moon Dog rode the streets and sidewalks of L.A. in an electric wheelchair. An eight-foot whip antenna sporting an orange safety flag ascended majestically from a metal bracket bolted to the frame. The back of the chair was devoted to the sticker collection that symbolized Moon Dog's unique take on not giving a fuck—peace symbol, marijuana leaf, Greenpeace, MIA/POW, Marine Corps, Friend of the San Diego Zoo, Bel-Air Homeowners' Association, Beware of Dog, Cthulhu Fish. The centerpiece was a red bumper sticker with large white print: If You're Close Enough To Read This, You're An Asshole.

I caught his eye and waved as I walked over to him. Moon Dog was on the job. He was holding a cardboard sign. The words Will Dance For Beer Money were written on it in black magic marker. I dropped the sack from the grocery store in his lap. Moon Dog looked in the bag. Inside were three porterhouse steaks, fresh off the cow.

"Angus?" he asked. Long, straight white hair was tied down with a red bandana, and bum-tanned cheeks peeked out from behind a scraggly beard.

"Yeah," I said. "How you doing, Moonie?" I refuse to call him Moon Dog to his face, on general principle.

"Grocery store?" asked Moon Dog.

"Yeah, real sorry, Moonie. You want it from the meat market or the pasture, you can get it yourself."

"Nah, it's all good, Domino. I dig the antibiotics and growth hormones. I think my legs are growing back in." He wiggled his stumps.

"That…really freaks me out, Moonie. Look, I need a favor."

"Sure, babe," he said. "What's up?"

"Follow me," I said, and led him over to the lot where I'd parked my car. I pointed to the front quarter-panel on the passenger side. "Take a whiff of that, Moonie."

Moon Dog wheeled up, leaned in and sniffed at the fender. "Smells like Turtle Wax, Domino."

I scowled. "What else?"

"That's about it." Moon Dog rubbed his nose and sniffed noisily. "This old nozzle ain't so good anymore. I think it's this fucking L.A. air."

"Maybe it's all the weed and blow, Moonie."

"Fuck that. They're the only reason I can smell anything at all, clear out my sinuses. So what is it you want me to smell?"

"Vampire," I said. "The prick was leaning on my car. I thought maybe you could pick up his scent, track him to his lair." I remembered the blanket I'd found in the canal, the one Fred had used to wrap up Jimmy Lee's corpse—the one with the vampire's juice on it. Damn.

"I can do that, but you got to get me something of his. Plus, I got to do it at night, once all the tourists clear out. I got to go doggy-style to track him. I go now, the assholes with the butterfly nets will be chasing me all over town."

"Okay. If I get something of his, could you track him later tonight? Maybe an hour or so before dawn, see where he goes to ground?"

"Yeah, Domino, I can do that."

"All right, I'll see what I can do. You going to be around here later where I can find you?"

"Sure, I can hang around."

"Okay, thanks, Moonie."

"No problem, thanks for the grub, Domino."

"Peace, Moonie."

"Fuck that, babe. I hope you stake his ass. I hate those undead cocksuckers."

★ ★ ★

Back at my condo, I paused at the door, keys in hand, and tried to prepare myself for what was coming. I took a deep breath, unlocked the door and went in.

"Hi, Domino," Honey said. She was wrestling with a gray squirrel on the sofa. The squirrel had one of Honey's feet in its mouth, and the piskie had an arm-lock on its bushy tail.

"Hey," I said. I went into the kitchen and set my remaining purchases on the breakfast table, taking care not to disturb the sizable nest Honey had made from grass, flower petals, newspaper and a couple strips of white cardboard.

The squirrel ran past me, leaped up on the windowsill and squeezed out through the crack.

I pulled the plastic-wrapped carnations out of the bag and went to look in the cupboard. I didn't have anything in the way of a vase, so I settled for a large sports bottle and filled it with water from the tap. Then I set the flowers on the windowsill where Mrs. Dawson could get a good look.

For a moment, it felt like someone was standing near me. I heard a delicate sniff, but whether it was the usual disdain or appreciation for the flowers, I wasn't sure.

I went back out to the living room, paused, looked around and then went back to the kitchen. I crossed to my bedroom and office and checked them, too. All of the walls had been painted in soft but vibrant shades—peach, mint-green, rose. A little girly maybe, but it was pretty. There was no smell of fresh paint. I went back into the living room.

"Nice paint job," I said.

"Thanks!" Honey said. "It's not really paint, just glamour. If you want, I can change it."

"Nah, it's pretty. Mrs. Dawson will love it. What's glamour?"

"Fairy magic." Honey threw out her hands and spun a circle in midair. A sparkling cloud of pixie dust winked and danced around her and then faded.

"Nice," I said. "Say, Honey, if you can paint the walls, why can't you use your glamour to give yourself some clothes? What was all that shit about fig leaves and garlands?"

Honey shrugged. "I like being naked. Anyway, you said I look good."

I nodded, threw open the French doors and walked out onto the balcony. Honey had started a garden. There was still room for one patio chair amidst the pots and planters of all shapes and sizes. There were flowers and herbs and other green things I couldn't identify. There were three healthy marijuana plants, each at least four feet tall. A dinner plate had been set out, and birds were flying onto the balcony and depositing seeds on the plate.

"Where'd you get the flowerpots and stuff?"

"Neighbors."

"They gave them to you?"

"Not exactly. I'm just borrowing them."

I nodded. "Okay, if someone calls the cops on us, you can deal with them. Same goes for the weed."

"Okay."

"I wasn't sure what you eat. Mostly I have alcohol and frozen dinners."

"Yeah, I saw that. I had a beer."

"Anyway, I took a guess and bought some honey."

"I want ice cream."

"Yeah?"

"Ben & Jerry's. Cherry Garcia or Chunky Monkey."

"Okay, I'll have to go back to the store."

"No hurry. I turned on the TV, but just to say hi. I told

Mr. Clean he should have told you about your spells in the Between."

"What'd he say?"

"He said you didn't ask."

I grunted. It was true, I hadn't asked. Sometimes Mr. Clean will volunteer information, but only if it isn't directly relevant to anything.

"So you'll be living in the nest?"

"Yeah, I'm still working on it. I could use some cotton balls."

"In the bathroom, drawer under the sink."

"Okay, thanks. Did you find the vampire?"

"Not yet. I have someone working on it."

"What then? You said he was protecting something."

I wasn't sure how much I wanted to tell Honey about what I was working on. The fact was, I could only afford not to distrust her because she wasn't part of my world and didn't know my business. Then again, I needed her and if she was going to be rooming with me and working with me in the Between, she'd probably have to know sooner or later. Plus, I liked what she'd done with the place. At least she hadn't trashed it or stolen all my stuff.

A decent human being would have left it at that. I spun up a spell and got inside Honey's head. "If you tell the truth you don't have to remember anything," I said.

The piskie's mind was an untidy place, but it was easy enough to find what I needed. She didn't know anything about the murders, or about Adan. She wanted to return to this world, and she wanted it with a fierceness that was almost overwhelming. She needed me, too. She wanted to be my friend.

She trusted me.

I dropped the spell. Honey wouldn't remember what I'd done to her. But I would.

"I think someone is being possessed by an evil spirit," I said. "Someone in the organization I work for."

"Your gang. You're a gangster."

"Yeah, I guess. Anyway, this guy in my outfit is being possessed. I think the vampire is protecting the spirit in the Between."

"A guy?"

"Yeah, my boss's son. It's pretty complicated."

"What's his name?"

"Adan."

"What's he look like?"

"I don't know. He's good-looking, I guess."

"You like him?"

"Yeah, he's nice. You know, he's my boss's son."

"Is he your boyfriend?"

"No. Maybe. I don't know. We just met. Really, I just have to keep an eye on him because of the whole possession angle."

"Why do you think he's possessed? Maybe he's just an asshole."

I looked at Honey. She seemed cross. "Are you jealous, Honey?"

Honey laughed. "Of course not! Why would I be jealous?"

I shrugged. "I don't know, you just seem awfully interested in Adan."

"You're my roommate. I just don't want you to be taken advantage of by some asshole."

"Well, I don't think he's going to take advantage of me.

He did threaten to skin me, but that was when he was possessed."

"Are you going to go out with him again?"

"Yeah, tonight. He's got to have something that belongs to the vampire. I need something of his to track him." I'd stopped by the canal on my way home, but there was no sign of Jimmy Lee's blanket.

"You need something for a spell?"

"No, it's hard for me to lock on to a vampire with my magic. Different kind of juice, I guess."

"Have you slept with this guy?"

"That's personal."

"You haven't."

I scowled. "Like I said, we just met. We've only had one real date."

"But you want to sleep with him."

"It's none of your business."

"You do. Even though he wants to skin you."

"He doesn't want to skin me. He was possessed by an evil spirit."

"Do what you want. I'm just saying, I don't think you should have sex with some asshole who wants to skin you. It's irresponsible."

"He's not an asshole. He's sweet."

"How many people has he skinned so far?"

"Just two."

"That's sweet."

"Possessed!"

Honey shrugged.

"So what about my training? Once I track down the vampire and take him out, then I can go back to the Between for the spirit. But I have to learn how to fight there before I can deal with it."

"We could cross over and start tonight."

"No, I have to meet Adan and get the thing from the vampire."

"Didn't you look for something when we were there before, in the Between?"

"Not really. I was looking for the spirit, or some clue that would lead me to it. I wasn't even thinking about Fred at the time."

"What kind of person hangs out with a vampire, anyway?"

"Yeah, I question his judgment on that one. He says Fred is cool."

"He murders innocent people and drinks their blood."

"Yeah. But I'm a gangster, so it's hard for me to win moral arguments."

"Still, Domino, don't you think it says something about him that he's friends with a vampire?"

I shrugged. "I guess vampires can be mysterious and intriguing, or whatever. Plus, his father is my boss. He had to be raised with a certain amount of ethical flexibility. Anyway, like I said, Fred is working with the spirit. I figure the spirit probably manipulated Adan into hanging out with him."

"Domino, seriously, what do you know about this guy? You're pretty hot for him. What is it about him you like?"

I shrugged.

"Well, what does he do?"

I frowned. "I don't know…he's taking some time off."

"So he's a bum?"

"No! He's got plenty of money. He's just between jobs."

"What did he do before?"

"He was in school."

"Has he *ever* had a job?"

I shrugged. "He's not a gangster."

"That's what you like about him? He's not a gangster?"

"Yeah, for one thing."

"Your standards are really low. Shouldn't be hard to find a guy who isn't a gangster."

"Yeah, but finding one who doesn't freak out every time I drop a spell is a little tougher."

"Oh, I get it."

I waited. Honey just hovered there and looked at me.

"What? You get what?"

"You're not falling for Adan. I mean, he's a bum—what's to fall for?"

"He's not a bum and I never said I was falling for him."

"You didn't have to. Anyway, you're not falling for Adan, you're falling for the idea of Adan."

"What the hell are you talking about?"

"You see it all the time in women who make bad choices about men. It's not the actual guy they fall for—he's just a blank canvas they can project their own needs onto."

"Another *Newsweek* article?"

"*Cosmo.*"

"Well, you're wrong, Honey."

"Yeah, see, you don't want a gangster and you don't think you can have a normal man, and then here comes this...boy... and he's neither one. He's perfect, even if he is a bum and a serial killer."

"He just needs to find himself."

"You're hopeless."

"Look, I'm not falling for him, Honey. But I do want to help him. And even if I didn't, it's my fucking job."

"Well, if you have to go on a date with your sweet, vampire-loving, serial-killer boyfriend tonight, we can start your training tomorrow."

"How long will it take? For me to learn the kung-fu magic, I mean?"

"I don't know for sure. It shouldn't take very long. It's just manipulating magic. You already know how to do it—you just don't know you know."

"What do you mean?"

"It's like what you do when you cast a spell. Only you're not tapping the juice. You are the juice. You control the juice, you control your construct."

"Sounds easy enough."

"Yeah."

"Okay, tomorrow then. After I track the vampire."

"What if you can't find something to track him with?"

"I don't know. I haven't thought that far ahead yet. I guess if I can't find Fred here, I'll have to deal with him in the Between."

"He'll probably kill you. He was just playing before."

"Yeah, well, then I better find something to track him. Don't jinx it. What are you going to do while I'm out?"

"Probably work on my nest."

"Okay. I'm going to grab a shower."

"Sounds good. I need one, too." Honey leaped into the air and flew to the bathroom.

"Honey?" I called.

"Yeah?" I heard the shower running.

"You know I'm not going to take a shower with you, right?"

She flew back into the living room. "Why not?"

"I'm just not. It's not appropriate."

"You don't want me to see you naked?"

"No, it's not that, it's just…roommates don't shower together."

"Why not? Come on, I'll do your back."

"Honey, you're a lot smaller than me. Don't you think that would take a really long time?"

"Remember how fast I knocked you down before?"

"Yeah."

"I work fast."

"That's not just in the Between? I thought that was your kung-fu magic."

"It is, but I can do it here, too. And use glamour. But I don't cast spells like you do, because I'm a piskie."

"Oh."

"So come on, it'll feel really good."

That's what I was afraid of. The whole Honey situation was pretty hard to figure out. I had no objections to a little harmless fun between girls. There'd been a few times with girls from the Men's Room, and I'd never regretted it. So how was I supposed to feel about a pretty, young naked woman who wanted to take a shower with me? What if she was eight inches tall? It was kinky, but more like a foot fetish. Not like bestiality or necrophilia kinky. And besides, it was just a shower.

Then I thought about Adan and what he would think of me showering with Honey. Well, he was a guy, so he'd probably be all for it as long as he could watch. But I knew I wouldn't like the idea of him taking a shower with some girl, no matter how short she was.

"Look, Honey, I just can't take a shower with you." Then I had a moment of real inspiration. "You're a very beautiful woman, you're very sexy, and I'm just not comfortable with that level of intimacy. We're roommates and I value our friendship."

"You think I'm sexy?" Honey beamed.

"Of course. You're hot. And I can't say the idea of some kung-fu scrubbing isn't tempting. But that's why I can't take a shower with you."

Honey sighed. "Okay, I'm first then." She flew off again. "You can come in if you change your mind," she called from the bathroom.

I dropped onto the couch and let out a deep breath. I felt like I'd either dodged a bullet or missed out on something so weird even the men's magazines wouldn't know what to do with it.

My preference for searching Adan's apartment was to do it when he wasn't there. I called him a little after ten and suggested we meet somewhere. My plan was to pick a place far enough away that I could break in after he left, search the loft and then make up for lost time with the traffic spell.

It was a good plan, but Adan invited me over instead. It was about ten-thirty when I got to his loft. He'd already had dinner, so we settled on coffee and shared a slice of take-out Washington. We finished the pizza and he let me smoke after I agreed to use my housecleaning spell to kill the odor.

"Tell me about Fred," I said, tilting my head away from him and blowing a line of smoke into open air.

"You picking a fight, Domino? You just got here."

"I'm not, but I work for your father and it's my job to look after his interests."

"And protecting little old me is part of that job?"

"I'm not trying to protect you, Adan. I know you can take

care of yourself." It was the exact opposite of how I really felt, but I couldn't very well tell him that.

Adan nodded. "He's German, but I think he's older than the country. He says it wasn't really unified when he was alive. He says he was a noble or a prince or something."

"They always are. You never seem to run across a vampire who came up a peasant."

Adan laughed. "Well, I told you I met him at the club."

"Yeah. I figure he hunts there."

"I think so. Actually, he owns the place. Anyway, we became friends before I knew what he was, and I've never been with him when he…did that. But I've seen him leave with women."

"And they don't come back."

"No, sometimes they don't."

I sank back on the sofa, smoked and thought about my next move. This was tricky. It was possible Adan could help me find the vampire, saving me the trouble of having to search his place. But if I asked the kind of questions I'd have to ask, he'd know what I was planning. Would he help me kill Fred? Or would he throw me out of his apartment?

My gut was telling me that his friendship with Fred didn't run too deep. He'd found out about him after they'd become friends. His father had him juiced-up with protective magic and spell talismans, but he was probably still a little intimidated by the vampire. Maybe he was worried Fred would come after him if he told him to get lost. Maybe I was right, and the spirit had even manipulated him into the friendship.

I just didn't know him well enough to make a read. Some people will remain loyal to a friend or family member no matter what they do. Even if he wasn't thrilled with Fred, that didn't mean he'd be okay with me taking him out. He might tell *me* to get lost. What I was most worried about, even though I didn't want to admit it, was that he wanted something from the vampire. Adan didn't have the juice to be a sorcerer, and he felt trapped between two worlds as a result. Maybe he saw vampirism as a solution to his identity crisis and he wanted Fred to turn him.

I didn't believe that, but I couldn't be sure. And again, I had to figure the spirit into this, whether it was responsible for the Adan-Fred connection or not. I didn't know all the details of how this thing worked, but it was a fair bet the spirit knew everything Adan did, even when it wasn't actively possessing him. It'd have to. I didn't like it, and I didn't blame him for it, but there was no way I could completely trust Adan, even if he would line up with me against Fred.

I couldn't read his mind, either, as I had with Honey. Even without his father's wards protecting him, I'd like to think I wouldn't have done it. Maybe it was even true.

"Are you going to kill him, Domino?" Adan asked. "Don't lie to me."

"No," I lied, "not unless you want me to. You had it right last night—I'm not really in a position to judge him."

He nodded, but I couldn't tell if he was relieved or disappointed. "I don't like what he does. It disgusts me. But he says he's a different species, that it's natural for his kind to prey on humans just like it's natural for us to eat cattle."

"Do you buy that?"

"No. I understand why he sees it that way, but I don't think it's the same thing."

"It's not," I said. "He's a monster. There's nothing natural about him."

Adan smiled an uneasy smile. "I told him the exact same thing once."

"What did he say?"

"He said cattle would have the same opinion of butchers."

I grunted. It was chilling, but it wasn't a big stretch for me to look at the world the way the vampire did. Maybe when I wasn't paying attention I *did* look at it the same way. I was a hell of a lot closer to human than Fred was, but I had to admit I usually didn't think of myself as one. Maybe it was the gangster thing, or the power magic gave me, but the same rules just didn't seem to apply. I was an outsider, and we made our own rules.

My attention turned from halfhearted moral angst to how I was going to search Adan's apartment without him noticing. He might make a move on me, and I was pretty sure I wanted him to. If I could get him in bed, there might be a shower later or he might fall asleep, and that would give me my chance.

I wasn't real comfortable with that approach. I've done much worse things, but the idea of trying to seduce Adan for any other reason than the honest one didn't sit right. I also had a feeling sex might bring the spirit back out to play, and I wasn't ready to risk my skin just to get laid.

It occurred to me that I might be more clever if I didn't always rely on magic to do anything remotely complicated. I finally gave up and decided I'd have to leave. Once he was safely tucked in bed, I could break in, find what I was looking for and get out with him none the wiser. It would have been a lot easier without having to break in, but I was sure I had the spells I'd need to do it without waking him up.

I stayed for another hour so it wouldn't look suspicious. We went into the living room and turned on the TV, cuddling up on one corner of his large sectional. Maybe I'd get lucky and he'd fall asleep, but he didn't really seem to be in the mood for channel surfing. The cuddling led to kissing, things started warming up and I had to keep my eyes open to see if Adan's went black.

The first real break in the action, I checked my watch and sighed. "I have to go to work, Adan."

"Now? It's after midnight."

"Gangster," I said and shrugged.

"Oh, yeah." He laughed. "Okay, that's cool, if you really have to go." We got up and he wrapped his arms around my waist.

"Yeah, I really do. Sorry. I mean, really sorry."

He smiled down at me and kissed the tip of my nose. "Thanks for coming over. This was nice."

"Yeah, it was," I said, kissing him again, and then I gently disengaged. He walked me to the door and a long kiss goodnight bought my way to freedom.

I sat in my car until the lights went out, first in the living room and then in his bedroom about twenty minutes later. I waited another hour just to be sure. Then I spun my wallflower and nightvision spells, got out of the car and walked back down the street to his building.

"Security is mostly a superstition," I said, and my B&E spell took down the alarm system and unlocked the door. I went in, shut the door behind me and climbed the stairs.

I stood outside his door for a few minutes and used a little juice to amplify my hearing. The open ductwork in the loft thrummed softly, and I remembered how silent it had been in the machineless world of the Between. I heard Adan in his bedroom loft, his breathing deep and even. I spun the B&E again, opened the door and slipped inside. As in the Between, Rashan's wards recognized me and let me pass.

I started on my left and systematically searched the large, open loft. I checked the pockets of the jackets hanging on the tree by the front door. I searched under the sectional and between the cushions. I rummaged through the DVDs in the rack under the flat-screen TV, and I searched every drawer and cabinet in the kitchen. Nothing.

I made my way over to the stairs leading up to the loft. I didn't like the idea of going up there with Adan sleeping, but not because I was afraid of being caught. I was pretty sure the wallflower would hold. It was too passive for Adan's wards to pick it up. I also knew his father hadn't given him a true seeing charm, or he'd have been able to see the ocean spirits on the beach. No, I didn't like the idea of going up to his bedroom loft because I felt like a fucking stalker.

I climbed the stairs slowly, treading as lightly as I could. The wallflower spell doesn't suppress sound, it just makes it easy to ignore, and I could hear the stairs groan and creak beneath my weight.

I found Adan snuggled in his queen-size bed, lying on his side with the flannel sheets drawn up to his chin like a little boy. He was sleeping deeply, peacefully, and his breathing was the only sound or movement.

I walked toward the bathroom, thinking to begin my search there, and then changed my mind. Even if he wouldn't know I was there, I didn't want to be in the bathroom if Adan woke up and decided to use it. That would push the creepy stalker vibe beyond tolerable limits, and I decided to stay out of there unless I had no other choice.

I crept back across the loft to the desk on the other side of Adan's bed. In the last drawer I checked, at the very back, I found the Vampire Fred's personal card. It proclaimed him Manfred von Hauptman, Proprietor, The Cannibal Club.

I used my witch sight to look at the card and found it dripping with the vampire's black juice. The scent should be strong enough for Moon Dog.

When I turned around, Adan was standing behind me wearing black boxer-briefs. His eyes were black and he was holding an expensive, titanium kitchen knife at his side.

I jumped back, banging into the desk, and fumbled the forty-five out of its holster. Adan just stood there, a flat smile doing ugly things to his face.

"Have you come to give me your skin, lover?" he asked in the same graveyard voice I'd heard the day before.

I brought the heavy gun up and sighted between those empty black, shark eyes. I willed juice and resolve into my arm to hold it steady. The eyes fixed on the stainless-steel barrel, and the motherfucker took a step back.

"Get the fuck out, or your host gets a lobotomy." I was bluffing, of course. I wasn't sure if I'd be able to pull the trigger on Adan, but I was sure the hollow-points wouldn't make it past his father's wards. I was just hoping the spirit wouldn't know that.

The eyes bore into me. I thumbed the hammer on the forty-five and stared back.

The eyes dropped to the gun again, and the creature took another step back. "Come to me in the spirit world, lover," he said. "I'll be waiting for you." Then the eyes cleared and the knife dropped to the floor point-first. It thunked into the hardwood and wobbled.

I stood perfectly still, holding my breath. Adan looked right through me, then turned and looked around. He saw the knife and jumped back. He backed into a corner near the bed, panic draining the color from his face, his breath coming in ragged gasps.

"What the fuck?" he whispered, his terrified eyes darting around the room. "Is somebody there? What's going on?" He moved forward, bent down and tore the knife out of the floor. Gripping it tightly in one hand, he checked the bathroom and the closet. I didn't move.

Finally, he crept downstairs. I heard him moving around the apartment, turning on every light in the place. He walked over to the front door, and I cursed myself for leaving it unlocked. I heard him lock the door and draw the chain, and then I heard him breathing heavily again.

Adan didn't come back upstairs. After a few minutes, he stopped searching the loft, and I heard him settle onto the sofa. I waited another fifteen minutes or so, and then crept to the edge of the loft and looked down. He was sitting on the couch, holding the knife at his side. I watched him like that for more than an hour before he finally fell asleep.

Moving as slowly and quietly as I could, every nerve on edge, I reached out with the juice and covered the nick left by the knife in the hardwood. My housecleaning spell wouldn't fix it, and I just had to hope the cosmetic job would hold up to scrutiny. I went downstairs and got the hell out of there, reversing the B&E spell to lock up behind me.

I was shaking as I drove out to Santa Monica. I could have used a little juice to make it all go away, but I just tightened my jaw and choked it down.

# nine

I found Moon Dog on the pier and we retreated to a low cinderblock building on the carnival side that was presently serving as his home. The building might have once been a concession stand or souvenir shop, but now it was just an unused storeroom. The security guys let Moonie crash there and even threw him a few bucks to watch the place. I guess he was cheaper than keeping a Doberman.

I handed Moon Dog the vampire's personal card. He sniffed at it, rubbed it against his nose, dabbed it against his tongue. Finally he nodded and handed the card back to me.

"Yeah, I think this will work. When I track, it's mostly the smell of the juice I'm following, and this has plenty on it. Probably gets his dinner all hot and bothered. I'll have to shift to track him, though."

"How's this going to work? You need me to drive you around, or can you track him on your own?"

Moonie shrugged. "I can probably pick up the scent anywhere in L.A. But if he's a ways off and you want me to find him before dawn, I'll need a lift. I move faster doggie-style than I do in the chair, but it'll still take a while if I have to hump it across town."

"How will I know?"

"Well, if I run off you know I don't need a ride."

"Okay, and how will I know where to go if I have to drive you?"

"Just drive, babe. One bark means next right, two means next left, three means turn around. If I lick my balls, that means stop."

"Jesus, Moonie."

"I'm just fucking with you, Domino. If I growl, that means stop."

I nodded.

"I can, though, lick my balls."

"Too much information, Moonie."

"Okay, babe, time to unleash the beast within."

I nodded and went outside for a smoke. I'd seen Moon Dog shift before, and it didn't bother me, much, but he would have to ditch his clothes. It turns out a naked sixty-year-old double-amputee bum is a far more horrific sight than the shapeshifting process.

Inside the building, clothes were discarded, the wheelchair creaked, skin stretched, bones popped and hair sprouted faster than Honey's cannabis plants. It took a couple minutes.

Moon Dog nosed open the steel door of the building and padded outside. In the movies, werewolves are always pony-size monsters with six-inch fangs and hell in their eyes. Moonie looked like a wolf. He was large for a wolf—probably a buck-twenty, buck-thirty—but he was still a wolf. He'd have been a popular attraction at the zoo, but he wouldn't have sent people away screaming. He was black, with a silver ruff and muzzle, and his eyes were a shining lupine-yellow.

He looked up at me and his tongue lolled out one side of his mouth. I crouched and offered him the card, and he sniffed at it. Then he raised his head and sniffed at the air. He turned in circles a couple times and then sank down on his belly, looking at me, and whined.

"Okay, you need a ride I guess," I said.

Moonie chuffed.

I got my car and brought it around. Moon Dog loped over and vaulted into the car. Just a girl and her wolf out for an early-morning drive.

I headed east on Santa Monica Boulevard. Moon Dog sat in the passenger seat, head out facing into the wind, tongue flapping like a wet flag. There wasn't much traffic at this time of the night, and we made good time. After about fifteen minutes, Moonie barked twice and I pulled into the left lane and stopped at the light. A young woman on a crotch-rocket wearing bright blue leathers pulled up beside us. She raised the visor on her full-face helmet.

"Nice dog," she said.

"Thanks," I said. Moon Dog chuffed at her.

"What's his name?"

"Moon Dog."

"That's cute," she said and smiled. Moonie whined. "What kind of dog is he?"

"Mutt."

Moon Dog swiveled his head around and looked at me. He growled.

The woman laughed. "He doesn't like that."

"He thinks he's a wolf."

"Aw, is she mean to you, puppy?" the woman crooned. Moon Dog whined and lowered his head.

"Don't feel sorry for him," I said. "He can lick his own balls."

The woman glared at me. "Bitch," she said. She smiled at Moonie, the light changed and she sped off, riding a wheelie down to the next light.

Moon Dog glowered at me and bared his teeth.

I shrugged. "See? Women just aren't that impressed with the ball-licking."

We got on the Harbor Freeway and drove into Watts. We exited at East Century and took a right on Compton and a left on East 108th. We drove past the graffiti-clad security doors of storefronts locked down for the night. We drove past rusted-out cars on blocks and brothers drinking forties around trashcan bonfires. I wasn't surprised we were heading deep into Papa Danwe's territory. It was late, and while the Haitian's juice was still raising hell in the streets, most of the civilians had retreated to their homes and barred the doors to wait for morning.

We were cruising through the ghetto version of a light industrial area when Moon Dog growled. I saw junk piled high beyond a line of corrugated fencing. A sign on the double chain-link gate read Luther's Salvage.

"This the place?" I asked. Moon Dog chuffed.

I parked on the street and got out of the car. I popped the trunk and fetched the Mossberg pump-action clipped in next to the tire jack. Usually, I don't bother carrying anything heavier than my forty-five, but I was behind enemy lines and the junkyard had the look of a place where a shotgun might keep you out of trouble. I pulled a handful of shells out of a tackle box and dropped them in my jacket pocket.

Then I closed the lid, perched on the trunk with the Mossberg across my knees and waited for dawn. Moon Dog hopped out of the car and sat on his haunches, staring at the junkyard.

"You don't have to go in with me, Moonie," I said. "That's not really what you signed on for. Anyway, once it gets light, Fred won't be much more than a corpse. I guess I can handle it."

Moon Dog turned and looked at me, yellow eyes shining like lanterns. He chuffed and turned back to the junkyard.

Another hour went by like that. The sky brightened, the ghetto went to sleep and the sun came up.

The salvage yard wasn't due to open for another three hours and it was quiet. I spun the B&E spell on the padlocked gate, and Moon Dog and I slipped inside. Luther apparently wasn't much on organization, and there was no apparent pattern to the shapeless piles of rusting junk scattered around the yard. Narrow, ragged paths cut between the twisted stacks, and the rising sun painted them orange.

Moon Dog found a path he liked and padded down it, his nose low to the ground. I went after him. We followed a bend around a tangle of rusting rebar and Moon Dog stopped, crouching low and raising his nose to the air. He sniffed and growled.

I don't speak wolf, but I guessed he was telling me we weren't alone. I didn't see the vampire out there taking a sunbath, so I expected we had company of a different sort. I spun the eye in the sky spell, then closed my eyes and pushed it up over our heads about twenty feet.

Up ahead, there was a clearing in the junk piles and a low concrete building squatting in the middle of it. It had a two-tone paint scheme at one time, light blue on the bottom and white on top, but now the building was mostly the color of graffiti. They were juice tags—I recognized some of the patterns from the factory site.

Two bangers were out in front of the building with submachine guns. Two more were lying on the flat roof with AKs. I spun the eye three hundred and sixty degrees and then circled it in a perimeter around the clearing. I spotted three more covering from the junk piles with open lines of sight to the building and the clearing around it.

Even in Watts, armed thugs don't hang out in junkyards at dawn just in case someone shows up for them to shoot at. They were waiting for me. Even if I hadn't known whose turf I was on, the tags and colors would have told me they belonged to Papa Danwe. That fit—Fred knew he had to have protection, and who else could he turn to?

The real question was what I should do about it. I could probably take them all out before they knew I was there, and I could probably do it without killing anyone. On the other hand, cooling things out with Terrence was about the only productive thing I'd really accomplished since this whole thing came down. I didn't really want to fuck it up by shooting in the dark.

"Hang back, Moonie," I said. "I'm going to try to talk these guys out of getting hurt."

I thumbed off the shotgun's safety, dropped it to my side and walked out into the clearing.

It turned out the bangers weren't really guarding the Vampire Fred. What they had working was more in the way of an ambush, and I walked right into it. They let me get about ten feet into the clearing and then they opened fire.

As soon as I saw the two out front raise their submachine guns, I triggered the defensive shield in the gold crucifix I wear around my neck. An invisible, spherical barrier winked into existence around me. Bullets rattled against the shield like hail against a storm window, and the shield spat raw blue energy like electrical discharges as it vaporized them.

The shield doesn't make me bulletproof forever, because I can't draw that much juice from a spell talisman. It gives me about ten seconds, and that's usually more than enough time to deal with a guy who's decided to take a shot at me. Unfortunately, it's not enough time to deal with half a dozen attackers or more.

I squeezed the shotgun to give them something to think about, mostly because it was faster than spinning a spell, then I turned around and ran back the way I'd come. Bullets rained against the shield and kicked up dirt around my feet, and it sounded like someone had lit the fuse on every firecracker in Chinatown.

I got back around to the other side of the junk pile and Moon Dog was nowhere to be seen. That was just as well—a wolf is out of place in a gunfight. I crouched behind an old refrigerator, leaning my back into it and trying not to flinch as a hailstorm of bullets tore into the junk pile behind me. I was considering my best course of action when the first ball of liquid fire exploded above my head and splashed down on me like napalm.

The spell caught too much of my cover or I'd have been dead. It engulfed the refrigerator and the rear half of an old pickup camper that jutted out from the junk pile to my left. Burning droplets spattered against the back of my head and neck and sprayed across my left shoulder and arm. My jacket lit up and I was on fire.

As quickly as my mind registered that I was under magical attack, the spell talisman on my left ring finger activated another shield that was the antimagic analog of the one that saved me from the gunfire. It flared up around me just in time to catch the second, more carefully targeted spell that poured fire down on me in cascading sheets.

I moved. I ran back down the path I'd followed to the clearing, bent low and burning as I went. I took the first fork to the left and kept going until I had another junk pile between me and the clearing. Then I dropped the shotgun, stripped off my jacket and spun a spell to put out the fire that was still nibbling hungrily at my exposed skin.

"God is a scientist, not a magician," I said, and juice coursed through my body. It attacked the fire and killed any other hostile magic that might have been affecting me. As soon as I stopped burning, I used some juice to block the pain and spun my wallflower spell. Then I retrieved the Mossberg, hunkered down and threw up the eye in the sky again.

The two bangers on the roof were still there, their AKs panning back and forth across the clearing. The others had left cover and were fanned out, moving in a ragged skirmish line in my direction. There were a lot more of them than the seven I'd originally spotted. I counted at least a dozen. Most of them had guns, but a few were obviously flowing juice, preparing combat spells.

When they reached the edge of the clearing, the thugs split into two groups, one moving down the path I'd taken, the other a path that would bring them up along my flank. They obviously had a pretty good idea of where I was—there just weren't that many places I could have gone. I was sure they wouldn't be able to see through my wallflower, but with automatic weapons and explosive spells, they wouldn't have to.

I let them come. One group came around the right side of my junk pile, and the other came around the left. When they were all more or less where I needed them to be, I dropped the eye and let the Mossberg slip to the ground. I drew in a breath, reached out and sucked down all the juice I could handle, taking it in until it felt like I was burning again.

"To every action there is an equal and opposite reaction," I said. Sometimes you have to quote the rulebook to produce the most fundamental physical effects.

The spell was essentially the same magic that was in the repulsion talisman I'd used at the Cannibal Club—the one that had turned Fred around and thrown him into the flower shop. This time, though, I spun the repulsion field into a vertical plane, like a wall about ten feet high and thirty feet long. I positioned this wall of repulsive force so that it neatly bisected the junk pile the bangers were flanking.

When the sheet of arcane energy snapped into place, the thousands of pounds of twisted, rusting metal to either side of it had to move. There was the hellish sound of a suspension bridge collapsing in an earthquake as the junk pile parted like the Red Sea, and the paths to either side of it were buried in a crashing avalanche of wreckage and debris.

I picked up the shotgun, pumped a shell into the chamber and dropped the wallflower, then I walked toward the clearing along the new path that had been cleared through the middle of the junk pile. There were screams and moans from buried survivors, but I tried not to hear them.

I wasn't sure if the gangbangers with the AKs had seen enough or if they would open fire, so I spun up another defensive shield. I needn't have bothered, because Moon Dog had seized on these new developments as an opportunity to get involved in the fight.

I couldn't see much through the enormous dust cloud that had enveloped the area, but I heard a snarl and a choked scream when the werewolf appeared on the roof. One of the thugs managed to crawl over the edge, drop to the ground and scramble away while Moonie was tearing the other one's throat out.

When I got to the edge of the clearing, the dust cleared well enough for me to see through the haze to the other side. Another dozen or so thugs had left cover and moved into position on either side of the clearing. I noticed they got well clear of the junk piles, but I didn't think I could handle enough juice to spin the spell again anyway.

The door of the low building opened and Terrence Cole stepped out. He raised his left hand and spread the fingers wide, like a starfish on the move. His other hand was gripping an M-16 with a grenade launcher slung under the barrel.

"Enough," he said, and his voice was deep and smooth. "Let's cool this shit out before any more brothers get themselves killed."

I saw Moon Dog creeping to the edge of the building above him, but I gave my head a little shake and he backed off.

"I thought we already cooled this shit out, Terrence. In case I wasn't specific enough, that means you and your fucking gangbangers don't go shock and awe on me."

"I know what you came here to do. I'm just here to tell you it's not going to happen. Not here, not today."

"You're protecting that cocksucker?"

Terrence shrugged. "It is what it is, Domino. It comes down from Papa Danwe, and I do what I'm supposed to do. This here's a line I can't cross, even if I wanted to."

"Fuck your line, Terrence. I came to talk and you tried to dust me."

Terrence shook his head. "That was righteous, Domino,

if a bit excessive. This is my ground. You come up in here heavy. I got a right to do it that way."

"Yeah, maybe, and now you have a dozen gangbangers you have to dig out. Some of them might even be alive."

Terrence shrugged. "You know I didn't see it going that way. It was a nice trick with that repulsion spell. You must have had to flow a lot of juice, though, must have been hard to pull it on my turf. You can't be feeling too good right now."

Terrence was right—my vampire-hunting expedition was over. I'd flowed too much juice and I was just about done, not to mention I'd almost had an arm cooked. I probably had enough left if it was just the thugs, but there was no way I could handle Terrence at the same time. I didn't really know what he could do, but he had the same job description as me so I could make a close enough guess. I also liked him for the napalm spell that almost cooked me.

The clincher, though, was that Terrence was also right about the political situation. The ambush had been excessive, but warranted, even considering our little agreement. I'd come onto another outfit's territory with the idea of killing some-body under their protection. It didn't really matter that I had a legitimate beef with the vampire.

As it stood, I was probably okay, too. They'd attacked me without warning and I'd defended myself. I probably hadn't gone too far to restore the fucking peace with Terrence—what there was of it. But now that I'd been given the opportunity to walk away, I'd have to take it.

"I'm going to have to stake him, Terrence."

"I understand that. It just can't happen here."

I let him think I was mulling it over and then nodded. "I guess I can see that."

"We can still hold it together, Domino. Like I told you before, some of this shit's already in motion, ain't nothing I can do about it. But it doesn't have to go any further than that. Doesn't have to be any war."

"Let's keep it that way. You take care of your business and I'll take care of mine."

"Always, Domino," he said, and he smiled a wide smile.

I turned around and walked away. When I reached the edge of the clearing I stopped and turned back halfway. I gestured at the wreckage.

"Sorry about your boys, Terrence. I hope everyone's okay." I tried to make my smile as wide as his.

On the way back to Santa Monica, my juice buzz warred with the adrenaline crash. My vision was almost painfully sharp and the wind whipping through the open car roared in my ears like storm surge. My skin felt tight and itched, and I could feel my hair growing. At the same time, the burn I'd felt when I cast the repulsion spell had softened to a warm, euphoric afterglow that was making me wet. In short, I was fucked up.

Most of the time, flowing juice doesn't have that kind of effect. I might get a pleasant tingle, just enough to look forward to the next time, but I'd flowed too much at the junkyard. When Rashan had brought me into the outfit, he'd warned me that juice can be addictive. I'd seen enough crackheads and junkies in the neighborhood to take him seriously, and I always tried to pull my juice in small doses. Most of the everyday spells I used—like the traffic and parking spells— were just like that. A heroin addict would call them bumps or taps.

For larger spells, I had my little rituals, and I had Mr. Clean to take some of the juice. The spell talismans were handy, too. Not only did they allow me to trigger an effect more quickly, but I was also able to charge them with a little juice at a time.

At the junkyard, I'd been rushing, hard. I'd flowed enough juice to toss around a couple tons of scrap metal like LEGOs. The gangbangers had been trying to kill me and I did what I had to do. Some of them were dead—probably all of them—but I wasn't planning to stop by their funerals or anything. Bad guys die. Someday I'd be on the wrong end. And *goddamn* that juice had felt good. Even the burn had been a good pain; the kind of pain you get from doing something your body needs but doesn't like.

I threw my head back and let the wind thunder over my face, and laughed. Outside of the bosses, there probably weren't five gangsters in L.A. who could have handled that much juice. Terrence probably couldn't. Fuck him—he was pretty good, but I doubted he could've moved that pile.

"I am a fucking monster!" I yelled, and laughed again.

Moon Dog whined and stared at me with those fucked-up yellow eyes. He'd been lying on the passenger seat with his muzzle tucked between his paws all the way from the salvage yard.

I looked over at him. "What? Look, Moonie, you don't got to worry about those fucking guys. I'll set you up, you can lay low for a few days if you want, but no one's going to fuck with you. Not after that, they ain't gonna fuck with you." What I meant was they wouldn't fuck with *me*.

Moon Dog just whined again and dropped his nose to his paws.

When we got back to the pier, I waited outside the building while Moonie changed back. When he came outside, he was trying to wipe away the blood matted in his beard with a dirty rag. For whatever reason, I hadn't even noticed the blood on the werewolf's muzzle.

I pulled out my roll and peeled off five bills. "Moonie, thanks for helping me out back there. You didn't have to get involved, and I want you to know I appreciate it." Moon Dog grimaced and took the money like it was a job application.

"That was fucked up, Domino."

"Fuck those guys, Moonie. I went out to talk and they tried to put me in the ground."

Moon Dog didn't seem to want to look at me. He was quiet for a minute. "I did a lot of fucked-up shit in the Nam," he said finally. "Had to, or thought I did. I didn't have to like it, though. Thing is, some guys did." He looked at me then— more like squinted at me.

"Jesus, Moonie, I didn't like it," I said, trying it out. It didn't sit quite right.

Moon Dog nodded. "That's good, babe. Most of those guys never made it home. They just kept going back, one tour after another, until they finally got to stay there. Some of them came back when the government made them, but their minds are still in the bush. Always will be."

"And you, Moonie?" Without the juice buzz, it probably would have seemed like a rude question.

Moonie chuckled. "I guess I made it out of the bush but never quite made it home. That's all right. I got no complaints."

"Well, me, either. I guess I won't turn into some psychotic baby-killer just because I decided not to let a few gangbangers shoot me."

Moon Dog flinched at the term "baby-killer," but he seemed to have put in enough words for one day. He just nodded, told me to be careful and wheeled himself back into his hole. The whole experience hadn't been too good for him. His PTSD was probably acting up.

By the time I got home, the buzz was gone and my mood was foul. I slammed the door, slammed myself onto the couch and stared at the peach-colored wall. Then I got up and went to the kitchen, grabbed a beer and slammed the refrigerator door. When I got back to the living room, Honey was hovering there.

"Bad day?" she piped. Her cheerfulness was annoying. I dropped back on the couch and drank my beer.

"What happened?" Honey landed on the coffee table and looked at me, concerned.

"Nothing much," I said, and glowered.

"It doesn't look like nothing much."

That pissed me off. "I don't want to talk to you right now, Honey."

"Yes, you do."

That really pissed me off. I thought about yelling, but I couldn't work up the energy for it.

"You're hurt, Domino," Honey said. She lifted into the air and hovered near my shoulder. She started to reach out, and then drew back.

I craned my neck to look at my shoulder. I'd forgotten about it. "Thanks for reminding me. Now it hurts like hell." I got up and went to the bathroom, grabbing the bottle of aspirin from the cabinet. I returned to the couch, reached for the juice and chased down a handful of the pills.

This time, the spell didn't come together at all. The juice and the tablets both made it halfway down. The juice burned off and faded away, but the tablets stayed there and I damn near choked on them. I finally forced them down with beer, and then slammed the empty bottle on the table, coughing.

"Let me, Domino." Honey flew over to the French doors and wrestled with the doorknob. She pulled open the door to the balcony and went out to her garden.

"What are you going to do, roll me a joint?"

"Don't be sarcastic, Domino. Take off your shirt." Honey came in with an armful of green stuff and flew off to the kitchen. I wasn't in the mood to be helped, but I wasn't in the mood to hurt, either. I stripped down to my bra, wincing and cursing.

I heard cabinets opening and closing and pots rattling in the kitchen. Then Honey started singing. It might have been chanting, but it sounded like music. I didn't recognize the language. It was either something humans didn't speak anymore or something humans had never spoken.

After about ten minutes, Honey came back in carrying a saucer that was almost as big as she was. She set it on the couch beside me and I saw there was some kind of yellowish paste on it.

"Looks like honey, Honey."

"I used honey for the base." She rubbed her hands in the paste and then held them up, like a surgeon who had just finished scrubbing. Pixie dust drifted down from her hands. "Now relax," she said. "This isn't going to hurt, but it might feel a little strange."

I grunted. Honey came to me and started rubbing the salve into my wounds. It didn't hurt, but I still flinched the first time she touched me.

"Jesus, that's cold!"

"Relax, Domino."

And it did feel weird. It felt like my flesh had gone as liquid as the salve, like Honey was moving it around, smoothing it out with her hands. She went back and forth to the saucer, working on my shoulder, arm, neck and scalp. I didn't look until she was finished. When I did, my skin was liberally coated with the salve, but it was a healthy, undamaged pink underneath.

"Jesus," I said. "That's a hell of a lot better than my aspirin spell, even when it works."

Honey shrugged. "It's glamour. I'm pretty good at it."

"Glamour," I said. "You mentioned that before, about the walls. What does that mean, exactly?"

"It means the magic will come undone if sunlight touches it," Honey said.

"Really?"

"No, I'm just kidding," she said and laughed. "It's just what we call fairy magic. It's as real as yours, just different." I relaxed my eyes, unfocused my vision and looked at my shoulder.

"I can't see it," I said. "I can't see the magic." I looked at the walls Honey had painted, and I couldn't see any magic in them, either.

"It's not the kind of magic you can see. You can't see it any more than a normal human can see yours."

The pieces finally clicked together in my mind. "Honey, that's why I couldn't see the magic the spirit used to squeeze my guys! The killer didn't clean it up, I just couldn't see it."

"Of course you couldn't," Honey said. "The spirit would be channeling magic from the Beyond, not from Arcadia."

"Huh," I said. "Well, I can see what you did with it, and I can feel it, and it rocks. Thanks, Honey." I tried a smile.

"No problem."

A thought occurred to me, and I frowned. "Any, uh, charge for that?"

"Yeah, you have to take a shower with me."

"Honey—"

She laughed. "I'm joking. That was on the house, just because we're friends."

"Yeah, okay. Well, thanks." I looked around. "How are you doing, settling in, I mean? You got everything you need?"

"Yeah, it's great! Did you see my place?"

"What place?"

"In the kitchen. You know, my nest." I hadn't even noticed it when I got my beer. I shook my head.

"Come on, I'll show you!" Honey flitted into the kitchen and I followed.

The nest looked like Barbie's Fantasy Island, if there'd been such a thing. The entire kitchen table was covered with what looked like a miniature forest. There was a sparkling pool in the middle, and a rocky hillside climbed away from it and into the kitchen wall. A shimmering waterfall tumbled down from it and splashed into the pool.

"Jesus Christ, Honey. This is amazing." The trees and foliage looked like they were alive. Everything was perfect, right down to the moss and lichen growing on the rocks.

"Thanks, I really like it. I wanted to make a cave behind the waterfall, but I'd have to cut a hole in your wall."

"Screw it," I said. "Go ahead. This is incredible." I didn't ask where the waterfall was coming from, or why the pool didn't fill up and overflow its banks.

"Okay, thanks. And I'm sorry about your table. It kind of got out of hand."

I shrugged. "I never use it anyway. Mrs. Dawson is probably freaking out, though."

"She probably can't even see it. I think maybe she sees this place like it was when she lived here."

"She tries to, anyway. She doesn't like the condos much."

I went back out to the living room and Honey followed.

She sat on the arm of the couch, her legs tucked under her, and watched me brood for a while.

"So tell me," she said finally. "Maybe I can help."

"I tracked down the vampire. He's being protected by another outfit. It got ugly."

"How ugly?"

"I have a lot more guys to search on FriendTrace, and I don't even know their names."

"FriendTrace?"

"Yeah, what I use to contact the dead."

"Oh. Well, I'm just glad you weren't hurt worse."

"The thing is, I think I screwed up. I'm not sure where exactly. When this thing came down, I had good reasons not to disclose all the details to my boss. I thought I did, anyway. But I think I should have, sometime between then and now. Probably when I caught on to the possession thing. At the time, it seemed like it had an easy solution. Go to the Between, deal with the spirit, problem solved."

"But now?"

I sighed. "Now, it's getting out of control—like your nest." I smiled weakly. "I feel like a degenerate gambler who's dug herself a hole and just keeps laying bets to try to get flush."

"So get out of the hole. Go to your boss."

"Now I don't think I *can* go to my boss. I withheld crucial information from him—namely that his own son is involved. I've been…socializing with him, and what's worse, I've been lying to him. I broke into his house and scared him half to death. I've been doing all this while the outfit is more or less at war."

"It's gotten pretty complicated," Honey said.

I laughed. "Yeah, but that's not the bad part. The bad part

is that I'm no closer to solving the problem than I was when I started."

"And that's why you don't want to go to your boss."

I nodded. "At this point, I can't undo anything. I think I just have to try to make it right. He's still not going to be happy when he finds out what I've been up to, but if I can solve the problem…at least that's something. Like I said, I have to keep laying bets to try to get flush."

"So what are you going to do?"

"I have no idea," I said, and laughed. "The vampire's protection isn't going to last forever. The problem is, I don't have that kind of time. I'm still convinced I'm not going to be able to get at the spirit in the Between without first getting through Fred."

"So you'll have to deal with him in the Between. He won't have protection there."

"Yeah. But I already know he can kick my ass in the Between. The spirit probably can, too. Which means I need you to train me, pronto."

"So let's get started."

I nodded. "I'm worried about what's going to happen in the meantime. I'm worried that by the time I'm ready to deal with the vampire and the spirit, it's going to be too late. When I broke into Adan's apartment, the spirit possessed him again. I put a guy on him yesterday, for a while, but Anton would be fucking useless if it came to that."

"You need to buy some time," Honey said.

"Yeah. I need a way to slow the spirit down, make it harder to possess Adan. I'll talk to Mr. Clean about it, but he seemed to think the only way I could protect Adan was by destroying the spirit. That's why I went into the Between in the first place."

"He's right. You don't have any magic that can stop the spirit from possessing Adan."

"That's what I was afraid of. If the spirit was powerful enough to defeat all the wards his father has on him, there's nothing I can do about it—short of abducting Adan and locking him up inside a protective circle somewhere. That seems like it might be digging the hole a little deeper than I want to."

"You don't have the magic to do it, but I do," Honey said.

"You do?"

"Yeah, and frankly, Mr. Clean might have mentioned it to you in the first place. How well do you know him, Domino?"

I shrugged. "He's a jinn. He's my familiar. He can be an asshole sometimes. That's about it, I guess."

"He's dangerous, Domino. He's not evil, exactly, not like your spirit from the Beyond. But there's nothing human in him, either—nothing at all. He's been here since the world was made and he'll be here still when the stars wink out and the skies go dark. He's your familiar, yes, but he hates it."

"Well, I knew he wasn't very happy about it."

Honey shook her head. "You've made him a slave, Domino. It's not the same as making a person your slave—he doesn't suffer from it. He can't suffer. But he hates it all the same. It's ego. Really, that's all he is—an ego so strong, and powerful, and willful that it will endure until the end of time."

"So you're saying he doesn't necessarily have my best interests at heart."

"He wants you to die, Domino. More than that—he wants to be the one who tricks you into getting yourself killed.

That's the game, to him, and it's the only thing that makes his servitude bearable."

I frowned. "I don't know about that. I owe him a lot of favors. I'm pretty sure he intends to cash in someday."

Honey laughed, but there was no humor in it. "Of course he does! He intends that you die, and when you do, you'll serve him until your debt is paid off."

"After I'm dead? He never said anything about that."

"That's because—"

"I didn't ask," I finished. "Well, this is good to know."

"You don't seem all that mad about it."

"I guess I'm not surprised. I can't really call myself his master and then pretend I didn't know what it meant." Mostly I was thinking about Rashan. He hadn't told me any of this, and he must have known. I could only think of one motivation for that. He'd wanted me to figure it out on my own, and if I didn't, I'd have been an acceptable casualty. I wasn't really surprised by that, either. I'd always known I didn't work for a saint.

"Well, I'd be pissed," Honey said. "Mr. Clean sent you into the Between knowing you wouldn't be able to handle what you found there. The only reason he even told you about me is that it indebted you to him further."

"Yeah, nice play. So tell me what you can do for Adan. You have magic that can protect him?"

Honey nodded. "I'm basically a spirit, too, you know. Not like the one that's possessing Adan, but still a spirit. Predators like that are common where I come from, and we have ways to protect ourselves from them. If we didn't, there wouldn't be any of us left."

"So what can you do?"

"I can make you a potion. It won't be much, like a

thimbleful. You can put it in Adan's food or drink. He won't even have to know about it."

"Will it drive the spirit out or whatever?"

"No, it will only make it harder for the spirit to possess him. Ordinarily it would make it hard enough that the spirit would be better off looking for a different host. But this spirit has a lot invested in Adan already, so I'm not sure it will want to start all over."

"But it will buy me some time."

"Yes. It should make the possessions less frequent, and if we're lucky it will prevent the spirit from possessing Adan for a long enough period of time to complete another ritual. At least for a few days."

"That's good enough. It should give me enough time for you to train me in the kung-fu magic so I can destroy the spirit in the Between."

"I think so," Honey agreed.

"What's it going to cost me, Honey?" I looked at her, hard.

"I'll do it as a favor, no strings attached," she said.

"Why?"

"Because I like you. Because I want to be here, in Arcadia. I belong here, Domino. My people weren't born of this world, but we long for it. We made ourselves its first children, spirits of tree and stone and brook."

"You must hate what we've done to the place."

"Cities are good, too," she said, laughing. "It's the magic of this world that we crave, and there's magic in the streets as well as in the groves and the hills. I want to dwell in this world again, and if I'm going to do that, I need your friendship more than I need to nickel and dime you for favors."

I laughed. "If friendship is all you want, you've got it,

Honey. I'm not in a good spot, but I don't even want to think about where I'd be if it weren't for your help."

"Good. Then come take a shower with me."

"I, uh…I'm not sure we—"

"I'm still kidding," she said, giggling. "I know humans have strange ideas about such things. I can wait." She winked at me and I blushed. "Go boil some water in a large pot—one of the copper ones I used for the healing salve. I'll get some things from the garden."

I boiled water and watched Honey brew the potion. It wasn't like any magic I did, and by the time she was finished I was nodding off in my chair. I'd been awake for a long stretch, and even without the events at Adan's loft and the junkyard, I'd have been exhausted. As it was, I barely managed to stumble into my room and collapse on the bed before I was out.

# ten

I woke up at about five in the afternoon. I had a hangover from my overindulgence at the salvage yard, and I used a spell to nuke a burrito and get the juice flowing. The hair of the dog smoothed out the throbbing in my temples and steadied my hands, but the burrito didn't do much for my stomach.

I spent some time with my head in the toilet and took a shower. By the time I was dressed, I felt just about good enough to go back to bed.

Instead, I called Adan. I had a small glass vial loaded with the potion, and I needed to hook up with him long enough to deliver the goods. I was thinking dinner, since I didn't have much to show for the burrito and it would give me the best chance to dose him.

"Not dinner," Adan said when I made my suggestion. "I don't want us to get predictable."

I rolled my eyes. This thing was complicated enough without having to worry about rules of dating etiquette. I mentally ran through other options that would involve the ingestion of food or drink. "We could go to a club, do some dancing, have a few drinks."

"I've had enough of nightclubs for a while. How about the Commerce?"

"Poker?"

"Yeah, they have decent no-limit games."

"You play poker?"

"Sure. Everybody with too much money and no job plays poker these days...people like me and Ben Affleck."

"Okay, that sounds fun. Do we have an angle?" All the big poker rooms in town have spotters with a little talent whose only job is to make sure people like me aren't juicing the games. We could still cheat the old-fashioned way, though, playing partners and working the rest of the table as a team.

Adan laughed. "I'm dating a thug. We're just playing for fun, Domino." Cheating *is* fun, but I was secretly relieved. I'd be better off playing it straight. I'd be able to sit next to Adan, and it would make it a hell of a lot easier to slip him the potion.

"All right, sounds good. Pick me up at eight."

"You pick me up. I tend to drink a little when I play cards. And bring plenty of money—I'm pretty good."

"You shouldn't have told me that. You might have been able to hustle me."

"Now I've got you thinking about it. You're doomed."

"True. See you at eight."

"Later."

The Commerce Casino opened in 1983, about ten miles from downtown L.A. just off the Santa Ana Freeway. It had expanded a couple times, and now it was the largest card room in California. I've heard it's the largest in the world.

It's also one of the largest juice boxes in town. With over two hundred tables and all the cards and chips and probabilities dancing twenty-four hours a day, it's like a numerological ritual the size of an amusement park. Rashan didn't have a piece of it, though. If anyone was tapping it, they were much bigger fish than the L.A. outfits.

The City of Commerce itself isn't much to look at, and the casino sticks out like the proverbial twenty-dollar necklace on a two-dollar whore. It's supposed to be Vegas glitzy, I guess, but doesn't get all the way there. There are cheap red lights running up to the entrance to let you know you're on the right track. A garish statue in the lobby that might be a female sphinx is about the only thing suggestive of a theme.

I surrendered my car to the valet and looked at him long enough to make sure he'd be nice to it. We went in, and the floor manager I knew got us adjoining seats at a no-limit table with a four-hundred-dollar buy-in. I had an idea to show off a little, but he seemed to know Adan better than he knew me. He seemed to like him better, too.

I'm a decent player, even when I can't cheat. I'd been playing since I was a kid, so I'd seen enough hands to feel comfortable with most of the situations that come up. In most of those games I was using enough juice to know what the other players were holding, but even without the juice, I can usually tell if a guy is strong or weak, and I can usually figure out what he thinks I'm playing.

In this game, I just wanted to loosen up the table and make sure Adan was having fun. I ordered drinks and kept them coming often enough to set a fast pace.

For the first hour or so, I played just about any two cards and I played passively enough that everyone was eyeing me like a malfunctioning ATM. I handed out my four hundred pretty fast and bought in again. I did it with such good humor that everyone had a nice time.

When I felt like Adan had to be feeling the drinks, I switched gears. I was sitting to his right, and I started to put some pressure on him. I wanted him thinking about his cards and his chips more than what I was doing with the drinks I was passing him.

Finally a hand came along that allowed me to get heads-up with him. I drew jack-ten of hearts on the big blind, which meant Adan was the first to bet. He stacked off four ten-dollar chips. That kind of bet in first position told the rest of the table he was playing a premium hand, probably a big pair. The guy on the button had been playing almost as loose as I had, and he cold-called Adan's open. I did the same, adding thirty dollars to the big blind that was already on the table.

The flop came down nine, eight, deuce, and the last two were hearts. This was just about the perfect flop for me. I had an open-ended straight draw and a flush draw, which gave me better than even odds to get ahead of Adan's big pair by the river. I'd also be the first to act and Adan would be sure to raise any bet I made. That kind of action would likely be too much for our third wheel, and Adan and I would play the rest of the hand mano a mano.

I opened for seventy dollars, a little more than half the size of the pot. Adan could see the straight and flush possibilities as well as I could, and he wanted to take the pot down right there rather than give them a chance to hit. He pushed all his chips in. The guy to my right pretended to think about it a while and then threw in his cards.

Now it was on me to either call Adan's bet or fold. It really wasn't much of a decision. I was almost certainly behind in the hand—Adan's bets told me he had a pair, and I had nothing. But I'd win the hand if I caught a heart, queen or seven on either of the last two cards. The rest of the table couldn't know I had so many outs, though, and that gave me license to stare at Adan a while.

I probably stared at him longer than I had license to—long enough for the dealer to remind me a couple times that it was my action, and long enough for the cocktail waitress to deliver another round. Everyone else at the table was staring at Adan, too, trying to pick up something on him. He stared straight ahead, looking at nothing.

I leaned back in my chair, tipped the waitress, took the drinks off her tray and poured the vial I was palming into Adan's Scotch.

"Well," I said, "at least I've got a fresh drink," then I pushed my chips in and called Adan's raise. Adan let out a deep breath and everyone laughed, then nodded sagely when we turned over our cards. Adan was holding kings. The eight of spades came on the turn and the four of diamonds on the river, neither of which was any help to me.

"You should have folded," Adan said, smiling as he raked in my chips. I didn't mind, because everyone at the table wanted to tell me I misplayed the hand.

"I thought you were bluffing, you bully."

"I never bluff," he said, and winked. Then he lifted his drink to his lips…and froze.

He frowned.

"Something wrong?" I asked. My blood pressure spiked a hell of a lot higher than it ever did during the poker hand. Did the potion have an odor? Honey hadn't said anything about it…

Then Adan laughed and took a drink. "No," he said, smiling at me over his glass, "I was just thinking that I'm getting drunk, but then I decided that was probably your plan."

I laughed, too. "Sure," I said, "that's obviously the only way I'm going to get my money back."

"You sure that's the only reason?" he said, and a boyish grin brought those dimples out.

"A player never shows her cards."

"I call," he said and drained his glass.

I woke up at about ten the next morning draped over Adan's chest. He was still asleep, and his soft breaths raised goose bumps on my skin.

We'd left the card room after one in the morning and gotten back to his loft about half an hour later. We'd started kissing before the front door was closed and we laid down a trail of clothes leading to the stairs up to the bedroom.

I'd mustered enough moral fortitude to mention the complexity of the situation we were getting ourselves into as I took off my clothes.

"This is probably a bad idea," I said as I sat on the edge of the bed and fought with my zipper. Adan was kneeling on the floor in front of me. His hands were on my breasts and he leaned in and kissed my neck.

"You should have thought of that before you got me drunk," he mumbled.

"Yeah, probably," I said, pulling off my jeans.

"Oh, well," he said, and nibbled my ear.

"Yeah."

"I'll still respect you in the morning."

"Really?"

"I mean, I won't respect you any less."

"Good enough."

We'd made love most of the night. We did it well enough that, like Honey's glamour, it didn't want to come unmade in the sunlight. Now was the time for morning-after regrets and self-recrimination, but I didn't have either. I was feeling pretty good about the world. After a few days of getting stuffed at the scrimmage line, I felt like I'd finally made some forward progress.

At the very least, we'd made it through the evening's activities without Adan's evil twin making an appearance. Maybe the potion was working, or maybe it was just dumb luck. Either way, I hadn't had any trouble falling asleep with him, and I still had all my skin where it was supposed to be.

Despite the weak protests of the night before, I'd blown by the point of no return in our relationship with a smile and a wave. Adan had been plenty of trouble already and he'd probably be even more when I told his father how it was. But I had the idea he'd be worth a lot more trouble than I'd actually get. I didn't feel inclined to worry too much about my boss unless and until.

There weren't many guys in L.A. I could ever have something with that amounted to more than a friendly roll in the hay. Most of the guys I met were interested in me because I was a gangster, and those were the ones I'd never take seriously. The rest weren't interested in me for the same reason, and those were the ones who made me feel sorry for myself. I couldn't hope for any better than a gangster's son who didn't care either way what I was. Adan, I knew, was a lot better than I deserved.

Adan stirred and then tilted my chin up to plant a kiss on my mouth. "Good morning," he said, grinning.

"One of the best," I said and kissed him back. "Sorry, my mouth probably tastes like I brought the casino home in it." Adan tasted just like he always did, like the apples and cinnamon on a freshly baked Washington. That didn't seem fair, and I wondered why I'd never worked up a spell for morning breath.

"It just tastes like you. I like it." As if to prove it, his head disappeared under the sheets and I stopped thinking for a while.

Later, we took a shower together, dressed and breakfasted on our cinnamon apple pizza. It tasted so much like Adan it was almost like making love again.

"Do you have to work today?" he asked when we were done.

"Yeah, actually, I have a lot to do." I looked at my watch. "I should get going."

"I want you to stay."

"I want to, too, but I can't. I still have a job, and it's more important than ever that I do it well. The only legitimate objection your father can make about this is that it interferes with my work." That wasn't the only reason it was more important than ever, but I didn't tell Adan that.

"You're a very responsible gangster, aren't you?"

I almost choked on my coffee. Spending the night with Adan was about as far as I could get from responsible. I wasn't going to feel anything but great about it but I wasn't going to call it responsible, either.

"This thing I'm working on," I said, "it's pretty important. About as important as my job ever gets. If it weren't for that, you'd have to kick me out."

"The murders," he said.

My eyes snapped up to him but I got a hold of them pretty quick. I shouldn't have been surprised he'd heard about it. The outfit is big for an outfit but small for anything else.

I nodded. "You heard about it, huh?"

"Yeah, and I heard you were working on it. I heard Jamal

was one of the guys that was killed." He was looking at me like we were playing a poker hand.

"Yes, he was. His parole officer said Jamal was hanging out at the club. That's why I was down there that night."

Adan nodded, but his eyes didn't leave mine. "And after that?"

"After that, what?"

Adan just looked at me.

"I'm not here because of work, Adan. Is that what you think?"

"Maybe you think I'm involved somehow, because I knew Jamal."

"Jamal and the other guy were squeezed, Adan. It was a ritual execution, a hit. The killer is a sorcerer. You couldn't have had anything to do with it, and if I thought you did, this isn't the angle I'd take." I wished it were true, all the way around. I hoped my wishing would make it sound less like bullshit than it did to me.

"Yeah, okay. I didn't really think so, obviously, but I wanted to hear you say it."

I nodded as small as I could and smiled, and felt like shooting myself.

"If you want to ask me anything else about Jamal, I don't mind."

"If you know anything you think might help, I'll listen."

"Well, it's like I told you, I really didn't know him very well. Maybe a little better than I told you, that night."

I just nodded.

"We hung out after the club closed sometimes."

"You picked up girls at the club."

"Yeah, I guess. Jamal showed me his graffiti, too. He tried

to explain how it worked, but I couldn't understand half of it. It was cool, though."

He looked up at me and I nodded again. "Jesus, Domino, you're still not going to ask any questions?"

"Nope."

"Okay. The thing is, I was at his apartment the night he was killed. Earlier, I mean. We were pretty drunk and we wanted to smoke some weed."

"What happened when you got to his apartment?"

"Finally a question. That's the thing, though, I don't know. I guess I drank too much and I blacked out. I woke up here the next morning and I couldn't remember much about it."

"You must have been pretty drunk," I said. "Shouldn't have been driving. Do you think Jamal drove you home?"

"I just don't know, and you're right, that's never happened to me before. I don't see how I could have made it home by myself."

"Maybe he drove you home and caught a cab back to his place."

"Yeah, I guess. When I heard about it, though—Jesus, it was like a bad movie. I thought maybe I did have something to do with it, you know, and just couldn't remember. Like temporary insanity or something."

"What did you do? Did you go to your father about it?"

"No fucking way. I only found out about Jamal yesterday. One of the guys called me. He said there had been two murders, and I knew I didn't have anything to do with the other one. Anyway, I didn't really think it was me. It was just weird, you know?"

"Yeah, I'll bet." I remembered how freaked out he'd been after the episode in his loft the night before, when I'd broken in. He'd had plenty of weirdness the last few days, and I was amazed how well he was holding it together.

"That's about it," he said. "You know, I just didn't want there to be any secrets."

"I'm glad, Adan," I said. "No secrets." I almost gagged on the words.

"So do you have any idea who did it? I mean, if you don't mind me asking. Do you think it was those guys I told you about? Papa Danwe's outfit?"

"I don't mind, but there isn't much to tell. That's what I'm working on, and that's why I have to go."

The look in his eyes said he'd noticed I didn't answer his question. "Do you think Manfred is involved? The reason I ask is, you know, he didn't like Jamal very much. And he could have followed us that night."

"It's possible. He couldn't have done the ritual, but he might have been involved. Either way, it wasn't your fault."

He nodded uncertainly.

"Jamal wasn't a random victim, Adan. Whether Fred was in on it or not, Jamal got squeezed. You don't set something like that up on a whim. Whoever did him had a reason for it, and that's what I'm trying to find out."

"I hope you do. Jamal was a cool guy. It's fucked up what they did to him."

"Whoever did it, I'll find him," I said, standing up. "I don't have the juice to bring Jamal back—no one does—but I can make sure it doesn't happen to anyone else." I sort of did have the juice to bring him back, as it turned out, just not in the way I meant.

"Be careful, Domino. Look, I know you can handle yourself, and it'd be pretty ridiculous for me to get protective. But be careful. Promise me."

"I promise," I said, and kissed him goodbye.

The promise was broken when it came out of my mouth. It was too late to be careful. I had to stick with reckless and try to finish the job before anyone noticed.

When I got home, Honey was waiting for me with an interrogation lamp and a rubber hose. We went through twenty questions and I ignored the ones I didn't want to answer. That was most of them. She was concerned or jealous or both, but she wasn't angry. I told her the potion seemed to have worked. I told her I was ready for training.

I went into my bedroom to change clothes and was momentarily defeated. What exactly is proper attire for shadow world training in kung-fu magic? Finally, I decided it didn't matter since my clothes wouldn't really exist in the Between anyway. I opted for running shorts, a sports halter and cross trainers. Honey said I looked like I was ready for yoga class.

If I'd have known where we were going, I'd have chosen a different outfit. Honey wouldn't say. After we crossed over and were ignored by Mrs. Dawson, Honey told me to follow her into the mist.

"How do I follow you? We don't actually go anywhere, as far as I can tell."

"If we both have the same destination in mind, we'll show up there together. Otherwise, we have to stay in physical contact and you have to focus on staying with me. Think of this as the first part of your training."

Honey zipped off down the street and I went after her. When we reached the mist, she grabbed my ear and pulled me in after her. I focused on staying with her.

The L.A. Coliseum didn't suffer much in the Between.

It didn't seem to be missing too many colors, the way other buildings might. It was drab and ugly in both worlds.

"The Coliseum?"

"Sure. What better place to learn how to fight? It's kind of a neutral ground and there are real fights here sometimes, but usually at night. Let's go!"

Honey zipped through the north entrance of the sprawling stadium, down a couple of ramps and out onto the field. There wasn't much grass to it, just hard-packed dirt. There were certainly no yardlines or goalposts anymore.

The stands were filled with ghosts. I stood in the middle of the field and turned a full circle. They were different from the ghosts of the Goth kids I'd seen standing in line at the Cannibal Club. They were loud, belligerent and I saw more than one brawl rippling through the densely packed crowd.

"What's with the peanut gallery?" I asked.

Honey shrugged. "Raiders fans. They're always here. I guess they're waiting for the team to come back."

"The Raiders went back to Oakland in ninety-five."

"Yeah, I guess that's why they're so pissed."

Before long, the ghosts sitting nearest the field noticed me and the abuse started. Shouted hoots, whistles and catcalls rained down on me. When I gave them the finger, I was answered with intermittent showers of litter, beer bottles, batteries and generic debris that seemed to have been liberated from the stadium itself. A three-hundred-pound guy whose shaved head and naked torso were painted black-and-silver nailed me in the ear with a half-eaten hot dog.

"Real nice choice, Honey," I said, mining mustard from my ear canal with my pinkie.

"Yeah, like I said, it's a good place to fight. Nice energy. Plus, do you see the kind of distance they're getting on those throws? They're just ghosts, but they've learned how to use their juice."

"Well, they've had a lot of time to practice." I picked up a rough chunk of concrete that looked like it had come from the mezzanine facade. I hurled it at the fat guy, but it didn't make the stands.

"Let's get started," Honey said. "Do you remember when I knocked you down yesterday?"

"Yeah, both times."

"And the vampire basically did the same thing, only he hit you a lot harder."

"I guess."

"Well, I didn't really use any kung-fu magic. I just moved really fast and ran into you."

"So…"

"So that's really all there is to combat in the Between—speed and power."

"Isn't that all there is to kung-fu fighting in the real world?"

"Speed and power are good, sure, but the physical world is a lot more complicated."

"How so?"

"Well, for example, there are those pesky laws of physics and biology. You have to worry about things like mass, and momentum and conservation of energy, and if you want to hurt someone, you have to worry about things like anatomy."

"And here?"

"There aren't any such laws here. There are other laws, I guess, but they're very different. Anyway, in the Between, you don't have any mass, you don't have any anatomy, and neither does your opponent."

"I just have juice."

"Right. Juice and thought. Magic and mind. That's what you are."

"Okay, I'm made of juice. What do I do now?"

"Magic and *mind,* Domino. You have to learn to control the magic part with the mind part."

"So it's like a 'free your mind' thing."

"Yes, exactly like that," Honey said, and smiled.

"Are you saying I can dodge bullets?"

"It's just a movie, Domino."

"Sorry. How do I do it?"

"I'll try to hit you again, and you try to dodge out of the way."

"Don't you have any other training methods?"

"It won't hurt if you don't let me hit you."

"That's brilliant, Honey. Why didn't I think of that?"

"Okay, on the count of three. Ready?"

I shrugged.

"One…"

"Two…"

Honey blurred, I felt the now-familiar burst of pain in my chest, and then I was hurtling backward through the air. The packed earth of the Coliseum surface was nearly as rough as the pavement I'd spent so much time on the last couple days. I couldn't be sure with no lines on the field, but I must have been good for at least fifty yards. My chest felt like I'd taken a major-league fastball in the sternum. I lay on the ground and tried to find my breath.

Honey flew up to me. "Oh, stop that. You don't even really breathe here, remember?"

I stopped gasping for air and tried it out. Honey was right— despite what my brain was inclined to think, there didn't seem to be much point in breathing.

"You cheated," I wheezed. I sat up and rubbed my chest.

"Your bad guys probably will, too."

"Yeah, I guess."

"Anyway, it shouldn't matter. You should be able to move out of the way as quickly as you can trigger one of your spell talismans."

"Maybe I don't have enough juice for this."

"It's not your magic that's the problem, it's your mind. You're a little slow."

"Fuck you, Honey."

"I don't mean you're stupid. You just have to realize you can move as fast as you can think. The juice will do the rest."

"Okay, let's try again." We did, and on the last take—I'm not sure how many it was, but we were well into the teens— I managed to flinch before Honey hit me. By this time, the stadium was filled with the dull roar of the ghosts' laughter. The fat guy was rolling in the aisle.

"That was better, I suppose," said Honey when she flew over to me.

"Fuck this, Honey." I looked down and saw I was sitting in a rough depression, like a small crater, that my body had eroded into the hard earth over the course of the training exercise. I wrapped my arms around my throbbing ribs and winced. "I think you're using some kind of secret fairy juju on me. This is bullshit."

"I am. I already told you, I *am* fairy juju."

"Well, it's no fair. I don't have to fight you, just Fred and the spirit."

"And what makes you think you can handle the spirit juju if you can't handle the piskie juju? It's not that different—it's all magic from the Beyond, just not from Avalon, where I come from."

"What's Avalon?"

"Faerie, the Otherworld, Anwnn, Tir na Nog—it has a lot of names. Avalon is the place where fairies were born and where we retreated as magic faded from Arcadia."

"And it's in the Beyond? That's why I can't see your glamour, just like I can't see the spirit's magic."

"Right."

"So the spirit can school me just like you can."

"If the spirit just wants to hit you, yeah, it can do that. Probably harder than I can. The vampire, too."

"Well, then, we have to keep trying. Let's go again."

"I don't know, Domino. You're not really getting any better at this. I think you only flinched that time because you knew what was coming."

"What are you saying?"

"I'm saying I don't think I can train you. I'm hurting you, even though I'm trying not to."

"You're pulling your punches?"

"Of course. If I wasn't, I'd have killed you already."

"Well, that sucks. What am I going to do?"

"You could get a gun."

"What? I thought guns didn't work here. Nothing seems to work here."

"They don't, usually. Some events, though, usually murders and suicides, create echoes in this place of the weapons that were used."

"Okay, that works."

"Is your gun, the one at home…?"

I shook my head. "No, it's clean. I'll have to find one here."

"Most of the guns that become real in the Between are controlled by a spirit called the Burning Man."

"I thought that was some kind of party out in the desert."

"This guy's no party. He's a spirit from the Beyond, probably a lot like the one that's possessing Adan. He's very dangerous. He's the boss of a gang in this place and he's basically cornered the local weapons market."

"Can I deal with him?"

"I think so. He's a businessman, after all. But be very, very careful what you promise him, Domino."

I nodded.

"This isn't a very good solution. You're still really slow. I'm not sure you'll be able to see the vampire long enough to shoot him."

"I can handle Fred if I'm carrying."

"I'll help you. I'll try to keep him busy, give you time to get a clean shot."

"Thanks, Honey, but it could be dangerous. It *will* be dangerous."

"Warrior-princess."

"Oh, yeah. Okay, thanks. So where do I find this Burning Man?"

"I'll take you, but I don't want to go with you to see him. He doesn't like me. Plus, I need to visit my family and let them know where I am and that I'm okay."

"No problem. I guess I can buy a gun by myself."

We left the Coliseum and headed north on Vermont a short distance into the mist before the world shifted. We arrived at a run-down warehouse in Van Nuys that had probably been built sometime during the oil boom of the twenties. It seemed a little clichéd that the arms dealer was shacked up in an old warehouse, but it also struck me as practical. Then, too, my gangster boss held court at a strip club, so who am I to cast stones at clichés?

I made arrangements to meet Honey at the condo after I'd done my business. She left, and I walked up to the office door of the warehouse. There was a guard out front, an Asian gangbanger who might have been eighteen when he died. He was holding a Kalashnikov.

"Hi," I said. "I'm Domino Riley. I need to do some business with your boss."

The kid's eyes moved down my body and got stuck somewhere around my waist.

I snapped my fingers. "Up here, Romeo. I'm in Shanar Rashan's outfit. I want to buy a gat."

He looked at me a moment longer and then jerked his head in the direction of the office door. I went in and found five ghosts sitting at a table playing seven-card stud. They looked up at me when I closed the door behind me and I repeated my business. There was a door leading into the warehouse and a stairway to a second-floor office.

One of the ghosts motioned me to a chair. He was a Mexican kid in a wife-beater and chinos. Just about every square inch of exposed skin was covered with gang and prison tats. I sat down and he went upstairs. A few minutes later, he returned and waved me up from the stairway. I squeezed past him and he followed me up the stairs. I really wished I'd put some sweats on over the shorts.

The Burning Man was seated behind a large banker's desk that might have been vintage but just looked worn-out. There was a chain-link cage behind him filled with boxes and crates. There were two padded chairs in front of the desk, one of which was occupied by a young woman. She was blonde and pretty, with the best skin you could get in a place where everything is yellow. She looked like a starlet from the black-

and-white days, like an Ingrid Bergman type. She smiled at me and showed me a vampire's fangs.

The Burning Man was an Anglo, tall, black hair slicked back, dark eyes glittering at me under narrow eyebrows. He gestured to the remaining chair and I sat down.

"Welcome, Miss Riley," he said and offered his hand. I leaned up out of my chair and reached across the desk to take it. It started burning and I gave it back to him. The flames just licked at him at first, then they caught and began to devour his fine old suit.

"Pay no attention to the special effects, Miss Riley. I assure you it's quite beyond my control. A bit of a nuisance, really." The fire had eaten away his clothes and was working on his flesh, blackening it and peeling it away from his bones. I forced myself to watch. I gave a little nod to let him know it didn't bother me if it didn't bother him.

"Tell us what we can do for you, Miss Riley."

"I need a gun. I heard you were the man to see."

"I am," said the Burning Man. "I am, indeed. Well, I know of you and your outfit, of course. I know of your boss. I'm very pleased to have your business. What manner of firearm are you in the market for?"

I thought about it. "Something I can use in a tight spot, but with enough pop to leave an impression. A forty-five or a three-fifty-seven should fit."

The Burning Man smiled and Vampirella stifled a laugh. I stared hard at her but she didn't seem to mind.

"Weapons are a little different in this place from what you're used to, Miss Riley. They're not truly real, of course, in any physical sense, and so characteristics such as caliber and muzzle velocity are of little consequence here."

I looked at him like I look at Mr. Clean and waited for him

to tell me something. It was a little disconcerting, because he wasn't much more than a smoking skeleton at this point.

He nodded. "Yes, you see, in the Between, a firearm's capabilities are more related to the…event responsible for its instantiation in this place." He stood up and opened the cage behind him. The fire was gone and he was clad in healthy flesh and well-tailored summer wool again. "In other words, Miss Riley, the size of the weapon doesn't matter here. It's what is done with it that counts."

"Well, like I told you, I need a handgun with some muscle."

"Indeed." The Burning Man nodded thoughtfully. "The best weapons are typically those used in mass murders and spree killings. Such weapons are regrettably rare, of course, and highly prized." He turned from the product he was considering and looked at me. "Do you mind if I ask about the nature of the job the weapon is intended for? You understand there is no law here and any information you provide is strictly confidential. My interest is motivated solely by my desire to provide the best possible service."

I looked at him and then at Vampirella. I shrugged. Fred already knew I'd be coming for him. Even if word got out, that would cost me less than going up against him with a gun that couldn't do the job.

"There's a vampire I need to shoot," I said. I smiled at Vampirella and winked. She still didn't seem to mind.

"I see. Well, vampires don't have a lot going for them—no offense intended, Sophia, my dear—but they are remarkably difficult to kill in the Between." He considered, curling the fingers of his right hand and pressing his thumb to his lips. He started to burn again. He turned back to the cage and lifted a rectangular box of dark wood from a crate. He brought it out of the cage and placed it on the desk, smoothing it with his burning hands.

"I have a weapon, Miss Riley—well, an artifact, really—that would be ideal for your purposes." He turned the box around and opened it. "It's known as the Dead Man's Gun."

It was a Colt Peacemaker. I'd seen enough Westerns to recognize the type. It had a polished walnut grip and the black steel barrel was half again as long as Honey.

"This gat's probably a hundred and thirty years old. And it's a six-shooter. It looks nice enough, but I had more modern technology in mind."

"It belonged to Wyatt Earp, Miss Riley. Its power lies not only in the number of men it killed, but also in the legend that is woven into it. As I said, the Dead Man's Gun is an artifact."

"Well, it's an artifact that holds six rounds and will probably choke on half of them."

"Again, Miss Riley, physical characteristics are irrelevant here. You will never have to worry about the Dead Man's Gun running out of ammunition. You will never have to worry about jams or misfires, I assure you."

I reached for the Peacemaker and then looked at the Burning Man for permission. He nodded and kept burning. I lifted the gun out of the case.

In the ordinary world, a gun is just a gun. The only thrill you get out of fondling one is a little boy's power fantasy. This wasn't the ordinary world. The Dead Man's Gun had juice. It tingled along my hand and up my arm, spreading out through my body. It whispered to me with the calm, comforting voice of a killer.

The Peacemaker was a rocket launcher in a compact five-pound package. Well, it wasn't that compact. It was about eighteen inches long from the tip of the barrel to the back of the grip. Not exactly built for a woman, but it felt comfortable in my hand.

"Says here its name is Ned," I said, studying the gun. The name was engraved in the walnut grip.

"Ned Buntline," said the Burning Man. He was nodding and smiling with the enthusiasm of a boy talking baseball cards. "He commissioned these long-barreled Colts and presented them to several peace officers in Dodge City in 1876. It was Earp's favorite firearm."

"Single action?" I asked. I released the cylinder and looked. It was loaded with five cartridges, the hammer resting on an empty chamber.

"Yes, the action is the only element of the firing mechanism that is functional in this place. I think it is part of its personality."

"So I have to cock it before it will fire."

The Burning Man nodded. "You can also thumb-fire and fan the weapon, if speed is more important to you than accuracy. You'll find that the action is very smooth and the gun enjoys such treatment."

"But it doesn't need reloading?"

"That is correct, Miss Riley."

"How much?"

The Burning Man spread his burning hands and sighed. "As I said, the Dead Man's Gun is a unique and valuable artifact. It is very difficult to put a price on it."

"But you're going to, just the same."

"Indeed, Miss Riley. My price is an exclusive arrangement with your outfit. If, in the future, your people need weapons in the Between, you will do business with me. Do you have the authority to make such an arrangement?"

I nodded. "Assuming my boss doesn't have an existing agreement with a supplier, sure."

"He does not. It is my business to know these things, you understand. Very well, Miss Riley, do we have a deal?"

"Yeah, we have a deal. I'll need some kind of rig for this thing." The Burning Man nodded and went back into the cage, returning with a black leather gunbelt. He handed it to me and I took it. The initials *WBSE* were tooled into the leather in silver.

"I must place one condition on this sale, Miss Riley. You understand that different rules must, of necessity, apply to property in the Between. On the event of your death, ownership of the Dead Man's Gun reverts to me, so that I might pass it on to another worthy warrior. This is its nature."

Well, what's one more spirit that wants me dead? I was assembling quite a collection. "Not on the event of my death," I said. "On the event of my passing into the Beyond, permanently, the gun goes back to you. It's mine as long as I have business in the Between."

The Burning Man stared at me. His skull burned and an eye popped. I didn't blink. Finally he nodded and smiled. "You are a shrewd negotiator, Miss Riley. I believe that weapon will make you a formidable opponent indeed. Very well, then, we have reached an agreement." He extended a blackened claw to me and I shook it. The bone was cold and charred.

I stood up and buckled the gunbelt around my waist. I thought it would be way too big for me, but the last hole on the belt was a perfect fit. I slid the Peacemaker into the holster, then nodded at the Burning Man, winked at Vampirella and left.

Honey was waiting for me when I got back to the condo. She looked at the Peacemaker swinging on my hip, back at me and then back at the pistol.

"I didn't know you were going to buy a cannon," she said.

"Wyatt Earp's gun."

"The cowboy in the movies?"

"He was a lawman, not a cowboy. In the movies, at least."

"Well, did you know his gun was cursed?" Honey was staring at the Peacemaker, frowning.

"They call it the Dead Man's Gun. I guessed it probably was. Anyway, I call it Ned." I turned sideways and showed her the engraving on the grip.

"It doesn't bother you that it's cursed." Honey was staring at me in disbelief.

"Well, it beats toting a gun some psychotic teenager used in a school shooting. Anyway, I think it likes me."

"It likes you."

"Yeah," I said, patting the Colt. "I guess it'll put a big enough hole in Fred."

"Well, it looks a little ridiculous."

I looked down at the holstered gun. It reached most of the way to my knee. "It doesn't really go with running shorts," I allowed. "I'll have to change into something more somber next time."

"It's a little…oversized, don't you think?"

"No," I said, "watch this." My right arm blurred and the Peacemaker came out of the holster like it didn't even notice it was there.

"It's very impressive, but that's not what I meant. Don't you think the length is a little pretentious?"

"I didn't put a foot-long barrel on it," I grumbled.

"Freud would have loved you, Domino. Are we going after

the vampire now, or do you need some time to practice with that thing?"

"I'm ready. I did some target shooting on the way back here."

"What did you shoot?"

"Stop sign. There's no traffic here, so you might as well shoot one."

Honey and I traveled south and the mist delivered us to Watts. It was a short walk to the salvage yard. The loitering ghosts were no more hostile than the living in the juiced-up ghetto.

We advanced through the yard. It was quiet. It was still a junkyard, but it was easier to look at it in the Between. The faded colors and vague light softened it and smoothed it out. It was almost peaceful, like an old cemetery.

I was sure Terrence had cleared the debris and dug out his gangbangers in my world, but the work hadn't gotten done in this one. The path I'd created with the repulsion spell was still there, and we followed it into the open lot. The Vampire Fred was polite enough to come out and meet us before we made it to the building.

He stepped outside and stood watching us, his hands at his sides. He left the door open behind him. I guessed the spirit was back there somewhere in the darkness.

I stopped about thirty feet away. Honey hovered at my side, pixie dust falling from her in agitated clouds. The sword was back and she held it in both hands, the blade dipping toward the ground in front of her.

It occurred to me to shoot Fred and cut the visit short. I decided not to, because I thought he might say something worth listening to. I heard metal shift and grind against metal behind me. I turned. The ghosts of the gangbangers I'd killed were pulling themselves out of the twisted and tangled debris. They weren't much to look at, with shattered bones, torn flesh and caved-in skulls. There were only eight of them, so Terrence must have gotten a few out alive. I turned back to Fred.

"You are extremely persistent for a woman," he said.

"I'm easily distracted when I don't stay focused."

Fred gave an exaggerated sigh. His shoulders humped and then collapsed like someone put a lead chain around his neck. "What precisely have I done to attract such devoted attention?"

"You know why I'm here."

"Yes, I suppose I do. You believe I had something to do with the murders of your men. The question is, why?"

"One of them told me." It was an irritating game, but I had to play if I wanted to learn anything.

"Ah, that is unfortunate. We had hoped the ritual would preclude such an eventuality."

"How's that?"

"My...client was confident that their souls would be cast into the Deep Beyond and lost forever."

I laughed. "Your client didn't want you to know how expendable you are. It needed to keep an easy target in front of me."

"You are right, of course. And, so, here we are."

"Here we are. How's it going to go?"

The vampire arched his eyebrows in surprise. "Is it up to me?"

"You're not the one I want. You're just in my way."

Fred chuckled. "Two things," he said. "First, I see that you have brought a weapon this time, but the outcome of any confrontation between us is hardly a foregone conclusion." I could hear the ghosts spreading out behind me at the edge of the lot.

"It's a really big gun," I said.

The vampire nodded and smiled. "Second, what makes you think I could give you my client, should I be inclined to do so?"

"I'm optimistic. Maybe you're protection and not just a dead guy with a target on his back. Maybe your client is hiding in the building back there."

"Sadly my client is not here."

"Where is it?"

"If I tell you, where does that leave us?"

The question had some thorns on it. If the vampire sent me off chasing shadows, it might give him time to find a new lair, even blow town.

"We'd all go see your client. I'd have my gun keep a close eye on you. If the spirit is where you say it is, we're done. If it's not, you're done."

Fred nodded sadly. "I see. That wouldn't do at all, then. I'm afraid I don't know where my client is."

The vampire was probably telling the truth, and that didn't leave us many options. Fred knew that, too.

The vampire moved.

I didn't see much of it, but I didn't have to. The Dead Man's Gun was in my hand. I thumbed back the hammer and my arm jerked to the right. Electric-blue juice arced and twisted in the cylinder. The trigger pulled back, though I'm not sure it was my finger that pulled it.

The gun fired and kicked sweetly in my hand, like a healthy baby in its mother's womb. The sound of the report was a hollow sound, like it had been fired into a long tunnel. A wisp of vapor coiled from the barrel, pale as a ghost.

Fred had leaped about twenty feet to his left and ducked behind a rusting forklift. A bullet as real as a bad dream passed through the machine with a sharp hiss and struck the vampire in the shoulder. The impact spun the vampire around and black juice sprayed the wall of the building behind him.

Honey let out a war cry that sounded like the high note of an opera. She flew toward Fred with her sword poised above her shoulder like an angry snake.

I turned to face the advancing ghosts behind me and fanned the Peacemaker's hammer with my left hand. In my world, it would have been an impressive waste of ammunition, even if I could have handled the recoil. Ned trembled gently in my hand as it panned along the line of mutilated shades. I don't know how many shots I fired, but three of them found targets. Ragged holes of azure energy burned through the ghosts. The holes widened as the juice chewed at ephemeral flesh, devouring the ghosts like a hungry fire.

The remaining five stopped and stared. They were armed only with anger and vengeance, and neither was as strong as their fear. They scrambled away, fading when they reached the rusting and twisted metal of their tomb.

I turned and saw two blurred forms dueling atop the squat concrete building. Honey spun and darted and dived, thrusting and swinging at the vampire with her tiny silver sword. Fred leaped and circled and clawed at her, but his left arm hung limply from the wounded shoulder.

I brought Ned up and pulled back the hammer. I aimed low along the hog wallow trough that served as a rear sight. The blue juice flared in the cylinder and I squeezed the trigger.

The shot hit Fred in the gut just above the waistline and knocked him off the roof. Honey darted after him and I moved up along the side of the building to the rear. The vampire was lying in a scatter of garbage in a spreading pool of black magic. It pumped out of the hole in his stomach like oil. Fred pulled himself to one knee and flailed at Honey. She buzzed around his head and her sword was a silver blur as she traced his pale flesh with bleeding black lines.

I thumbed back the hammer again and nodded for Honey to back off. The vampire looked up at me, his dark eyes glittering with hate. He sneered and spat. The black juice spattered and smoked on the yellow-brown dirt.

"You weren't muscle and you weren't just a target, were you, Fred? You were hired to find the spirit a host. You knew Adan from the club. You picked him out and gave him up to that…thing."

The vampire laughed, and a fine spray of black juice followed the sound.

"Tell me where it is," I said. I gave him the words without any feeling in them.

The vampire laughed. "You're a fool, Riley. You know how to stop him and you don't have the stomach for it. He doesn't need any protection because he knows you're too weak. He owns you, you pathetic little cunt."

It was an impressive speech. When he'd finished delivering it, Fred sprang at me. The taloned claw at the end of his one good arm reached for my throat. I pistol-whipped him in the face with the Peacemaker's twelve-inch barrel because that's what it seemed to have in mind. Fred's jaw shattered under the steel and he collapsed at my feet.

I leaned down and pressed the muzzle into his forehead. I thought about all the people the Vampire Fred had murdered in all the centuries of his unnatural life. I thought about Adan.

"Tell your master I'm coming if you see it out there," I said.

This time, Ned didn't have to help me squeeze the trigger.

# eleven

We searched the building and the rest of the salvage yard for the spirit, even though I knew we wouldn't find anything. Fred had served his purpose. He was more use as a distraction than he would have been as protection.

"Are you okay, Honey?" I asked as we wandered the yard, looking for nothing. She was quiet and seemed a little agitated.

"I'm fine. The vampire didn't even touch me. He was finished when you hit him with that first shot."

"Well, that's good. I'm glad you weren't hurt."

"Yeah, I'm great." Honey landed on the air cleaner of an old car engine and sat down. "What are we looking for, Domino? There's no stupid spirit here."

"I know. I just need to be sure."

"So what are you going to do now?"

"I don't have many options. I just have to stay close to Adan. Eventually the spirit will try to possess him again. When it does, I have to be ready."

Honey threw up her hands in exasperation. "You should

go to your boss, Domino. The vampire was right. You're too close to that…man. You don't think straight."

"Let's not start this again, Honey. I can't go to my boss until I deal with the spirit."

"Oh, fine. Do what you want, Domino. You're going to anyway."

"What the hell's the matter with you, Honey?"

Honey laughed and I didn't like the sound of it. She put her head in her hands and looked like she wanted to pull her hair out. She took a deep breath and let it out slowly. Red pixie dust danced in the yellow light.

"I'm sorry," she said finally. "It's my family. They gave me trouble when I went to see them, when you were talking to the Burning Man."

"What kind of trouble?"

"They're just worried about me." She shook her head and sighed. "They say I shouldn't be crossing over to Arcadia by myself. But really, they just don't like the idea of me making deals with sorcerers. They say it's too dangerous."

"They don't even know me. Did you tell them we're friends?"

She nodded. "They just don't trust sorcerers, Domino. Our kind has never really gotten along."

"Why not?"

"Sorcerers have a habit of imprisoning us, binding us—like you did with Mr. Clean. Or using us in other ways."

"You know I don't mean you any harm."

"I told them it's not like that with us, that you're my friend. But they're worried that I could get trapped in Arcadia with no way to cross by myself. Really, they're just worried it gives you too much power over me."

I nodded. "I guess I can see their point of view."

Honey smiled and shook her head. "You're sweet, Domino. I mean it."

"What can we do about it?"

"You could make me a gate," she said. "It's just like a spell talisman. You work the magic to bring me across, and then you bind it to a physical object. It wouldn't hold up forever, but it would allow me to cross back and forth on my own for a while. Long enough for my family to get used to the idea. I told them I'd ask you, but I understand if you don't want to."

"I'll do it, Honey. I trust you."

"Thanks, Domino. You're a good friend." She hovered near me and then darted in and kissed me on the forehead. She flew away before I could react. Blue and violet pixie dust trailed behind her.

We went back to the condo and I hung the gunbelt in the closet by the front door. I crossed over and went into the kitchen and poured myself a tall glass of tequila. I went out on the balcony and stood with Honey's garden pressing in on me from all sides. I drank the tequila and chased it with a cigarette.

Then I went back to the kitchen and called Honey. When the threads of magic snapped into place, I tied them to the sports bottle that held the wilting carnations I'd bought for Mrs. Dawson. The world stretched thin and Honey came through.

"Thanks, Domino," she said, but she didn't seem too happy about it. She disappeared into her cave behind the waterfall on the kitchen table.

I poured some more tequila and thought about getting drunk. Then my cell phone beeped, letting me know I had a voice mail message. I got it out and listened.

"I have to go out, Honey," I said in the general direction of the kitchen table. She didn't answer.

Rick Macy lived in Pasadena near the campus of Caltech. He was in grad school, particle physics, but he worked for the outfit on the side. I'd never met him, but I knew of him. He had more juice than Jamal or Jimmy Lee. He was a theorist, a designer. In the real world, he might have been something like a systems engineer. He was valuable.

I parked on the street outside his little two-bedroom rambler. Vernon Case was sitting on the front steps looking like he'd rather be somewhere else. Case was a veteran. He'd hooked up with the outfit in the early sixties and made a career of it. He had enough juice to stick but not enough to go all the way up. He looked old and tired.

"Hey, Case," I said, "what's the story?"

He looked up at me and jerked a thumb over his shoulder. "More of the same, I guess. You might as well see for yourself. I was just told to lock the place down until you could get here."

"Okay," I said and walked up to the door. "Thanks for your help. You find the body?"

Case shook his head. "No, his girlfriend. They pulled her out already. She went a little nuts about it. University student, no connection to our thing except Ricky. We're just lucky she called us before she called the cops. Hell, we're lucky she didn't go bat-shit seeing that thing in there."

I nodded and went in, and Case came in behind me. Rick Macy was in his bedroom, his arms duct-taped to the headboard. He'd been skinned, but at least they hadn't nailed him down first. I went through the motions, just like I'd done at

Jamal's apartment. The only thing I found was a black stain left by the soul jar, this time on Rick's bed.

"You on this thing, Domino?" Case asked when I was finished. "Everyone knows what's happening in South Central. Hell, most of us have been down there to see for ourselves. The word is, Papa Danwe is moving on us and we're doing jack-shit about it. Everyone says we're at war, which no one minds too much, but it seems like only one side is fighting."

"We're fighting. Rashan just doesn't want to fight blind."

Case nodded. "That's good. I knew Ricky pretty well. I helped bring him in, you know. Hell, I guess I recruited him. The guy was a fucking genius, Domino. I was supposed to train him." He laughed and shook his head. "I had to turn him over to Rashan because he was way ahead of me, even at the start."

That got my attention. "Rick was trained by Rashan?"

"Sure he was. Ricky didn't have your kind of juice, but he was brilliant. He got it, you know? He understood how all this shit works." He shrugged. "Me, I do what I do but most of the time I don't really understand it. I don't have to—I just do it."

I nodded, thinking. "You've been around the outfit a long time, Case. You know everyone. How well did you know Jamal and Jimmy Lee?"

"I knew them well enough, I guess. I watched them come up, tried to help out where I could. They were good boys."

"Who trained them, Case?"

He pursed his lips and rubbed his chin. "Jamal got some basics from Rafael Chavez. Jimmy Lee was brought in by Frank Seville...you know him?"

I nodded and waited for the rest of it.

"But both guys were specialists, you know. Most guys in the

outfit don't do one thing any better than another. Hell, most of us don't do anything all that well. We've got lots of guys who can lay down tags, but most of them aren't really *taggers* like Jamal was. You know what I mean? Him and Jimmy Lee didn't have a lot of juice, maybe, but they had one thing they did well. That made them different."

"They needed more training than most," I said. "Advanced training in their specialty. Who gave it to them?"

"Well, Rashan did. He always does that kind of thing himself."

"I was afraid you were going to say that."

I told Case to keep the place locked down until nightfall and then to get rid of the body. Then I got on my cell and called Rashan. He was on his way home from the strip club. He agreed to meet me at his house.

I ran to my car and spun the traffic spell, and I kept the speedometer above ninety most of the way out to the hills. I pulled up in the circle driveway in front of the house just as Rashan was getting out of his Mercedes.

I'd never been invited to Rashan's house before. It was pretty typical for the filthy rich in that part of town. Hillside. Boxy modern architecture. Lots of glass. Wide balcony. Stilts.

"Stilts, boss?" I asked, looking up at the house. "That doesn't seem like a good idea."

Rashan smiled. "The stilts are very strong, Dominica."

"How strong?" They looked pretty spindly to me.

"It would be easier to move the hill than to move the stilts."

"This is L.A., boss. Mudslides, earthquakes. It wouldn't be that surprising if the hill decided to move someday."

Rashan shrugged. "It's L.A."

"Yeah, what are you gonna do?"

The boss smiled. "I'm not afraid of earthquakes. We had some big ones back home. Biblical ones. We took pride in them. We thought even the gods had taken notice of our great works and mighty deeds."

"Alas, Babylon," I said.

"Close enough, Dominica," Rashan said quietly. "Close enough."

We climbed the stairs to the front door and went inside. Rashan led me to his study and closed the door behind us. I sat in one of the leather chairs in front of his desk and he poured us both a Scotch.

"You've been to Rick Macy's house?" he asked, settling in behind the desk.

"Yeah," I said, "I was there. Same story."

"And do you have a theory?"

"I've been chasing a theory, but I think I got it wrong."

"Why don't you tell me."

I nodded and took a deep breath. "I was able to bring Jamal back from the Beyond. He told me who the killer was."

"You neglected to report this development. You must have had a reason for that."

"Yeah. The killer was your son, Adan."

"But Adan is not a sorcerer. He could not have done these murders." He didn't seem terribly surprised by my revelation. I'm not sure why I thought he would be.

"Right. I could see he wasn't a sorcerer, but Jamal pointed to him. Based on what Jamal said about the ritual and something that happened when I was with him, it looked like Adan was being possessed."

"Is that why you've been staying so close to my son?"

I looked down at my glass and took another drink. "Yes

and no. At first, I just needed to stay close to him, like you say. But…it got complicated. It *is* complicated."

"And if you believe he is the victim of possession, what have you done about it?"

I told him about my plan to find the spirit in the Between and destroy it. I told him about the vampire. I gave it all to him.

"But now you are questioning your theory?" Rashan asked.

I nodded. "Mr. Clean speculated that a spirit might be using the rituals to prepare a host, Adan, to move in permanently. He admitted it was just speculation, but I took it and ran with it."

"And now?"

"There's a connection between the victims that doesn't fit with that angle. You trained them all. You don't train many guys, and I don't think it's a coincidence. I don't like that connection, and I don't see what difference it would make to a spirit."

Rashan leaned back in his chair and looked at me for a long time. "Do you have a new theory?" he asked finally.

"Maybe," I said. "It's the Papa Danwe angle. I don't have any proof—I don't think I'll ever have any proof with this thing. But it fits. You've got three sorcerers who all received training from you. One is a tagger, one is a warder and one is a designer."

Rashan nodded. "Go on."

"We know that there's no point in squeezing these guys— unless you need their unique arcane talent. Well, what do they all have in common? They all learned their craft from you."

"And so what would squeezing them accomplish, in this case?"

"It'd be like getting inside your head, wouldn't it? I thought about this all the way over here. Jamal was a tagger. He created arcane symbols that tapped and rerouted juice. Jimmy Lee was a warder, a specialist in defensive magic. And Rick Macy was a theorist, a systems guy.

"When Jimmy Lee first turned up dead, I thought it was someone going after our defenses. At the time, it didn't make any sense because he wasn't doing anything important. But he was working *your* magic, boss. It didn't matter that he wasn't doing anything important—it wasn't what he was doing, it was how he was doing it. If I could get inside your head and figure out how you did that kind of magic, I'll bet I could reverse-engineer your personal defenses. I'll bet I'd know enough about your wards and protections to take them down."

Rashan arched his eyebrows. "You would, yes. Anyone else would still be missing a piece of the puzzle."

I frowned and shook my head. "I don't get that."

"You would have all the knowledge you needed—the craft, just as you say. But as you've learned, Dominica, magic isn't a science. It isn't engineering, even though sorcerers such as Mr. Macy try to approach it that way. Sorcery is an art. There is a practical aspect, technique, certainly, which the killer could have gotten from the three victims. But there are a thousand different ways a sorcerer can approach any given magical task. That's why magic is fundamentally a creative endeavor."

"So the missing piece is creativity?"

Rashan nodded. "The missing piece is *style*."

I stared at him and swallowed hard. "That's what I learned from you. I already had the nuts and bolts. You showed me how to bring it all together." I thought back to those days, when Rashan had trained me. It had been…intimate. Not sexually, not exactly, but it had some of the same vibe to it. In a very real sense, Rashan had shared his juice with me.

"I'm afraid so. And more to the point, you're the only one with whom I've shared this most intimate aspect of my art. In other words, I suspect you're next, Dominica."

"I think I would have been next anyway," I said. Maybe I should have been shocked or angry, but I wasn't. Mostly I felt like I should have seen it earlier.

Rashan continued. "So Papa Danwe isn't after territory, at least not directly—he wants to take a shot at me. He knows he has no hope of succeeding with my magical defenses in place. The question is, why bring this spirit into it? Why bring my son into it?"

"Before we get to that, I need to ask you a question." I looked up at him and he nodded. "What's it all about?"

"I'm afraid you'll have to be more specific, Dominica."

"All of it. The juice, the outfit—everything. I've been thinking about it since Jamal's body first turned up. It doesn't make any sense."

"Why not?"

"There's too much juice. All the things we're into. We have Jamal's tags and others like them pumping juice from crack houses. We have gambling and prostitution rackets that are just cover for numerology and sex magic rituals. We're on the verge of war with Papa Danwe, and half of South Central is drowning in juice. Even without all of the outfit's operations, there's more juice running through this city than anyone could ever use.

"That's one reason it doesn't make any sense that Papa Danwe is trying to move on you. What would be the point? To get more juice? Everyone already has more than they know what to do with. I asked Case, and he said there's never been a war in the forty years he's been with the outfit. There's no real conflict between the outfits because there's nothing scarce for them to fight over."

Rashan nodded and smiled. "It wasn't always so, you understand. I came to L.A. in the twenties with the bootleggers. It was a different time. There was a lot less juice and a lot more violence."

"But now there's plenty of juice."

"Yes. Every year, every day, it gets stronger. I take it you realize there is far more magic in the world today than there used to be."

"Yeah, I guess I knew things had been a little dry for a few hundred years."

"Indeed. Some will try to tell you the Enlightenment was responsible for the decline of magic. This reverses cause and effect and ignores what was happening in the rest of the world, beyond the borders of Western Europe. Magic was already fading and men simply turned their attention to other pursuits."

"But now it's coming back."

"Yes. It isn't the first time this has happened. Magic is rather like global temperature. It follows a cycle, it waxes and wanes. Humans can influence the cycle, even catastrophically, but there isn't any ultimate cause of it. It's just the way it is."

"So magic is on the rise again and that's why we have more juice than we can ever use."

Rashan shook his head. "That's why we have more juice than we can use today. You asked what this is all about. Simply put, it's preparation for what's coming."

"A war," I said.

"Yes. And other instabilities, before it comes to that."

"What kind of instabilities?"

"The kind you get when six billion human beings wake up to a world of magic, the unreal made real, things they can't possibly understand."

I had a sudden vision of the Four Horsemen riding through the streets of L.A. It would be like riot weather in Inglewood, but on an apocalyptic scale.

"And then war," I said. "Who is the enemy?"

"Monsters, of course. Things that can't exist in this world without magic, things human beings haven't had to face in hundreds or thousands of years. Things they don't even remember."

"So we're the good guys?"

Rashan laughed softly and shook his head. "Our interests coincide with those of the rest of humanity, at least insofar as this is concerned. We're all threatened by what is to come. But we share their interests only by virtue of knowledge they do not possess, and there is an inescapable arrogance and elitism in that. We certainly can't expect them to thank us for it. They will see us as secretive criminals with powers that are forever beyond their reach, criminals who play by their own rules. That is how they have always viewed sorcerers. To them, we will be no different from the monsters."

"But we aren't monsters. We're human, too."

"Are we? In the biological sense, certainly. But we aren't part of their community. We exist at the margins of their society, and they're right—we don't play by their rules. The truth is, Dominica, whether we are or not we don't think of ourselves as merely human and we certainly don't act like it."

"Speak for yourself," I said angrily. "I'm not six thousand years old. I'm still human."

"Really? Tell me something, Dominica, when was the

last time you considered the effects of your magic on other people?"

"What do you mean? I never use sorcery to hurt innocent people." There it was again—the gangster's code.

"Not intentionally, I'm sure, and not with violence. Unfortunately it goes much deeper than that. When you confronted the vampire at the nightclub, did you consider the owners of the businesses you destroyed? I suspect it never even occurred to you. When you use your traffic spell to make better time on the freeway, do you think about the effect it has on others? What if your tampering with probability slows down an ambulance just the few seconds it would take to safely deliver a critical patient to the hospital? Even the most trivial magic you use for simple convenience can have life-and-death consequences."

I didn't have anything to say. I kept my mouth shut and worked at flattening my teeth.

"You don't think about such things, because it would make your life impossible. You'd find yourself unable to cast even the simplest spell for fear of the unforeseen consequences for innocent people. You'd have difficulty getting out of bed in the morning."

"Maybe I shouldn't. Maybe the juice does make us monsters."

Rashan shrugged. "That's something you'll have to decide for yourself, Dominica. You wouldn't be the first to turn her back on her gift. But if you decide that you are a sorcerer, you will have to accept that you can never be fully human. You'll have to realize that you do not—you cannot—play by the same rules as those who do not share your abilities."

"That's a pretty good description of a sociopath."

"Yes, it is. And that's all we'd be if this thing of ours, this thing that sets us apart, were just in our minds."

Neither one of us spoke for a long time. Everything Rashan had said was true. I didn't go out of my way to hurt people—I just didn't think about them at all. I shared space with them, but I wasn't really part of their world and they weren't part of mine. I lived in a secret world, a world of magic, and most of the time I forgot the mundane world was even there.

"I don't know what to do with this," I said finally. "I don't want to be a monster, and I don't want to take the coward's way out and pretend to be just like everybody else."

Rashan started to say something, but I waved him off. "No, don't. This is something I have to figure out for myself, boss, if I get the chance. But first I have to finish what I started."

"I understand," Rashan said.

"Tell me about these things that are coming, and I'll tell you what I have to do."

As Rashan started telling me about my future, my mind kept wandering to my past. I thought about the things I had done, the things that had made me what I was. I remembered driving back to Santa Monica from the junkyard, and the way Moonie had looked at me. I'm a fucking monster, I'd said.

Sometimes the truth hurts.

# twelve

I drew my forty-five as I walked into the kitchen. I set it on the counter and poured a glass of tequila. I drained it and poured another one. I tore loose the threads binding Honey's gate to the sports bottle and let the magic escape out the open window like a bad smell. I turned to look at the nest. There was no sign of Honey, but I knew she was in there, hiding in her cave.

"I trusted you," I said. "I thought we were friends."

Honey walked out through the waterfall, parting it like a curtain. The water didn't seem to touch her skin. Her wings drooped and blue and violet pixie dust fell from her like tears. She sat down on a rock by the lagoon and put her head in her hands.

"We are friends, Domino. You're my only friend in Arcadia."

"You betrayed me." I turned and picked up the gun from the counter. "I know, Honey."

The piskie nodded. "They made me, Domino. I was ordered. I had no choice. If I hadn't asked you to make the gate, they would have punished me." She looked up at me, and her cheeks were wet. "My *family*, Domino."

"The gate and what else, Honey? How far does it go? You were supposed to play along, right? Keep me focused on the vampire? Make sure I was buying the Evil Spirit act? And what about Mr. Clean? Did you both set me up?"

"No!" Honey shouted. "I didn't know any of it, Domino! The jinn didn't, either. I'm not saying he wouldn't betray you if he got the chance, but we didn't know."

"How long have you known?"

"When you went to get the gun from the Burning Man, I went to see my family. They were waiting for me, in my home."

"Who was waiting for you, Honey?"

She didn't answer for a long time. I guess some choices are hard to make. Finally she looked at me, and I saw resignation in her eyes.

"My king. In Arcadia, he is called Oberon."

I'd known the answer before I asked the question. I'd probably known before I went to see Rashan. In the cop movies, the moment when the detective solves the mystery is always a decisive one. It hadn't been that way for me. It started as a question I couldn't answer and gradually became a suspicion. But despite everything that Rashan had told me, I probably couldn't have really owned it until I heard Honey say it.

I couldn't pretend there hadn't been plenty of clues—enough to get me close, if not all the way there. Even if there hadn't been, Honey should have been enough. The first thing she'd asked of me—the only thing she'd ever asked of me—was to help her cross over to my world, to Arcadia. She told me the fairies were born of a different world, a world in the Beyond.

She told me they longed for this world and its magic. They needed that magic, that juice, to survive here.

I'd been so focused on the Evil Spirit act, on my obsession with saving Adan, I hadn't connected the dots. I wanted to be the white knight riding to the rescue, right out of a fairy tale. I should have remembered that in *real* fairy tales, the white knight is always a sucker.

"Adan is a changeling," I said.

"Yes," Honey said. "He's a shapeshifter. He can be anyone or anything he wants, and he's a born liar. That's his glamour. But you almost destroyed their whole plan when you brought Jamal back. King Oberon didn't expect that. The changeling had to improvise all that stuff about the evil spirit when he realized his part in the murders had been revealed."

"It was a good act," I said. "Good enough for me, anyway. The lie really wasn't that far from the truth. The killer was a spirit from the Beyond. It used magic from that place, magic I couldn't see. The only question was what kind of spirit from the Beyond? Well, the kind that didn't like the railroad spikes Fred used to crucify Jamal—cold-iron railroad spikes. The kind of spirit with a preference for titanium over steel in kitchen cutlery. The kind that seemed, just for a moment, to sniff out your potion when I dosed his drink with it."

"It doesn't seem like much to go on."

I scowled. I didn't think Honey was really in a position to question my investigative technique—or lack of it. "More than anything, it was the juice. This whole thing was always about the juice. Papa Danwe doesn't need Rashan's territory. Neither would a spirit that's just looking for a vacation home in the mortal world. It had to be something that needed a lot more magic—needed it just to exist in this world. From there, the details pointed to your people. Rashan just confirmed my suspicions."

Honey shook her head. "I didn't even know about the conspiracy, and I gave it away."

"Yeah, I guess you did," I said. "So I'm next, right?"

Honey hesitated before answering. "I'm not sure, but I think he would have killed you already if he didn't need you. He needs your juice, Domino."

"And he's the assassin? Once he has the juice he needs, he's going to kill Rashan?"

"No, he can't. Remember, he's not a sorcerer. He can't use the juice himself."

"I guess that makes sense. If he could do it, he wouldn't need the soul jar. His job is to get the juice and give it to the assassin, and then help the assassin get close to Rashan. Papa Danwe. That's the only reason they really needed him."

Honey shook her head. "They needed him to build the gate, too."

"In Inglewood. The gate I was so sure was the World's Largest Magic Wand."

"Yeah, but Domino, it's actually in Hawthorne."

"So what? It's all Inglewood to me."

"In the old days, hawthorn trees were doorways between Avalon and Arcadia."

"What the fuck? Is that important?"

"No, King Oberon just thinks it's funny."

"Yeah, I can't stop laughing." I shook my head. "The one thing I don't understand is why use sorcery at all? If Oberon wants to take down Rashan, why not just nuke him with *fairy* magic?"

"They know each other, Domino. I think they've known each other a really long time. They aren't friends, obviously.

I think your boss has defenses against glamour, but that's not the only reason. There are stories. It's said the last time they faced each other there was a treaty, and King Oberon promised to never again use his magic against the sorcerer."

"Seems like your king broke that promise when he sent the changeling after him."

Honey shrugged. "I guess it depends on what his definition of 'his magic' is."

"He's worse than a fucking politician." I wondered why Rashan hadn't bothered to mention any of this. Then again, I'd learned not to waste too much time on that kind of wondering.

"He *is* a politician, Domino. A really good one."

"Well, he hasn't changed my opinion of them much."

"So what about us?" Honey was looking at the gun in my hand. I put it back in its holster.

"I guess I probably won't shoot you."

"Maybe I deserve it. I'd rather die than betray you." She started crying, and I didn't like hearing it. "Maybe that sounds stupid, but it's really true. I'll do anything if you can just forgive me and we can still be friends."

"Take a shower with me?"

The crying stopped, and Honey blushed.

"Just kidding," I said. "But I'll think about it." I winked at her and smiled.

Honey laughed and shook her head.

"The thing is, Honey, I don't have many friends in Arcadia, either." I swallowed hard. "And I betrayed you, too. When we first met, I used a spell to read your mind."

"What did you see?"

"Enough to know you're not to blame for any of this.

Enough to know I'd be lucky to have a friend like you. And I'm sorry."

Honey started crying again, but this was a different sound, one I could live with. "Thank you, Domino," she whispered.

I nodded. "Okay, just two more things. What's Adan planning to do with your gate, and what are we going to do about your family?"

The piskie smiled, and there was an evil gleam in her eye.

Adan arrived at my condo right on time. I buzzed him up and went to meet him at the door. When I opened it, he was standing there wearing faded jeans and a snug white T-shirt, with a sports bag slung over his shoulder. It was the kind of unremarkable image—just a guy standing in a hallway—that nevertheless breaks over a girl and pulls her in, making her feel that all is right with the world. It made me think of razor blades and sleeping pills.

I let him in and he gave me a quick kiss. He set the bag by the couch and went into the kitchen to fix us some drinks. I sat down on the sofa to wait. I'd like to say I didn't feel anything, but I guess I'm not that tough. I hurt like hell, and just like in the Between, I couldn't tell exactly where the pain was coming from.

Adan came out of the kitchen with two glasses and a bottle of tequila. He smiled at me. I looked at him, and for a moment, he was all I'd ever wanted. He smiled again and came to me.

When he reached the middle of the living room, he crossed the circle I'd laid down with saltwater. I'd been a little apprehensive about it, but I followed Honey's directions to the letter. The changeling never even noticed, never sensed the trap until it was much too late. I tapped the ley line running under my building and channeled it into the circle.

When the circle closed, Adan noticed. His eyes narrowed and the beginnings of a snarl tugged at his mouth, but he quickly controlled it. He kept walking and a few steps brought him up against the other side of the circle. He bumped into the magical barrier and stepped back. He looked confused. It was very convincing.

"Domino, what's going on? There's an invisible wall in your living room!"

I considered playing along, letting him have his moment. I decided I had better things to do.

I picked up his sports bag. I set it on my lap, unzipped it and pulled out the soul jar. Its magic was strong, old and black. Holding it was like telling a secret.

"What is that? I didn't put that thing in my bag. Domino, strange things have been happening to me. You'll probably think I'm crazy, but…I think something is inside me. I think maybe I'm possessed. Is that possible? Is this… Can you help me?"

"Yeah, I can help you, Adan. But I won't lie to you. It's gonna sting a little bit."

Right on cue, Adan called out in the lilting pre-Celtic language of his people. The spatial fabric of my living room stretched and thinned, and two fey warriors came through the gate. They had long, perfectly straight, silken hair, and their features were far too fine and sharp to be human. They were very tall, and their bodies were heroin-chic thin but bound in corded muscle that made them look dangerous rather than delicate. They were dressed more like street kids than elf lords, with battered jeans, T-shirts and trench coats. They held long, straight swords like they meant to use them.

While impressive, all of this was little more than a fleeting image. As soon as the fairies stepped through the gate, they were bound to Honey's nest on the kitchen table. The audible pops as they disappeared were followed by two tiny splashes as the miniaturized elf warriors were dropped unceremoniously into Honey's lagoon. That had been the piskie's idea.

Adan screamed and threw himself at the magical barrier, clawing at it like a wild animal at the bars of its cage. He stilled himself quickly, though, and his look of rage and madness was replaced by one of quiet terror when he saw what I was doing.

I got up from the couch and knelt on the floor before the circle. I set the soul jar in front of me and placed my hand on the lid. Then I lifted my head and locked eyes with Adan. To his credit, I suppose, he didn't beg for his life. He stared back at me defiantly, but the fear still gnawed at the edge of whatever sanity he'd been given when he was made.

"It doesn't matter anymore, lover," he said, his voice a harsh whisper. "You can't change what is happening. The Shining Host of the Seelie Court is coming, and this world will have a new king."

I nodded. "You're probably right. Your death probably wouldn't serve anything. It won't bring back the guys you killed."

"I can *be* him, Domino. I can be anything you want." The words were soft and seductive.

"So this is really just payback."

I tapped the line and poured juice into the circle and the soul jar. "And your very flesh shall be a great poem," I said. It was more power than I'd ever wielded. I didn't really tap the ley line—I just opened myself to it. The tidal wave of power broke over me, and for a moment I feared the magic would unmake me. The juice gave birth to the ritual, and the ritual slouched toward Adan like a wolf taking a helpless lamb. I couldn't do it exactly the same way the changeling had. The juice was different, and so was the spell. The soul jar came as advertised, though.

When I removed the lid, a black cloud, like thousands of tiny flies, swarmed out of the jar. An insectile droning filled the room, but there were no real insects in the swarm. They were too indistinct, shapeless, like figments of void suspended in the air.

Adan fought. The circle prevented him from using his magic against me, but he could still use it to protect himself. He began to sing in that musical tongue, and a silver glow, like moonlight, surrounded him and held the dark swarm at bay. The song was beautiful, and so was the monster.

His form began to change, slowly at first, but then faster and faster. He was a child, perhaps three years old, Adan as a little boy with curly hair and eyes large enough to swallow the world. He was something ancient and glorious, with leaves and vines woven through the long, straight hair of the elf lords, crowned with the antlers of a great stag. He was an old woman and a young mother, a blood-drenched warrior and a shining prince.

The silver glow pulsed and pressed against the swarm, and the changeling's magic warred with my own. The ritual broke against Adan's will like surf against the rocks, and it retreated, flowing into me, immersing me in juice as cold as space.

Adan's form was again as I had known him. He threw out his arms and his chant rose until it thundered in my ears. He smiled. I felt the life and heat leached from my body as the dark magic inundated me. My sight blurred and narrowed, and I thought I would sink into that cold river forever.

"You really are an asshole, Adan."

I opened myself wholly to the flood of magic, and I fed it with hurt, and betrayal, and loneliness and rage. I spiked it with everything in me that was still human. My body warmed and my vision sharpened. The swarm pressed against Adan's halo of moonlight, and the light dimmed. Then it darkened. Then it was gone.

The swarm moved to Adan and settled around his head. Then it began moving down the length of his body. He fought and screamed as the swarm devoured his flesh. His struggling didn't move me, and my dampening spell swallowed the sound of his death. Whatever he had been, in the end Adan died just like anything else.

When its work was done, the black cloud floated back to the jar and disappeared inside. I replaced the lid and the hellish droning subsided. I collapsed onto the floor and gasped for air as the juice burned through me. Finally, I raised my head and looked at what I had done.

What was left of the thing that had been Adan looked more like petrified wood than human remains. I struggled to my feet and walked slowly over to the body. Adan didn't smell like apples and cinnamon anymore. That wonderful smell hadn't been real, anyway. It had just been the changeling's glamour. Just another lie.

"I'm sorry, Domino," Honey said.

"I told you, we're good. Don't worry about it."

"That's not what I mean."

"I know." I stood there and looked at her. I didn't say anything else and I didn't turn away. Finally, Honey flew to me, perched on my shoulder and wrapped her arms around my neck.

"I can't cry," I whispered.

"I'll do it for you," she said, and I felt her tears on my skin.

After a few moments, Honey disengaged, wiped her face and hovered in the air beside me. "What will you do with it, Domino?"

I didn't have the energy to haul the corpse into the desert and bury it, and I didn't really want to make Anton do it, either. This was my mess. I lifted the body and was astonished at how light it was, despite my exhaustion, as if the remains were little more than a husk or shell. From what Honey had told me, I knew that fairies were really just corporeal spirits. The changeling had been more juice than mass, and now all the juice was in the soul jar.

I carried the corpse across the room and set it down in front of Honey's gate. I went back into the living room, sprawled onto the couch and crossed over into the Between.

Mrs. Dawson was standing in the middle of the room with her hands covering her mouth. She was sobbing quietly.

"It's okay, Mrs. Dawson. Everything is going to be all right. I'm sorry you had to see that. Really, I am."

"You murdered him. Right there, in the middle of my living room. You're a monster."

"Maybe you're right, Mrs. Dawson. But he wasn't human. He killed three of my men and he came here tonight to kill me. I did what I had to do. I'm just sorry it had to happen here."

"It was so horrible."

"You're really not going to like this next part. Maybe you should go into the bedroom for a while." The ghost left the room and closed the door behind her. I could still hear her crying.

I went to the gate, reached through, and pulled the changeling's corpse into the Between. I went to the closet and took a hammer, nails and a box cutter from the toolbox. I dragged Adan's body out into the hallway, stood it up and nailed it to the front door.

This was probably enough of a message for any fairy assholes who stopped by, but I wanted to make sure nothing else would be able to use Honey's gate. I sliced the palm of my hand with the box cutter and incandescent blue juice began to spill from the wound. I used the juice to paint warding sigils on the door frame. I couldn't actually spin the wards in the Between, but I could power them up when I crossed back to my world.

I opened and closed the door a few times to make sure the corpse would remain in place, and then went back inside. There was no sign of Mrs. Dawson. I had a feeling I wouldn't see her for a while. I let the spell unwind and crossed back into my world.

Honey was there, waiting for me to finish the cleanup. "What are we going to do with those guys in my nest?"

"I don't know, Honey. It was your idea to put them there."

"Yeah, but I really didn't think about what to do with them, after."

I went to the closet and replaced the tools, then drew my forty-five from the shoulder holster hanging there. I didn't say anything as I walked to the kitchen. I was thinking about what a forty-five caliber bullet would do to a body that was eight inches tall and change. I was way too tired to spin a spell, though, so the gun would have to do.

"Wait, Domino," Honey said. She hovered in front of me, blocking my way. "I don't want you to kill them."

"Why not? My outfit is at war, and they're enemy soldiers. You don't want them in your nest, and I can't think of anything else to do with them."

"I'm on your side, Domino, but they're still my people. Not exactly the same, I mean, but they're still fey folk. Anyway, they're not just soldiers, they're sidhe."

"She who?"

"Not she, *sidhe*. They're like the nobility. And I think they could be useful. The Seelie Court will want them back. You can hold them hostage."

I had to admit, it wasn't a bad idea. The two fairies didn't seem like a lot of leverage, but they gave me more than I'd have without them. Besides, it wasn't like Honey would have to share her nest with them. Her family—all twenty-seven of them—was busy building a new one in my office. I'd moved the laptop and Mr. Clean into my bedroom.

"Okay, they can live. But they have to stay in your nest. I don't have anywhere else to put them." I grabbed a beer from the fridge, returned the gun to the closet and retreated to the couch. Honey flew over and landed on the coffee table.

"We need to talk about what's going to happen next. We need to plan our next move."

"It's over," I said. "The good guys won. Papa Danwe is going to have a big fucking problem, but that's just a loose end. The changeling is dead and Rashan is safe. Your king's invasion has no chance with Rashan still in play. He knew that—that's why he had to take him out." I shook my head. "He had to have been planning this for more than twenty years. He planted the changeling on Rashan and then waited all this time to make his move."

"King Oberon is immortal, Domino. He takes a very, very long view of things. It's been more than five hundred years since fairies were able to dwell in Arcadia. What's another twenty?"

"Okay, but that brings up another question. Why here? I get why the Seelie Court wants back in. I get that they've been thinking about it for a long time. But why L.A.? Why Rashan's territory? Shouldn't they have their hearts set on Ireland or something?"

"We're drawn to the magic, Domino. The magic of that place was strong once, but now it's stronger here. And your boss controls more juice in L.A. than anyone else."

"It just seems like it would have been easier and safer for this Oberon to start small and work his way up. Why come straight for Rashan?"

"King Oberon can't start small. The Seelie Court needs a lot of juice just to survive in this world. The magic is like oxygen for us."

I nodded. I'd known that, and it was one of many little hints and clues that eventually came together in my subconscious and led me to the truth. The talk with Rashan had just confirmed my suspicions. Honey had filled in the details.

"Well, that's just it. The fey can't start with just a little magic, any more than you could make do with a little oxygen. They can only survive in a place that's filled with it. You said it yourself—your enemy had to be something that needed a lot more magic than a spirit would."

"Well, anyway, it's over now," I said. "Your King Oberon failed. His changeling is dead. Rashan is alive. I guess he'll just have to wait a little longer and try somewhere else."

"He won't stop, Domino. Killing Rashan would have made it a lot easier, but he's still coming. It takes a while for his plans to unfold, but once they do, he sees it through to the end. To tell you the truth, despite all his lore and wisdom, he's a lot like a little boy with a one-track mind."

"Then Rashan will crush him. Not only that, we'll rally all the outfits to our flag. Maybe not Papa Danwe—he probably can't come back to Jesus now, even if he wanted to. But all the others. We'll be unified. There will be no power vacuum for Oberon to move into. He's screwed."

"Don't underestimate him, Domino. Don't underestimate any of the fey. You've seen what I can do, and I'm among the least of my kind."

"I doubt that, Honey. Warrior-princess, remember? Anyway, I'm not underestimating anyone. I know it won't be easy. War never is. But it's a war we can win."

"So what will you do?"

"Right now, I've got to report in and get my marching orders."

I got on my cell and went into my bedroom, closing the door behind me. I trusted Honey, but I still didn't feel comfortable talking business in front of someone who wasn't part of the outfit.

Rashan had been prepared for what had to happen by the time I left his house, and he listened to my report without emotion. That's pretty much the way he did everything.

"Honey is convinced King Oberon is still coming," I said when I'd finished.

"She's right. We might be able to defeat him, but he won't stop without a fight. It's not his way."

"We *might* be able to defeat him? Don't be so modest, boss. We just need to get you down to Crenshaw and you can open up a can of Sumerian whoop-ass on him."

Silence.

"Boss? You there? You can take this guy, right?"

"I'm here, Dominica. But I'm afraid I cannot participate in the coming battle."

"You got something more important to do?" Maybe Rashan had agreed not to use his magic against Oberon.

Rashan sighed. "You're aware of the effect juice has on sorcerers."

"Yeah, I guess. It gives you a buzz, maybe it's a little addictive."

"It's very addictive, and I've been using it for more than six thousand years. The addiction itself isn't the problem—it's the effect repeated use of magic has on the human mind."

"What effect is that?"

"It drives us mad. Sooner or later, it breaks whatever part of us is left that is still human. Surely you've seen hints of this in your own practice of the art."

Again, I recalled how I'd wigged out after trashing Terrence's gangbangers at the junkyard. I'd felt like a monster then, and I was feeling it now. I'd been at the edge of collapse after squeezing the changeling, but now I felt like I could do it all over again. Worse, I felt like I might want to.

"I guess I never thought about it much. You never really mentioned it would get worse."

"Now you know. It's no coincidence that there are so many legends of mad wizards in human folklore. In the mythology of every culture on Earth, secret and forbidden knowledge always has a price for the mortals who seek it. Dominica, I haven't cast more than one spell at a time in fifty years. I haven't used magic seriously, for an extended period of time, since the sixteenth century. If I start using it now, I will become as great a danger to this world as King Oberon."

"Well, ain't that a bitch." It was like finding out your role model, someone you idolized, was kind of a loser. I hadn't been this disappointed in someone since Michael Jordan tried to hit a curve ball.

"I didn't intend for you to find out like this. Things are moving faster than I anticipated. I'd hoped for more time to prepare you." He sighed again, and for the first time he sounded old and tired. "There is never enough time. One thing you learn after six thousand years—there's never enough time."

"What are you saying, boss?"

"You're ready, Dominica. You've proven that. You un-covered this plot. You revealed and defeated King Oberon's agent. You did that. I didn't lift a finger. I've been searching for someone who could lead us through the approaching storm for more than half a century. I finally found that person, in you."

"Just like that? I'm the new boss?"

"Don't be presumptuous. I'm not dead. As long as I'm alive, I remain the boss of this outfit. Your boss. And should you grow weary of that arrangement and begin to think ambi-tious thoughts, remember that I've survived for six millennia. I enjoy being alive. If forced to choose, you'll find I choose madness over death."

"Jesus, boss, I wasn't planning to rub you out. It's just…I'm not sure what to say. I'm not even sure I want this."

Rashan laughed. "Bullshit, Dominica. You want it bad. Even when I made you my lieutenant, you felt sorry for your-self. You always felt like you were just a serving girl, always running around doing things I could just as easily do for myself. Well, now you know the truth. I need you, Dominica. I always have."

"So what is my role, exactly?"

"You're my wartime captain. In the old days, I would have called you my champion. As far as the coming war is concerned, you're in charge. You make all the decisions, you give the orders and your word is final. I'm available to advise you, at your discretion."

"My discretion?"

Rashan sighed again, but this time he sounded more impatient than old. "Yes, your discretion. As I said, your word is final. Even if I'm the one disagreeing with you."

"What if I want to change the name of the Men's Room?"

"Don't even think about it. That has nothing to do with the war."

"Just kidding, boss. Okay, I'm in. So advise me. What do I do next?"

"You tell me. You're in charge."

"Okay, I'm in charge." It felt good. I took a deep breath. "Well, the Seelie Court is still going to try to come through. We don't know exactly when, and we don't know exactly what they'll do when they come, but at least we know where. The gate in Hawthorne is the key. That's where we have to attack."

"And how will you attack?"

"I'm too tired to dick around with them. We mobilize in Crenshaw and fight our way into Hawthorne. We hit the gate. If we can take it down, the Seelie Court can't come through. That way we don't have to fight them block by block, house by house, down on the street."

"Yes," Rashan agreed. "But you have to move quickly. King Oberon will send small tactical teams through to seize territory and lay down their own tags. He won't send an army at first, and you must use the window of opportunity that gives you."

"Why won't he send an army?"

"For the same reason we avoid such overt action. Think, Dominica. This world is changing, but it's not ready for that change. How do you imagine the U.S. government would react if a fey army invaded L.A.?"

I didn't know. I couldn't even imagine it. It would escalate slowly, because the politicians and generals wouldn't be able to make any sense of it. Maybe just the National Guard at first, to deal with a wave of "illegal immigrants." The Marines would follow, and then…who knew? What would happen when they had to admit the illegal aliens weren't human and they were using magic? What would happen when the lid was finally popped off the underworld for everyone to see?

"It could get pretty ugly," I said finally. "Like, total break-down of society ugly. But it would get even worse. Once it became clear L.A. had really been invaded by magical beings from another plane of existence…no options would be off the table."

"Exactly. And King Oberon didn't wait all this time to eat a nuke the moment he finally makes it back."

"So, no army."

"Right. Not at first, anyway. Not until he's established himself here and consolidated enough power to sit down at the negotiating table as an equal among the nations of this world."

"That's what he wants?"

"Of course. Long ago, even before my time, Arcadia was an empire that stretched from what is now Greece to the British Isles."

"Arcadia. I thought that was just the fairy name for our world."

"It is. For King Oberon, our world and his rightful kingdom are one and the same."

"That's ambitious."

"Yes, but he has to bide his time. His kingdom will not be built in a day. As you've discovered, he is exceedingly patient."

"Is he evil, boss? I mean, what he did to you..."

Rashan was silent for a time. "You will drive yourself mad trying to answer such questions," he said finally. "You've learned how difficult it is to apply such categories even to sorcerers. Let it suffice that different rules apply to King Oberon, just as they do to us. Never doubt, he is capable of great cruelty—but also great kindness and beauty. Perhaps such balance is the only thing to which any of us can aspire. Perhaps we must leave good and evil to mortal men."

"If you say so. Anyway, we just have to take out the gate. That's his Achilles' heel. It's the only reason he really needed Papa Danwe. For everything else, he could have used his own minions if he'd had to. But he needed someone in this world to throw open the door and let him in." Just as Honey had needed me.

"I concur," Rashan said.

"I'll take a few guys to hit the gate. I'll mobilize the rest of our soldiers and hold them in reserve, just in case some of those tactical teams slip through."

"I think I chose well, Dominica."

"I better get down to Crenshaw, boss. When he finds out his changeling is dead and his plan has gone sideways, Oberon will move fast."

"There's one other thing."

"What's that?"

"Perhaps you didn't tell me the truth about your relationship with Adan, with the changeling, because you thought I
wouldn't approve."

I didn't say anything.

"You should know that if you're good enough to be my
champion, you're good enough to be my daughter. It would
have made me proud."

"Thank you, sir." I had to fight against the sudden tightness
in my throat to get the words out. I thought there might be a
lot of other things I wanted to say, but I didn't have the guts.
I switched off the phone and put it away.

# thirteen

"I'm coming with you, Domino!" The pixie dust was flying off Honey like Kansas topsoil in a tornado, and most of it was deep red.

"I said no, Honey. This isn't your fight. I could never have made it this far without you, and you know how much I appreciate it. But I'm going to war with your king. I can't let you put yourself in the middle of that."

"I'm already in the middle!"

"You can stay here—all of you—for as long as you want. I'll protect you and your family. But you're not coming with me."

Honey started singing in that strange language of hers. I couldn't understand any of the words, but suddenly I understood why she had to come with me.

"Oh," I said. "Yeah, I guess you're right. You have to come with me. You can help. If I try to do this without you, I'll just get myself killed."

Shaking her head in disgust, Honey flew up to me and blew green pixie dust in my face. Why had I just agreed to let her come with me?

"I just put a glamour on you, Domino."

I shook my head, trying to clear out all the pixie dust that seemed to be dancing around in there. "Jesus. Kinda like the Jedi mind tricks I use on bouncers."

"And I didn't have to release you from it if I didn't want to. I only did that because we're friends."

"Yeah, thanks. So like I was saying…"

"No, Domino. Don't you see? You had no protection from my glamour. You'll be helpless against the Seelie Court. You're not prepared for fairy magic. You need me."

Honey had a point. How was I supposed to fight the fairies if the bastards could drop spells on me right through my defenses? I looked over at the soul jar where it still sat on the living-room floor.

"Don't even think about it, Domino!"

I went over and picked up the soul jar and sat down on the couch. I looked at it. I looked at Honey.

"No, Domino!" Honey screamed.

I shrugged and opened the lid. I let the juice of my three fallen soldiers evaporate out into the air. I only took the changeling's juice. I tapped it just as I would tap the ley line under my building, but I didn't spin it into a spell. I just took it all in, letting that bone-cold juice seep into my mind and soul.

I knew how to do it, but I'd never squeezed anyone before. It had never come up. It wasn't like learning a new spell, or even learning to use magic for the first time. It wasn't like learning at all. When it was over, when I'd sucked every last drop of the changeling's juice out of the jar, I just had his magic in me.

"Cool," I said, and tossed the soul jar onto the couch.

"That should have killed you, Domino," Honey said. Her face was pale and she was trembling.

"Didn't."

"I can see that. I don't understand it."

"I am Dominica Riley, called Half-elven. My father was a fairy prince exiled to this world long ago, and he hooked up with Mom when he was passing through L.A."

"Really?"

"No. He was a deadbeat drunk. Split on us when I was two."

"Not funny. So did it work? Can you…"

I nodded. "Yeah, I have it all, I think." I pictured Anton in my mind, and just like that, I was an obese Russian man.

"That's disgusting, Domino."

"I am becoming to be hungry," I said in my thick Muscovite accent. "You have chips?" I laughed. The word sounded like "cheeps." It sounded exactly like Anton. "R-r-ruffles have r-r-ridges," I said, rolling the Rs dramatically.

"*Ya umeu govorit' po russki,*" I said in Russian.

"What are you saying, Domino?"

"I said, 'I can speak Russian.'" I laughed again, and shifted back to my own, more feminine Mexican-Irish form.

"That's great, Domino, but you still have to let me come with you."

This time, I actually saw the cloud of pixie dust come billowing toward me. It was golden and glowing, like sunlight through a window, and I knew I was only seeing it because of the fairy magic inside me. I took a deep breath and blew. My breath was laced with sapphire juice. It cut through and dispersed the cloud of pixie dust.

"Damn," Honey said.

I looked at the walls of my living room, and now I could see

Honey's paint job wasn't real. I saw the magic pulsing there, and I could see through it to the white drywall.

"Okay, Honey, you can come with me."

"What changed your mind?"

"Now I know what you people can do, I'm going to need all the help I can get."

Mom still lived in East L.A. in the house where I was born. I'd offered to buy her a condo in a gentrified neighborhood in Eagle Rock or Highland Park, but she said she'd never leave the barrio. As an outfit girl, I've learned to pick my battles. This was one I'd never win. Anyway, the barrio was still on Rashan's turf—she was probably safer there than she'd be in Beverly Hills.

Honey was nervous about coming to dinner. I guess fairies are a little skittish about revealing themselves to humans— unless they're playing an angle.

"You want to come with me? Okay, this is my first stop," I said.

"I could be invisible," Honey suggested, a worried frown tugging at the corners of her mouth.

"Mom's a medium. She'd probably sense you anyway. Better if you just play it straight. Besides, I already told her I was bringing someone."

"You did?"

"Yeah. She probably thinks you're a new boyfriend."

Honey mumbled something I couldn't quite make out.

"What?"

"Nothing. Jesus, Domino, you could have told her what I am. She's going to be really disappointed."

I shrugged. "I couldn't think of a good way to tell her you're a piskie. Better she just sees for herself."

"You don't think it's going to freak her out?"

"It's not like she's never met a spirit before, in her line of work. She met Mr. Clean, once. Didn't care for him much."

"She probably won't like me, either."

"She'll like you fine. You might want to glamour up some clothes, though, just this once. Mom's pretty conservative."

"You're a gangster and she accepts you."

"Yeah, but I'm her daughter, so I have to work pretty hard at it to do anything wrong. Besides, the way Mom sees it, living a life of crime and violence is one thing. Naked women are something else entirely."

"That doesn't make any sense."

"Well, maybe you want to explain that to her. Just let me know so I can go somewhere else."

Honey sulked most of the drive out to the barrio, but she dusted up a pretty little floral sundress before we pulled up outside the well-kept bungalow. Mom was waiting for us at the door when we stepped onto the porch.

"I've been waiting for you, Dominica," Mom said.

"You can see the future, Mom. I guess you knew we'd be late."

Gisela Maria Lopez Riley was fifty-four years old, but she looked at least ten years older. Life in the barrio raising a juvenile delinquent tomboy as a single mother will do that to you. There was as much silver in her hair as black, and the deep creases in her face spoke of hard years. But she was still just as slender as she'd been as a young girl when she met my father. They'd been the kind of Roman Catholic couple that ordinarily has at least eight kids, but then Dad took off. I had the feeling Mom would have gladly traded her figure for another half dozen *niños*.

"Where is your friend, Dominica?" Mom asked, as she

led me into the house. The living room was where she conducted her business, and it was filled with the trappings of the Mexican *bruja*. Portraits of Jesus and the Madonna shared space on the darkly painted walls with crucifixes and indio art. Statues of the saints and candles of all sizes and colors huddled on every horizontal surface. A dramatically hideous beaded curtain set off the room from the rest of the house.

"She's here, Mom." I turned and looked behind me, but there was no sign of the piskie. I patted the front of my jacket and lifted the lapels to look inside. *Nada.* "Honey, come on," I said. "This is ridiculous."

Honey dropped her invisibility glamour and materialized right in front of my mother. She'd brought a tiny flower from her garden, and she offered it shyly. "Hello, Mrs. Riley. It's very nice to meet you. I'm Honey."

Mom's eyes grew wide, and for a moment I feared cardiac arrest was imminent. Then she laughed, and it was a sound I recognized very well from my childhood—the sound of simple delight in small things. She took the flower and set it carefully in her hair.

"Thank you, Honey," she said. "It's a pleasure to meet you, too, and welcome to my home."

After that, I didn't get in another word until we'd finished dinner. I helped clear the table and then went out on the porch to smoke while Mom and Honey took care of the dishes. Yes, I offered to help. No, they didn't let me because I'd just be in the way. Both were familiar with my housekeeping skills.

When they were finished, they came out to the porch to join me and enjoy the cool evening. We sat on the swing together, with Honey perched between us. They chatted like they'd lived next door to each other all their lives. Mom was telling Honey about a client of hers, an elderly widower who had—to hear my mom tell it—more or less ignored his wife for the fifty years of their marriage. Now that she was gone, he was distraught and desperate to contact her in the Beyond. The overall theme seemed to be the general pigheadedness of men.

After an hour or so, they'd said all they could say about that. Their attention turned to me.

"Why are you so quiet, Dominica?" my mother asked. I thought about mentioning that I couldn't get a word in edgewise, but I didn't think about it long. I generally keep the sarcasm holstered when I'm talking to Mom.

"I'm fine," I said. "Great dinner, Mom, thanks." I'd never found a better tamale, and I'd been all over L.A. looking for one.

"She's not fine," Honey said. "But she'll never admit it. She's very stubborn."

"She certainly is that," my mother agreed. She looked at me, and covered my folded hands with one of hers. "Your world is changing, Dominica, and you're not sure about your place in it anymore."

I nodded. There wasn't any point denying it—you give up a certain amount of privacy at a young age when your mother is a fortune-teller. Besides, this was why I'd come. I needed her. Chavez was pulling everything together in Crenshaw, and this was my last chance for a reality check before I went to war.

"It's the magic. I'm not sure I can handle it. I'm hurting people, Mom, you know? I don't mean to, but I do. But it'll hurt people if I stop, too."

My mother was silent for a time. I was afraid of what she would tell me—I wasn't expecting any sympathy. Finally, she spoke. "Every night, when I was a little girl, I prayed to the

Madonna and begged her to take this burden from me. Surely what I do is a sin! Am I not interfering in God's plan? Who am I to look into the future, to try to change it by telling others what I see? When I commune with the spirits, am I damning my soul and those of the petitioners who come to me?"

I started to speak, but Mom shushed me. "No, let me finish, Dominica. The truth is, I don't know. I can't know. But when someone comes to me, and they are in pain, is it a lesser evil to just let them suffer, even though I have the power to help them?"

I shook my head.

"No!" my mother said, and there was strength and conviction in her voice. "What do I know of God's plan? The real arrogance is in thinking I *could* interfere with it. The universe, God's plan—these things are too big for me, Dominica. I am just a woman and God has given me a gift. I don't know why. I don't know why He chose me. But if one of His children comes to me, and I have the power to help them, I will *do* it. And now when I pray to the Madonna, I thank God for His gift and I praise Him for allowing me to serve Him in my way. Everything else—all these big questions—I leave that to Him."

"You help people, Mom. I'm not reading palms and telling fortunes. I kill people. It's not the same."

"Your path is harder than mine, Dominica. Your burden is heavier. I won't lie to you. What you do puts your soul in peril of Hell."

"Thanks, Mom. I feel a lot better now."

"The question is, are you willing to risk damnation for what you do? Is it that important? And if it is, do you have the courage to sacrifice your soul to do what must be done?"

At first, it didn't make any sense to me that God would

expect that kind of sacrifice. If you were doing something that doomed you to Hell, you probably weren't doing God's will, whatever that might be. Then I remembered Mr. Clean's account of Lucifer's Fall. Was this the sacrifice the Morning Star—the most exalted of God's angels—had been expected to make? What if God's plan really did require some to be damned in order to serve it? And even if that were true and not just the heretical ranting of a spirit with a questionable pedigree, what did I ever do to deserve the short fucking straw?

I shook my head. "I don't know, Mom. I hear what you're saying, but it sounds like a rationalization. It's just 'the ends justifies the means' wrapped in convenient theology."

"Of course it's 'the ends justifies the means,' Dominica!" Mom seemed agitated. "Grow up, girl. Life isn't fair, and the right choices aren't always easy to come by, especially for a woman. If the ends we seek don't justify what we do, what else possibly could?"

I didn't have a good answer for that, but then I'm a gangster and not a philosopher. I was a little out of my depth. I didn't really care about the philosophy, anyway. What mattered was that it made sense to me. I was a criminal, and a killer. I had power that other people didn't, and using that power meant I would affect the lives of others in ways I couldn't even guess. Should I choose to wield it anyway?

It depended entirely on what I was wielding it for. It depended on what I was fighting for. Was it important enough?

I realized the gangster code wasn't going to cut it anymore. I couldn't take a life and then shrug it off because of my victim's choice of profession. *That* was just rationalization. It always had been, and I'd always known it. If I was going to call myself a soldier, I'd have to start acting like one. I didn't believe I was an instrument of God's plan. God didn't speak to me and He never had. But I had a righteous cause, just the same. I was willing to die for it. I was willing to burn for it, if it came to that. I had a battle to fight. Now I just needed an army.

I hugged my mother, tightly and for a long time, before Honey and I left. And for the first time in my life, I was at peace with myself as we drove toward Crenshaw. I felt like a faithless Abraham climbing up the mountain with his son in tow, but I was at peace.

Chavez had set up our field headquarters in a vacant suite in a strip mall on La Tijera. The suite was the only space in the mall that was open for business. The taggers had moved in over the last couple days, and the building had become a complex nexus of converging lines of magic that now criss-crossed the neighborhood. Outfit gangbangers stood watch outside the entrance, and they all had enough juice that they didn't need any heavy weaponry.

Honey had replaced the summer dress with a biker-girl ensemble—black leather from head to toe, including the cute little hat. It was bound to cause a stir, but I was glad she wasn't going in naked.

The suite was large for that part of town, but it was still a tight fit for the twenty or so outfit guys milling around inside. Vernon Case was there, and Chavez, of course. Rashan was there, too. Sonny Kim and Ilya Zunin stood to one side, keeping to themselves. I saw a few of the big hitters I'd asked Chavez to bring in. Even Anton was there, but probably only because he'd been in it from the start, when he found Jamal's body. It was a courtesy—his juice would have never gotten him in the door.

When I walked in, Rashan started clapping and everyone else quickly joined in. There were cheers and such witty salutations as "Long live the queen!" I blushed and tried to cover it with a scowl. In the outfit, promotions are typically private affairs between you and your boss. They're usually met with more resentment than praise, at least until you've busted enough heads to make it stick.

A few of the guys started yelling "Speech! Speech!" I started to tell them to shut the fuck up, but then I saw Rashan nod. "Do it," he said, mouthing the words. Honey flew over and hovered near him, whispering something in his ear. She drew a few stares, but mostly everyone's attention stayed on me.

Jesus Christ. I walked slowly to the front of the room and looked out at the assembly of hardened career criminals while I tried to think of something to say. I had in mind to give them a rousing speech, do my part to rally the troops. Unfortunately I suck at inspiration.

"We've had a good run," I said. It was a great start—if that didn't get them fired up, what would? "All of us in this room, we have juice. We have power. We live a life normal folks can't even imagine.

"That life is over." I dropped it on them and let it sit there. I heard some whispering and saw more than a few unhappy faces, but mostly they just looked at me.

"Something's coming, and it's a lot worse than Papa Danwe. And after that, it's going to be something even worse…and it's never going to end." I was thinking about the Firstborn, demons, and their lust for dominion over the earth. I didn't think it was time to tell my soldiers everything I knew about what was coming. Not yet. "We're going to be asked to fight, and die, and not for our own wealth and power. That's something we've always been willing to do. We're going to be asked to die for the soccer moms and the welfare queens, the lawyers and the bums. You probably don't even like these people very much. We're not like them. We're not part of their world. We're the hidden masters of a secret underworld, and we ignore them because we can.

"We can't ignore them anymore. The world needs saving—but it's their world, not ours. It's always been their world. We've just been living off the crumbs.

"We call ourselves soldiers. Starting today, that's what we are. Starting today, we're not just an outfit, we're a secret army. We have to fight, because there's no one else to do it.

"No one's going to thank you for it. To the people you're saving, you're just another fucking monster. The only ones who are going to know you're a hero are the men and women standing beside you."

They looked like they wanted something more, but I didn't have anything else. "That's it," I said. "That's all there is. If you're thinking this isn't what you signed up for, you're right. You can leave, right now. No hard feelings. I just don't have the time to try to change your mind."

I stopped talking and pointed to the door. No one left, though a few of them shifted uncomfortably and stared at their feet. I waited long enough for it to get awkward, and then I waited some more. Now that I had them thoroughly demoralized, it was time to wrap up.

"Let's go to war," I said.

There were no rousing cheers, no oaths or vows, no dramatic salutes. They just stared at me. Then Anton waddled forward, a forgotten, half-eaten sandwich hanging at his side.

"Will we still get paid, Domino?"

There were a few chuckles, then a few laughs, and then the

whole room was roaring. Anton looked around, bewildered, an uncertain smile pulling at his cherubic face.

"Yeah, Anton, you'll still get paid. Matter of fact, I'm going to give you a fucking raise." Laughter coursed through the group like the Wave at a football game. Even Rashan was laughing.

I realized Anton had accomplished something I'd utterly failed to do on my own. That he did it unwittingly goes without saying, but that didn't make it any less important. The gangsters in the room had made their choice, and most of them would stand by it. But Anton had brought them together. Anton had made them feel good about themselves, and about each other, just by being Anton. I could give them orders— my rank and my juice gave me that right. But it would take more than rank to make an army out of them. It would take a lot more than juice to lead them.

Chavez called me over to a long conference table in the center of the room. A large map of L.A. was spread out on the table. Glowing lines marked our borders and those of Papa Danwe's territory, as well as the tag networks that snaked their way through South Central and converged on Hawthorne. The location of the gate was circled in pulsing blue light.

"The strike team is ready, boss," Chavez said. "We've still got taggers out there on the street, but we've got enough juice to go when you say go. We were even able to run a couple lines all the way up to the factory grounds."

"What's Papa Danwe doing?"

"We don't know, but the pot is boiling. He's got a lot of fucking juice in there. If we're going to hit it, we got to go soon."

"Okay, I want five guys. Frank Seville, Ismail Akeem, Amy Chen." I looked over at the big hitters where they huddled together trading gossip and lies. "Pick two more, but not Wale. I don't trust that guy." Simeon Wale probably had more juice than the others, but he had a bad reputation even in a hard crowd. He also ran a crew in South Central, and he'd been a little too friendly with Papa Danwe in the past.

"That makes five anyway, boss," Chavez said. He tossed his head in the direction of Sonny Kim and Ilya Zunin. "Those guys say they're in. They insisted." Chavez shrugged. "That don't mean anything, though."

"Yeah," I said, "that's good." I waved my allies over and shook their hands.

"Thing is, boss, why just five? Everyone here is ready to go. Let's call in the fucking cavalry. Why hold back?"

"Manpower isn't the problem, Chavez. You did great with the tags, but we're still going to be sucking a dry tit compared to what Papa Danwe has in there. What juice I've got, I want my best guys tapping it." We also needed the others with their own crews. They had to get their soldiers ready for block-to-block fighting if we failed and the fairies came through.

My boss knew what I had in mind, and he started clearing everyone out. Pretty soon, it was just Chavez, my strike team and me. And Honey. She mostly kept to herself, but she didn't leave my side.

I laid out what we were up against, even though I knew they'd all heard the story by now. We studied the map and planned our approach, following the tags that stretched into Hawthorne like a clawed hand.

"If everything goes just right, it's not going to be that complicated," I said. "We move in fast and take out Papa Danwe's soldiers. I take down the wards." I was pretty sure there were fairy wards on the gate—that's why I hadn't detected them.

But I was also confident the changeling's juice would allow me to take them down. I'd also have Honey backing me up.

"Once we crash the gate's defenses, any one of us should be able to destroy the hardware," said Sonny Kim. He looked at Zunin as if to say, "Even you."

"I don't like the juice situation," said Amy Chen. Amy was as petite as Terrence Cole was wide. She might have been five feet in heels, and she couldn't make a hundred pounds with a thumb on the scale. She looked impossibly young but her power was very old and very strong. The combination was exotic and sexy, but every guy in the outfit was scared shitless of her.

"I do not like it, either," Akeem whispered. He always whispered. He was Somali, some kind of witchdoctor or juju man back in the day. He said he always whispered so evil spirits wouldn't know what he was thinking. Rumor said the whispering was a side effect of repeatedly subjecting himself to ritual possession. "But what is worse? Do we attack with less juice than we would like? Or do we wait for more tags and give this King Oberon a chance to open the gate?"

No one had an answer for that. I realized that either course could be a mistake, and the mistake could be a disaster.

"I don't think we can assume Oberon will give us time to lay down more tags," I said. Akeem nodded in agreement. "But I'm also worried about the juice," I finished, and Amy winked at me. "Honey, what do you think?"

The piskie had been sitting on my shoulder, like a pirate's pet parrot, and she jumped to her feet. Maybe she was surprised I'd asked her opinion. Or maybe she'd fallen asleep.

"I wasn't told anything of King Oberon's plans. I don't know when he will come. But I think it will be soon."

"Okay, thanks, Honey."

"I'm not finished, Domino," the piskie said, sparing me an annoyed glance. Whatever else it had gotten me, it didn't seem like my promotion had earned me any deference from the people in the room. Then again, what could I really expect from gangsters and fairies? Hell, I'd been known to crack wise with Rashan from time to time.

"Like I was saying, I don't know when the gate will open. But maybe I can find out. I could go to the Between, you know, scout it out."

I smiled at her. "That's a good idea. It won't take long, and we'll be able to see what kind of force Oberon has deployed at the gate, maybe get an idea of when he will move."

"We?"

"Damn right, we," I said. "I'm coming with you."

Honey was right—even inside my condo, nighttime in the Between was really blue. An eerie, ghostly blue that cast a nimbus over everything, like the light from a TV set that's always just around the corner. I fetched Ned from the closet, then we hoofed it in no time to the Hawthorne city limits.

We materialized in an alley about a mile from the factory, right in the middle of an armed encampment of sidhe warriors. There were nine of them: six men and three women. They'd scavenged fuel from Dumpsters and old buildings, and they were sitting around an honest-to-God campfire. The fire didn't do much but brighten the ambient blue a little, but it did seem to be throwing off some heat.

The fairies were sitting there, at their fire, wearing silver chain and dark leather, whipping up a quick dinner in small copper pots and sharpening long, slender swords just like the ones the sidhe warriors had brought to my condo. Fey horses the size of Clydesdales were tethered in a line along the edge of the alleyway.

"The Renaissance Faire isn't for a few months yet," I said.

The elves froze and stared at me for a long moment. Then they leaped to their feet and attacked. Honey missed most of the fun in the early going, because she darted straight up and hovered over the alley, roughly parallel to the roofline of the adjacent buildings. That didn't leave the fairies with a whole lot else to think about, other than me.

Three of them came at me with the weed whackers, while the other six hung back and lobbed glamours at me. I still couldn't use sorcery in the Between, but my own glamour worked just fine. I huffed and puffed and managed to block most of the spells that floated toward me like bad air. One got through. It settled over me and worked its way inside, and it turned me into a toad.

This was a bad choice of spells to use on me, all things considered, though the elf had no way of knowing that. I just hopped around and waited while the sidhe warriors sheathed their swords and started laughing. Then I shifted back to the Domino-shaped body I prefer, drew Ned and gunned a couple of them down.

"Ribbit," I said.

Honey corkscrewed down toward us, dropping pixie dust on the elves like confetti at a parade. Three of them collapsed on the street, laughing uncontrollably, and I was pretty sure Honey's magic was the cause rather than my amphibian humor.

One of the warriors had gotten close enough to take a swing at me, and his sword lashed out, reflecting the blue night as it swung in a flat arc at my head. I brought Ned up and caught the blade on the barrel. When the silver touched iron, there was a flash of sapphire sparks and the sword shattered.

"Sorry about that," I said to the elf, who stood there staring dumbly at his broken sword. Then I shot him in the head.

As necessary as it may be, witty banter in the midst of battle is never the most efficient angle to take in a fight. While I was commiserating with the sidhe warrior, one of the remaining three drew a silver hunting horn from her pack and lifted it to her lips. I cursed and was just able to aim and fire Ned before the sidhe sounded the horn. The shot took the elf in the chest and she crumpled without a sound.

Honey's sword was out and she was dueling two of the sidhe. They looked like they were trying to swat a fly with machetes. I couldn't get a clean shot with Ned. The elves lunged at Honey, and her blade flashed, slicing open a slender throat. She spun in midair and planted her sword in the other sidhe's eye. The piskie flicked emerald juice from her blade as the bodies fell.

"Domino, follow me." Honey flew into a nearby building and I followed her up three flights of stairs to the roof. The piskie flew to the edge and looked back at me.

"I saw it when I flew up here at the start of the fight," she said. I came up beside her and looked out over the city. Our vantage wasn't that high and we were encircled by the pale mist. But I could see what I needed to. We hadn't been unlucky appearing in the middle of the fairies, because they were everywhere. Some of the sidhe were camped, but others marched along the streets in columns that trailed into the mist.

A fey army was mobilizing in South Central L.A.

# fourteen

"We have to go, right now," I said when we made it back to the field headquarters in Crenshaw. I briefed my team on what I had seen while they gathered the weapons and arcane paraphernalia they'd need for the attack on the gate.

"We stumbled on an encampment a mile from the factory," I said. "They're all over Hawthorne. It seems like the whole Seelie Court is encamped in the city."

Honey disagreed. "The Court is vast. It's a nation, Domino. What we saw is just an army."

"The point is, Oberon has moved an army into position around the gate. Rashan seems to think he won't send them through all at once, but he's obviously ready to send some of them. That gate is going to open soon, and we don't have time to wait for more tags."

"We will make do," Amy said. She already had her shit together, and she sat quietly, preparing herself.

We piled into Frank Seville's Hummer, and I rode shotgun while he drove. Literally—I'd grabbed the Mossberg out of the trunk of the Lincoln before we left. The weapon might come in handy if the juice ran low during the fight.

We'd done everything we could to keep a lid on it, but civilization was coming undone in Crenshaw, and things grew steadily worse as we drove through Inglewood toward Hawthorne. The orange glow of fires dotted the skyline in every direction, and the only people on the streets were looters and thugs.

Honey and I went to work on the other members of the strike team, putting glamours on them that would offer at least some protection from fairy magic. I was hoping it would be an unnecessary precaution. If we destroyed the gate quickly maybe we wouldn't even see a fairy, let alone have to fight one. I wasn't willing to bet on it, though. And I didn't want to think about what would happen to my team if they went up against the sidhe completely unprotected.

At Centinela and La Brea, a line of burned-out cars had been towed into position across the street, forming a makeshift roadblock. I was willing to bet we'd find more just like them blocking all of the major arteries into Hawthorne.

Seville stopped and began backing up, and then the Hummer was rammed from behind by a massive green waste management truck. We were thrown forward and smashed into the roadblock, just as a rocket-propelled grenade detonated against our left front fender and tore away most of the Hummer's front end. The airbags deployed as the ambushers unloaded on the mortally wounded vehicle.

I threw up both my physical and magical shields as I battled the front and side airbags. I couldn't see anything, and all I could hear was the cacophony of combat spells and automatic weapons fire tearing the SUV apart. My defensive shields wouldn't last long, and if we couldn't get clear of the ambush, we were going to die.

I've mentioned before that I can't fly, and this is true. I can use my telekinesis spell on myself, or, say, a vehicle I'm in, but I'd discovered soon after learning the spell that this isn't the same as flying. The telekinesis spell is simple force magic, and what control it offers is a little crude. It's great for tossing vampires around, and it serves as the basis of my levitation spell, but it's not so great for flying.

Given the circumstances, I realized crude was better than dead. "All movements go too far," I said, and hit the twisted wreckage of the Hummer with the telekinesis spell. I picked up the truck and threw it about fifty yards down the street, beyond the roadblock and the kill zone. It hit the street with a hellish crash, rolled a few times and smashed through the metal and glass facade of a dollar store. We finally came to rest upside down. I hung from my seat belt and looked over at Seville.

"That'll buff right out, Frank."

"Fuck it, Domino. I've got GEICO."

We piled out of the truck and staggered into the street, looking back toward the roadblock. Papa Danwe's gangbangers had left the buildings, rooftops and alleyways to either side and were strung out in a line, scrambling down the street toward us. There were at least a couple dozen thugs in the little mob, and they never had a chance.

All six of us, plus Honey, unleashed our nastiest combat spells on them simultaneously. This probably would have been the most impressive magical performance I'd ever seen, except it all happened at once and I didn't really see anything. Magic lit up the street in rapid-fire flashes, and a sound like heaven falling to earth crashed around us. There was a lot of smoke, and when it cleared, the gangbangers were gone. Most of the buildings and storefronts were gone, too. What was left looked like the streets of Dresden after an Allied bombing run.

We all stood there for a moment and looked at our handiwork. A brick fell loose from a demolished building and clattered down a pile of rubble into the street. A shard of glass dropped from a shattered window and smashed against the still-smoking sidewalk. Then all was silent, but for a lone dog barking somewhere in the night.

We covered the rest of the distance to the old factory on foot. We followed the path marked by the friendly graffiti our taggers had put down. There were three more ambushes before we reached the factory. They all ended like the first had, and a lot more quickly. I couldn't be sure because there weren't any bodies to count, but we must have trimmed the size of Papa Danwe's outfit by at least a hundred.

So I wasn't surprised when we arrived and I saw the factory grounds were only lightly guarded, about like they'd been on my first visit. The ward surrounding the site had been reinforced. The magic was much stronger, and a lot more complex. Papa Danwe had probably come down and done it himself, after my little incursion.

The team remained out of sight of the guards and split up. Honey and I stayed out front, along with Ilya Zunin and Sonny Kim. Ismail Akeem took the north side, Amy Chen the east, and Frank Seville the south. When everyone was in place, we all hit the ward's anchor points with chaos magic. It went down within seconds, and the alarm bell began to toll.

Sonny Kim chanted something in Korean, and a cyclone tore through the gangbangers positioned around the building. A few had time to get off a single spell or fire their weapons wildly before they were borne away by the wind, as if a giant had reached down and brushed them aside. We were joined by the other three as we walked across the lot to the factory.

As we approached the building, Zunin flung out one arm

and the tattoos inked into his skin burned red. The force spell hit the brick wall like a cruise missile and punched a hole in it large enough to drive a school bus through. The back-blast from the spell blew out all the windows on the west side of the building, and tiny, winking shards of glass showered down on us like rain.

Papa Danwe was waiting for us inside with his own posse of hard-hitting gangsters positioned around the gate machinery in a semicircle. There were a lot more of them than us, enough that I didn't have time to count them all. The Haitian stepped forward when we appeared out of the choking clouds of brick dust and smoke.

He was old and impossibly thin, like a skeleton draped in papery black skin. His eyes were as pale gray as Rashan's. He was stooped, his bony shoulders hunched forward, and his shriveled right hand clutched the silver pommel of a walking stick. A necklace of human finger bones rattled on his chest as he hobbled toward us. I waited for him to get within twenty feet, and then I brought the Mossberg down from my shoulder and leveled it in his general direction.

"That's far enough, old man."

The Haitian squinted at me, as if he wasn't sure what he was seeing. "Where is your master, girl? It is time we finish this." His voice was a dry rasp. Not as bad as Akeem, but still pretty damn hard to understand.

"He couldn't make it. It's amateur night at the strip club, and he's the judge."

"He too craven to face me, yes?" Papa Danwe laughed. It was more of an insane giggle, really.

I wasn't going to mention why Rashan hadn't made the trip. The vibe I was getting from Papa Danwe led me to believe he should have sat this one out, too. For all I knew, he'd been spinning spells as long as Rashan, and he was clearly on speaking terms with crazy.

"Anything he can do, the six of us can do almost as well."

"Seven," Honey corrected.

"Seven," I said. "Sorry, Honey."

Papa Danwe scowled. "None of you is welcome here. This is my ground. Go now, or I kill you here."

I just shook my head. Everyone knew the game, and the stakes. Why couldn't we just get an early start on killing each other? Why did we have to talk about it first? Probably because bad guys have limited educations and even worse social skills. They just don't know how to act. Once the Haitian started jawing, though, I felt like I at least had to hear him out. Maybe he actually had something to say. Maybe he wanted to back down, if I gave him a chance.

I sighed. "Okay. You and your boys walk away, and we'll take down this gate. There will still be some unfinished business between our outfits, but nothing we can't work out."

"Who are you to give orders to me, girl?" Papa Danwe spat. "I was a king on a gold and ivory throne when your people were still beating each other with sticks. You cannot dream so darkly to imagine what I will do to you."

I gave it due consideration. I tried to work it from every conceivable angle. "Yeah, that's what I figured." I shrugged. *"Vi Victa Vis!"* I shouted, and hurled a lance of kinetic energy at the old man's withered heart. His counterspell swatted it aside with a lazy wave of his left hand.

The plan was for me to handle the wards on the gate machinery, which meant I didn't have time to tangle with Papa Danwe. Fortunately, my team knew the plan, too. Frank Seville shouted something inarticulate and charged the Haitian. He was flowing all his juice into defensive spells as he barreled at the old man, and the malevolent energy that crashed over him from Papa Danwe's posse lit him up like a fluorescent bulb. He hit the Haitian's shriveled body like a train running down a deer on the tracks, and they tumbled out of sight and out of mind.

I started fighting my way toward the tower. I wasn't entirely sure how the gate apparatus worked, but I was certain I'd been more or less on the money with the Tesla machine theory, when I'd thought it was just a magic cannon. I was convinced the crystal suspended at the top of the tower was the business end, that it was the device that would tear a hole in the world and let the fairies in.

Images of the first few moments of battle were imprinted on my mind. I saw Amy Chen standing her ground, calmly casting spell after spell at the gangsters that tried to bring her down. The phantasmal shapes of serpents, dragons and lions sprung from her outstretched arms and savaged the ranks of her attackers like nerve agents carried on the wind.

Ilya Zunin waded in like a Russian bear, flailing about him with force magic that sliced through flesh and smashed bone. Sonny Kim stayed by his side, spinning protections and defensive spells with impossible precision, carefully deflecting the hostile magic that assaulted Zunin from all sides.

Ismail Akeem danced convulsively in a circle and writhed in pain as he disgorged one spirit after another from his tortured body. The spirits howled and wailed as they descended on their terrified victims and devoured them.

All of this I saw in those first few seconds. After that, the battle dissolved into chaos. There was so much juice coursing through the place and so many mind-twisting spells in the air it was difficult even to think, let alone make sense of what was happening around me. I would remember the sound. It was like the shriek of ravaged metal and lost souls, and it went on and on and on.

Honey stayed with me. She sang her wind-chime war spells and laid about her with her silver sword. We left a trail of the dead and dying behind us as we fought our way to the tower. I didn't feel like climbing it again, so I spun my levitation spell and fired the Mossberg down at the gangsters who came after us as I rose into the air.

I half expected to find another thug battalion on the roof, but I guess Papa Danwe was running low on guys who had enough juice to make a difference. The roof was deserted. I continued up to the small platform where the crystal sphere was suspended above the silver bezel. I could see the fairy magic warding the device this time, and I knew it would be impervious to both magic and physical attack. I landed on the platform, and Honey and I got to work.

It was a little like I imagined defusing a bomb would be. The warding spells were woven around and through the apparatus like tiny, intricate threads. I reached out with my mind and the changeling's magic and began unweaving the spells thread by thread. The terrible sound of the battle below cut through the roof and set my teeth on edge. The juice rose like heat from a burning building and lifted all the hair on my body like a static charge.

I'm not sure how long we were at it, but after a time we had undone most of the warding spells. As the threads were pulled free from the whole, they fell apart and the juice evaporated into the air. I'd just isolated the few threads that remained when Honey cried out in alarm.

"Domino, below you!" she yelled. I looked. Papa Danwe was rising through the hole in the roof on an unseen wind. His arms were stretched out to his sides, and he held his walking stick in one hand and Frank Seville's severed head in the other. Frank's head burst into flame, and the Haitian sorcerer hurled it at us. I got my shield up just in time as the fire exploded into us.

Sorcerers' duels are mostly a matter of who can flow more juice and who can spin that juice into combat spells more quickly. If anything, speed is more important than power. With each spell you cast, you have to decide whether to attack or defend, because you can't cast two spells at once. If you can spin attack spells quickly enough, you can force your opponent on the defensive, even if the spells aren't all that strong. All of this has to be done with spontaneous magic, of course— you can't recite quotations quickly enough to spin spells in a duel.

I knew Papa Danwe could tap more juice than I could in this place. In fact, I noticed immediately that our juice was running pretty thin. I also discovered in that first exchange that he was faster than I was. A lot faster. I had two things going for me, and I'd have been toast without either of them. The first was Honey and the second was the fairy magic I'd stolen from the changeling.

The Haitian had warded himself against fairy magic. I wasn't sure how he'd arranged it, but it seemed like a prudent thing to do given what he'd been up to. He'd cut a deal with the Seelie Court, but in the underworld any deal can go wrong. So the bad news was that Papa Danwe was protected. If he hadn't been, Honey and I could have swatted him around like two cats playing with a ball of yarn. The good news was that his protections against fairy magic weren't nearly as good as his defenses against sorcery.

I poured all the juice I could pull up from our tags below

into the bare minimum of static defenses that would prevent the Haitian's attacks from instantly reducing me to meat pudding. Whenever I got a second to go on the offensive, I picked away at his defenses, just as I'd been defusing the wards on the gate machinery.

That's what I was doing, but none of it was apparent to the naked eye. It *looked* like I was just getting my ass kicked. Even this was an advantage, though, because the sorcerer didn't know what I was doing, either. He was protected, but he didn't have any fairy magic of his own.

Papa Danwe's initial assault knocked me from my perch on the platform, and I tumbled to the roof of the factory some twenty feet below. He came after me like a seagull swooping in for a bread crumb on the pier. His attacks were relentless, pummeling me with spell after spell, knocking me from one side of the roof to the other. Honey did what she could, lighting him up with ineffective glamours and wailing away at him with her tiny sword. It was enough to occasionally distract the sorcerer, and I seized each opportunity to pull loose one more thread.

In the end, I just ran out of juice before Papa Danwe ran out of protections. It got harder and harder to keep my defenses up, until finally, I couldn't keep them up at all. The Haitian saw the moment when it came. He grinned evilly, picking me up with a telekinesis spell, lifting me slowly into the air about level with the sphere at the top of the tower. Then he slammed me down into the rooftop with all the strength he could muster.

I managed to get my legs under me before I hit. They shattered on impact, but better them than my back or neck. My body was completely numb from all the juice I'd been flowing, so there wasn't any pain. I levered myself up on one arm and tried to spin one last spell, but I was dry. I was done.

Honey screamed and dive-bombed the sorcerer, but he intercepted her with a writhing bolt of electricity that arced from his outstretched hand. The force of the spell sent the piskie cartwheeling through the air over the edge of the building, and she plummeted, smoking, to the ground below.

Papa Danwe was in the mood to talk some more. He hobbled forward and stopped about ten feet away. "I been looking forward to tasting your juice," he said, licking his cracked lips. It was pornographic, and my stomach turned. "I heard so much about you, that you become so strong." He spat. "I heard wrong. You are weak. You have nothing for me." He cupped his hands before him and they began to fill with baleful juice that sizzled like acid. He started giggling as he came for me.

Then a ball of liquid fire burst over his head and poured down on him, scouring the thin, dry flesh from the back of his skull and one side of his face. It would have devoured him completely, but he reacted quickly, extinguishing the fire with protective magic. He turned slowly and I followed his gaze to see Terrence Cole's wide head poking through the hole in the roof. Papa Danwe roared in pain and fury and unloaded on his erstwhile lieutenant.

Terrence didn't run. He came all the way out onto the roof and pushed forward, knocking aside his boss's attacks and pummeling the sorcerer with his own. He took one step at a time, bent forward as if battling a gale-force wind.

I reached out and untangled the last knotted threads that protected Papa Danwe from what I could do to him. When his defenses had burned away into the ether, I poured out the fairy magic inside me and turned him into a toad.

Terrence stopped and stared. I collapsed onto the roof and

rolled over on my back, staring up at the starless, electric-orange L.A. sky. Terrence started laughing. I tried to join in but I didn't have it in me.

After a while, Terrence's laughter subsided. "What you want me to do with the frog, Domino?" he asked. I turned my head and looked over at him. He'd caught the toad and was holding it up, peering at it curiously. It struggled in his wide hands and its mouth opened and closed spasmodically.

"Squeeze the motherfucker," I said, and Terrence did.

"Domino?" I opened my eyes and saw Honey hovering over me. I was still lying on the roof, and Terrence had covered me with his jacket. The juice buzz was gone, and the pain was welling up from my legs like bile in my gullet.

"Honey, I thought you were dead." She was burned, but it didn't look like anything her healing magic couldn't handle. "I guess you're pretty hard to kill."

"Warrior-princess," she said, and smiled. "Just like you, Domino."

Honey was able to finish dismantling the wards on the crystal sphere without my help. It was a good thing, too, because it took whatever reserves I had just to stay conscious.

With the wards down, the destruction of the gate was a little anticlimactic. Amy Chen hit the sphere with an entropy spell and it just came apart, melting like an ice sculpture in summer. She even captured some of the free juice and poured it into me, returning my body to blessed numbness.

All of them had survived—all except Frank Seville. I'd never gotten to know the man very well, and now I regretted it. I remembered what Vernon Case had told me, that Frank had brought Rick Macy into the outfit. I wondered what else he had done for us over the years. I knew what he'd done at the end.

Amy got on her cell and called Chavez to give him the news and request an extraction. I certainly wasn't going to be walking back to Crenshaw. She started issuing orders and then fell silent. Amy wasn't one for emotional displays, but she didn't look happy. Finally she handed the phone to me.

"You'd better hear this for yourself," she said.

I took the phone. "What is it, Chavez? The gate is down, the deed is done and I'm all fucked up. Send some guys out here to give us a ride back to town."

"They're already on the way, Domino, but that's not the problem."

"Spit it out, Chavez, or I'm likely to pass out before you get the chance."

"Reports have been coming in for the last hour, *chola*. Gates are opening all over South Central."

# fifteen

Honey's healing magic had me up and limping around with a cane within a couple days. I'd taken Papa Danwe's walking stick. The black wood was carved into the likeness of a cobra twining around the shaft, and its hooded head worked in silver formed the pommel. The stick had some juice, and I thought it was the least he could do.

A guerilla war had broken out all over South Central L.A. Our battle plan had become more of a counterinsurgency operation since the other gates opened, and near as I could tell, we were losing. I'd become so fixated on the Hawthorne gate that I'd never really considered the possibility of others. It had been an obvious, terrible mistake. It was even worse, because I'd known they didn't have to be huge, permanent structures like the one in Hawthorne. I had one of them tied off to a sports bottle in my kitchen.

In hindsight, it seemed a perfect match for King Oberon's way of thinking. Give your enemy a big shiny to focus on, and he won't even notice anything else you're doing. He'd been playing Three Card Monty with me since this whole thing started. I was getting hustled.

We'd lost a lot of soldiers in the past thirty-six hours or so. Our guys had no real protection against fairy magic, so even when we could find the sidhe and pick a fight, it usually ended the same way. I'd seen enough. The changeling had been right—King Oberon was coming, and there wasn't a hell of a lot I could do about it.

Our efforts hadn't been a total failure. It was looking like the Seelie Court would end up controlling most of Papa Danwe's former territory, but at least they wouldn't have ours. Not yet. And with a little time, I might be able to give my outfit the defenses they needed to make it a fair fight.

It could have been worse, but it still wasn't good. I couldn't see the future like my mother, but what I could see didn't look all that bright. King Oberon would bring in more and more of his sidhe, consolidating his power in Inglewood and Watts and slowly expanding from there. We'd be mired in a guerilla war for months, maybe years. That's what King Oberon had been trying to avoid. By decapitating our outfit, he'd have been able to move in and fill the power vacuum while seizing the largest territory and the deepest juice supply in L.A. Instead, he'd gotten a quagmire, but it was a quagmire he'd probably win, eventually.

I slammed my fists down on the conference table. I crumpled the map in my hands and swept it aside. I looked at Chavez, who had a cell phone glued to each ear, taking reports and issuing orders to the front. I looked at Amy Chen and Ismail Akeem, who were taking a breather and licking their wounds before heading back out to the war. Sonny Kim and Ilya Zunin were still out there somewhere. They'd brought in their outfits with us, as promised, and they were dying as fast as we were. Even Anton was in the trenches, doing what he could. I got up and headed for the door.

"Where are you going, boss?" Chavez asked, momentarily pulling himself away from the cell phones.

"China," I said, and walked out.

When I got outside, two men were standing by my Lincoln. Black suits, black ties, white shirts, sunglasses. One was medium height and build with a shaved head and a ruggedly handsome face. The other was larger, with close-cropped black hair, a square jaw and a dimple in his chin. The guy with the dimple was leaning against the trunk of my car.

"You should see the last guy who leaned on my car," I said as I limped up to them. His expression didn't change, but he stepped away from the Lincoln.

The bald guy came forward and flashed an ID at me. "Ms. Riley, I'm Agent Lowell and this is Agent Granato. We're with the Department of Homeland Security. Special Threat Assessment Group."

I peered at the ID and then looked at him. "Stag? Really? Are you guys serious?"

Lowell, the bald guy, flinched a little, but Chin Dimple didn't seem to get the joke. "Ms. Riley, we'd like to talk to you about the recent…disturbances…in this part of Los Angeles."

"What disturbances? It's always like this. The tourists mostly stay in Anaheim." I looked at the guys. They were both sorcerers, and both had a fair amount of juice. By the looks of him, Lowell could have been one of my big hitters.

"Ms. Riley, we know of your associations, and we know what's happening here. It's our job to evaluate the MIE, gather intelligence and recommend an appropriate response."

He was doing the Mr. Clean thing to me, so I just looked at

him. He didn't seem to know what I was waiting for, though, so I finally had to ask the question. "What's an MIE?"

"Major Incursion Event," Granato answered. "Our concern is the national security of the United States. And the welfare of its citizens, of course," he added, somewhat belatedly.

I nodded. "Well, what do you want from me?"

Agent Lowell answered. "Ms. Riley, the U.S. government—part of it, anyway—is aware that we're moving into a period of global instability. We're aware that we can't stop it. Our goal is to manage the transition as effectively as possible."

"Hope they pay you well for that."

Lowell shrugged. "It's a government job. Ms. Riley, are you aware of the role the Mafia played during World War II?"

"Yeah, I guess. They were recruited by the government to do their part for the war effort—use their influence, help gather intelligence, mostly in Italy."

"That's right," Agent Lowell agreed. "We'd like you to do the same."

"You guys have some juice," I said. "I guess the government can handle it." Maybe the outfit wouldn't have to save the world after all.

Lowell looked at Granato and then back at me. "Ms. Riley, as far as we know, Agent Granato and myself are the only two practicing sorcerers in the federal government. Our organization has compiled a great deal of information, but as you are aware, knowledge is not enough."

So much for the cavalry riding to the rescue. "Let's say I'm interested. What do I get out of this?"

Agent Granato scowled. "You get a chance to serve your country in a time of crisis. Isn't that enough, Riley?"

"Serving my country and serving my government—or part of it—isn't necessarily the same thing."

"I understand, Ms. Riley," Lowell said. "Uncle Sam's reputation isn't what it used to be."

I shrugged. "Everyone's got a crazy uncle in the family."

"Understand this, though. The government isn't some monolithic entity that speaks with one voice and acts with one hand. It's just people—people with different ideas, making difficult decisions that have pretty serious consequences. They need good information, good advice. It's our job to give it to them, and you can help with that. If they don't get it, bad decisions get made and really bad things happen."

I remembered what Rashan had told me, and an image of a mushroom cloud over Los Angeles sprung into my head.

"And of course," said Lowell, "we could ensure that your business operations are not a priority for the federal government."

"Done," I said. "But I'm not going to start voting Republican."

Agent Lowell laughed. "That won't be necessary, Ms. Riley. For now, we'd just like to know how this thing is going to go. Can you contain this MIE?"

"I don't know. But I'm about to find out."

When I got back to my condo, I pulled up a chair at the kitchen table. The tiny sidhe warriors were sitting at the edge of the lagoon. One of them was nibbling on a fruit, and the other seemed to be napping.

"Hey guys," I said.

"What do you want?" asked the one with the fruit. His voice sounded like one of the Chipmunks. The other opened an eye and looked at me.

"I want to arrange a sit-down with your boss. Thought y'all might be able to help me with that."

"A sit-down?"

"Yeah, you know, a parley. Negotiations."

Sleepy sat upright. "You would have to free us from this prison," he said. "We cannot contact our king from this place."

"I could do that," I said, "if you delivered the message for me. Just one of you, though. The other one has to stay in the nest."

Sleepy nodded and Fruity scowled. I had a pretty good idea who was staying. "I am Queen Titania's nephew, and I have rank," Sleepy said. "I will be your messenger."

I let the threads binding the elf to the nest unravel, and Sleepy appeared before me in the kitchen. He bowed. "On my honor, my lady, I will return when I have delivered your message to my king."

"Yeah, okay, sounds good. See you later."

The sidhe warrior strode proudly into my living room, stepped through the gate and was gone.

We met in the Between, at Temple Emanuel in Beverly Hills. Churches are neutral ground in the underworld, just like in *Highlander*. Whether in the physical world or the Between, you can't tap any juice in a consecrated place. Really, it works just like our thing. Churches are juice boxes—powerful ones—but someone else's lips are on the straw. I'd been angling for a Catholic church, but the sidhe insisted on something non-Christian. Something about old grudges.

The king's entourage stood in orderly ranks around the outside of the building. I had my big hitters with me, and I left them outside, too, when I went into the temple.

King Oberon was sitting alone in a pew toward the front. He stood as I approached and we shook hands. He looked absurdly young, maybe twenty, tops. Straight, luxurious auburn hair cascaded down his back, nearly to his waist, and his skin looked like it had been lovingly crafted from flawless porcelain. His body was slender and perfectly proportioned, and he was wearing an exquisite bespoke suit the color of pearls. He was the kind of beautiful boy that would be really popular in prison.

"Ms. Riley, thank you for arranging this meeting. I am honored." He smiled, and his face lit up like a child's on Christmas morning. It made you want to love him. It made you want to worship him. It made me want to punch him in the mouth.

"Thank you, uh, Your Highness. I wasn't sure you'd agree. It seems like this might have been worth a shot before you took the assassination angle." Oberon smiled and nodded, and we sat down.

"In hindsight, it was a bit of a miscalculation. I admit it. But you must remember, Ms. Riley, when I set this plan in motion, you were just a tomboy using your magic to steal cigarettes at the convenience store."

"What's that got to do with anything? You could have had a sit-down with Rashan. Instead, you decided to kill him and take his place."

"I had reason, based on long experience, to believe that I could not have reached an amicable agreement with Shanar Rashan."

"Why's that?"

"Pride, Ms. Riley. We both have far too much of it."

Was that supposed to mean I didn't have any of it myself? I decided to let it pass. "I'm not real happy about what you did, but I guess I wouldn't have asked you to sit down with me if I couldn't get over it."

"Indeed. So where do we go from here?"

"I understand you want in, and I can live with that. But I can't give you my outfit's territory."

"Certainly—I do not expect you to. Papa Danwe's territory will suffice, for now. I will eventually need more, but I will agree, by treaty, to refrain from further attacks on your organization."

I shook my head. "I can't give you Papa Danwe's territory, either. It's Terrence Cole's territory now—his outfit, what's left of it. Terrence is a friend of ours." I shrugged. "I owe, King. Anyway, that's the same deal you gave Papa Danwe, and I killed him for it. I don't think it would look very good if I agreed to it myself."

King Oberon sighed, and his shoulders slumped. "That is unfortunate. Perhaps one or more of the other outfits in the city, then? I have quite a lot invested in South Central already, you understand, but I am not unreasonable."

"Thing is, King, I think we're going to need the other outfits for what's coming. No offense, but you're not the worst of it."

"Indeed I am not, Ms. Riley. It seems we have reached an impasse, and for that I am deeply regretful."

"What do you think of Hollywood?"

King Oberon arched an eyebrow. Then he smiled and broke out the light show again. "Oh, Ms. Riley, I think that would do very well."

"Yeah. The way I see it, all the outfits nibble at the edges, but none of us control it. We'd all like to, but we've always balanced each other out. Hollywood is low-hanging fruit, Your Majesty. And it's got a lot of juice."

"So what is your proposal, in detail?"

"I build you gates in Hollywood. I convince all the outfits

in the city to play along. You get the juice you need and start rebuilding Arcadia, in Tinseltown."

"And you, Ms. Riley. What do you get?"

"I get an alliance with the Seelie Court. You and your people line up with me in the war that's coming."

King Oberon nodded. "We would likely have done that anyway, Ms. Riley." He looked at me, and a deadly serious expression hardened his face. "Whatever you may think of me, of us, understand one thing. We love your world. We even love humans, though it is, perhaps, not always the kind of affection mortals can appreciate. We are not monsters, Ms. Riley. We will fight for this place. We will fight, with you."

"That's good enough for me, King. There's just one more thing. Honey gets a full pardon. And her family."

"The piskie betrayed me," the king said, frowning. "Surely, in your position, you know how damaging that can be."

"I know. You have to protect your authority in order to run your crew. But the way I see it, you're a great king. You're strong enough to show mercy."

Oberon laughed. "There is nothing quite as charming as flattery from a beautiful woman, Ms. Riley."

"Besides," I added, "you had it coming."

"Perhaps I did. Very well. The piskie and her house are hereby pardoned. And I agree to your terms, Ms. Riley."

"Done," I said, and we shook hands to seal the pact.

King Oberon and his entourage returned to the mortal world through a gate I built on the dance floor of the Cannibal Club. The club's legal status was in limbo in the wake of its proprietor's disappearance. The law firm charged with handling the affair had been only too happy to sell the club to a blind holding company I'd set up for the king. Oberon had provided me with enough gold to buy half of Hollywood—it seemed gold was the only physical substance that existed on all planes of existence, and the king had a lot of it.

I'm not much for ceremony, but I'd brought in a few cases of Cristal so we could properly toast the occasion. Rashan was there, and my big hitters. And Honey. King Oberon arrived with a small entourage of the sidhe aristocracy, including Sleepy and Fruity.

He also brought his queen, Titania. She looked like a teenager, innocent and pure, and so beautiful she made me feel like an ugly cow. She had long red curls and skin like milk and honey. She was wearing a white dress with silver accents that looked like it had come from one of the designer shops in Beverly Hills. The silk clung to her body, and the promise of budding womanhood was almost overpowering, even for me. Despite her youth and beauty, she had a regal elegance and an air of command that even Mrs. Dawson couldn't match.

We made the introductions and shared several toasts. Finally, King Oberon set his glass aside and walked over to my boss.

"Master Rashan," he said, inclining his head, "there is one more matter to which we must attend."

"And what is that, Your Highness? I should think you've gotten everything you might have hoped for, and more." Rashan had supported my decision, but I had the idea he didn't like it much. I had the idea he didn't like the king much.

"Master, I took something from you. Something precious." The king paused and stared deep into Rashan's pale gray eyes. "And I would like to give it back to you." The king nodded to where Sleepy and Fruity stood in front of the gate, and they moved aside.

Adan Rashan stepped through the gate. He was just as I remembered him, in every detail. He was wearing a dark suit and ivory shirt, just like the one I'd seen him in that first night in the club. He was exactly the same—his hair, his lovely eyes, the line of his jaw, the way he moved, the little dimples when he smiled.

It was Adan.

My boss made a small, inarticulate sound as he rushed to his son. He wept openly as he embraced him. The rest of the crowd moved away to give them some privacy, but I just stood there and stared.

As I watched them, I realized this Adan wasn't quite the same as the one I remembered, the one that had been a lie. This Adan had juice. When I looked at him, I saw the magic in him, strong and vibrant. It was the magic both of this world and the other one, the place they called Avalon. It was the same magic of two worlds that was in me.

Finally Rashan released him and led him away. Adan must have felt my stare, because he turned and looked back, and our eyes met. And he must have seen something in the way I looked at him, because he smiled at me, uncertain but warm. Then he turned away again, and took his father's arm, and left.

On the way home, I stopped at Miss American Pie and went into the restroom. Jamal was gone, but the words "JJ was here" were carved into the door of the stall, as if with a very sharp knife.

"Peace out, Jamal," I said, and then I went out of there and into the restaurant. It smelled like apples and cinnamon, but that was just the fucking pizza.

★ ★ ★ ★ ★

*How did Domino get to this place?*
*Don't miss "Retribution" found in*
*HARVEST MOON in October 2010,*
*an anthology featuring*
*New York Times bestselling authors*
*Mercedes Lackey and Michelle Sagara*
*along with Cameron Haley*

# ackknowledgments

If writing a first novel is difficult, publishing one is even tougher. I wouldn't have accomplished either without contributions and support from a lot of remarkable people. I'd like to thank my two moms, Phyllis Benage and Louise Clark, for making everything possible. My friends Michael Born and John Cunnick for introducing me to fantasy and science fiction, and for sharing so many adventures with me. Jeffrey Barber and Christian Petersen for letting me make stuff up for a living. My agent, Shawna McCarthy, and my editor, Mary-Theresa Hussey, two very talented women who believed in this book and made it better. Tim Bradstreet, for the fantastic cover art. The entire community at Absolute Write, especially the squirrels in Query Hell and my crew in Purgatory. Most of all, I want to thank Maria Benage, who believed even when I didn't.

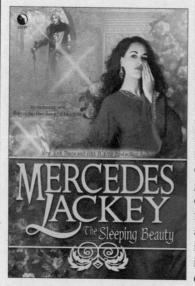

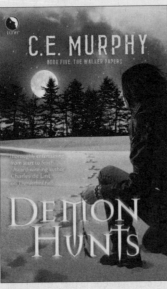